A MISSING PERSON . . .

"Mother Mastiff, open up, it's me, Flinx!" No reply from the other side.

Pip danced on his shoulder; the flying snake was half airborne and half coiled tight to its master. Flinx moved a dozen steps away from the door, then charged it. The door gave.

Inside, the stall looked undisturbed. Flinx tried the inner door. In contrast to the order behind him, the living area was a shambles.

The destruction was worst in Mother Mastiff's room. The bed looked as if it had been the scene of attempted murder. Across the bed, hidden from casual view, a small curved door blended neatly into the wall paneling. When it was shut, few visitors would be sharp-eyed enough to notice it.

It stood ajar . . .

FOR
LOVE OF
MOTHER-NOT

Alan Dean Foster

A Del Rey Book

BALLANTINE BOOKS • NEW YORK

A Del Rey Book
Published by Ballantine Books

Library of Congress Catalog Card Number: 82-90867

ISBN 0-345-30511-6

Manufactured in the United States of America

First Edition: March 1983

Cover art by Michael Whelan

For Michael and Audrey and Alexa Whelan;
good neighbors . . .

Chapter One

"Now there's a scrawny, worthless-looking little runt," Mother Mastiff thought. She cuddled the bag of woodcarvings a little closer to her waist, making certain it was protected from the rain by a flap of her slickertic. The steady drizzle that characterized Drallar's autumn weather fled from the water-resistant material.

Offworlders were hard pressed to distinguish any difference in the city's seasons. In the summer, the rain was warm; in autumn and winter, it was cooler. Springtime saw it give way to a steady, cloying fog. So rare was the appearance of the sun through the near-perpetual cloud cover that when it did peep through, the authorities were wont to call a public holiday.

It was not really a slave market Mother Mastiff was trudging past. That was an archaic term, employed only by cynics. It was merely the place where labor-income adjustments were formalized.

Drallar was the largest city on the world of Moth, its only true metropolis, and it was not a particularly wealthy one. By keeping taxes low, it had attracted a good number of offworld businesses and trading concerns to a well-situated but mostly inhospitable planet. It compensated by largely doing away with such annoying commercial aggravations as tariffs and regulations. While this resulted in considerable prosperity for some, it left the city government at a loss for general revenue.

Among the numerous areas that were rarely self-supporting was that involving care of the impoverished. In cases in which indigence was total and an individual was isolated by circumstance, it was deemed reasonable to allow a wealthier citizen to take over responsibility from the government. This thinned the welfare rolls and kept the bureaucracy content, while providing better care for the individual involved—or so the officials insisted—than he or she could receive from underfunded and impersonal government agencies.

The United Church, spiritual arm of the Commonwealth, frowned on such one-sided economic policies. But the Commonwealth did not like to interfere with domestic policies, and Drallarian officials hastened to assure the occasional visiting padre or counselor that legal safeguards prevented abuse of "adopted" individuals.

So it was that Mother Mastiff found herself leaning on her cane, clutching the bag of artwork, and staring at the covered dispersement platform while she tried to catch her breath. One curious attendee moved too close, crowding her. He glowered when she jabbed him in the foot with her cane but moved aside, not daring to confront her.

Standing motionless on the platform within the Circle of Compensation was a thin, solemn boy of eight or nine years. His red hair was slicked down from the rain and contrasted sharply with his dark skin. Wide, innocent eyes, so big they seemed to wrap around the sides of his face, stared out across the rain-dampened assembly. He kept his hands clasped behind his back. Only those eyes moved, their gaze flicking like an insect over the upturned faces of the crowd. The majority of the milling, would-be purchasers were indifferent to his presence.

To the boy's right stood a tall, slim representative of the government who ran the official sale—an assignment of responsibility, they called it—for the welfare bureau. Across from her a large readout listed the boy's vital statistics, which Mother Mastiff eyed casually.

Height and weight matched what she could see. Color of hair, eyes, and skin she had already noted. Living relatives, assigned or otherwise—a blank there. Personal history—another blank. A child of accident and calamity, she thought, thrown like so many others on the untender mercies of government care. Yes, he certainly would be better off under the wing of a private individual, by the looks of him. He might at least receive some decent food.

And yet there was something more to him, something that set him apart from the listless procession of orphans who paraded across that rain-swept platform, season after season. Mother Mastiff sensed something lurking behind those wide, mournful eyes—a maturity well beyond his years, a greater intensity to his stare than was to be expected from a child in his position. That stare continued to rove over the crowd, probing, searching. There was more of the hunter about the boy than the hunted.

The rain continued to fall. What activity there was among the watchers was concentrated on the back right corner of the platform, where a modestly attractive girl of about sixteen was next in line for consignment. Mother Mastiff let out a derisive snort. Government assurances or not, you couldn't tell her that those pushing, shoving snots in the front row didn't have something on their minds beyond an innocently altruistic concern for the girl's future. Oh, no!

The ever-shifting cluster of potential benefactors formed an island around which eddied the greater population of the marketplace. The marketplace itself was concentrated into a ring of stalls and shops and restaurants and dives that encircled the city center. The result was just modern enough to function and sufficiently unsophisticated to attract those intrigued by the mysterious.

It held no mysteries for Mother Mastiff. The marketplace of Drallar was her home. Ninety years she had spent battling that endless river of humanity and aliens, sometimes being sucked down, sometimes rising above the flow, but never in danger of drowning.

Now she had a shop—small, but her own. She bargained for objets d'art, traded knicknacks, electronics, and handicrafts, and managed to make just enough to keep herself clear of such places as the platform on which the boy was standing. She put herself in his place and shuddered. A ninety-year-old woman would not bring much of a price.

There was an awkwardly patched rip at the neck of her slickertic, and rain was beginning to find its way through the widening gap. The pouch of salables she clutched to her thin waist wasn't growing any lighter. Mother Mastiff had other business to transact, and she wanted to be back home before dark. As the sun of Moth set, the murky daylight of Drallar would fade to a slimy darkness, and things less than courteous would emerge from the slums that impinged on the marketplace. Only the careless and the cocky wandered abroad at such times, and Mother Mastiff was neither.

As the boy's eyes roved over the audience, they eventually reached her own—and stopped. Suddenly, Mother Mastiff felt queasy, unsteady. Her hand went to her stomach. Too much grease in the morning's breakfast, she thought. The eyes had already moved on. Since she had turned eighty-five, she had had to watch her diet. But, as she had told a friend, "I'd rather die of indigestion and on a full stomach than waste away eating pills and concentrates."

"One side there," she abruptly found herself saying, not sure what she was doing or why. "One side." She broke a path through the crowd, poking one observer in the ribs with her cane, disturbing an ornithorpe's ornate arrangement of tail feathers, and generating a chirp of indignation from an overweight matron. She worked her way down to the open area directly in front of the platform. The boy took no notice of her; his eyes continued to scan the uncaring crowd.

"Please, ladies and gentlebeings," the official on the platform pleaded, "won't one of you give this healthy, honest boy a home? Your government requests it of you; civilization demands it of you. You have a chance today to do two good turns at once; one for your king and the other for this unfortunate youth."

"I'd like to give the king a good turn, all right," said a voice from the milling crowd, "right where it would do him the most good."

The official shot the heckler an angry glare but said nothing.

"What's the minimum asking?" Be that *my* voice? Mother Mastiff thought in wonderment.

"A mere fifty credits, madam, to satisfy department obligations and the boy is yours. To watch over and care for." She hesitated, then added, "If you think you can handle as active a youngster as this one."

"I've handled plenty of youngsters in my time," Mother Mastiff returned curtly. Knowing hoots sounded from the amused assembly. She studied the boy, who was looking down at her again. The queasiness that had roiled in her stomach the first time their eyes had met did not reoccur. Grease, she mused, have to cut down on the cooking grease.

"Fifty credits, then," she said.

"Sixty." The deep voice that boomed from somewhere to the rear of the crowd came as an unexpected interruption to her thoughts.

"Seventy," Mother Mastiff automatically responded. The official on the platform quickly gazed back into the crowd.

"Eighty," the unseen competitor sounded.

She hadn't counted on competition. It was one thing to do a child a good turn at reasonable cost to herself, quite another to saddle herself with an unconscionable expense.

"Ninety—curse you," she said. She turned and tried to locate her opponent but could not see over the heads of the crowd. The voice bidding against her was male, powerful, piercing. What the devil would the owner of such a voice want with a child like this? she thought.

"Ninety-five," it countered.

"Thank you, thank you. To you both, the government says." The official's tone and expression had brightened perceptibly. The lively and utterly unexpected bidding for the redheaded brat had alleviated her boredom as well as her concern. She would be able to show her boss a better than usual daily account sheet. "The bid is against you, madam."

"Damn the bid," Mother Mastiff muttered. She started to turn away, but something held her back. She was as good a judge of people as she was of the stock she sold to them, and there was something particular about this boy—though she couldn't say precisely what, which struck her as unusual. There was always profit in the unusual. Besides, that mournful stare was preying unashamedly on a part of her she usually kept buried.

"Oh, hell, one hundred, then, and be damned with it!" She barely managed to squeeze the figure out. Her mind was in a whirl. What was she doing there, neglecting her regular business, getting thoroughly soaked and bidding for an orphaned child? Surely at ninety her maternal instinct wasn't being aroused. She had never felt the least maternal instinct in her life, thank goodness.

She waited for the expected rumble of "one hundred and five," but instead heard a commotion toward the back of the crowd. She craned her neck, trying to see, cursing the genes that had left her so short. There were shouts, then yells of outrage and loud cursing from a dozen different throats. To the left, past the shielding bulk of the ornithorpe behind her, she could just make out the bright purple flash of uniformed gendarmes, their slickertics glaring in the dim light. This group seemed to be moving with more than usual energy.

She turned and fought her way forward and to the right, where a series of steps led to the platform. Halfway up the stairs, she squinted back into the crowd. The purple 'tics were just merging into the first wall of office and shop complexes. Ahead of them a massive human shape bobbed and dipped as it retreated from the pursuing police.

Mother Mastiff permitted herself a knowing nod. There were those who might want a young boy for other than humanitarian purposes. Some of them had criminal dossiers on file that stretched as far back as her lifeline. Obviously someone in the crowd, a salaried informer, perhaps, had recognized the individual bidding against her and had notified the authorities, who had responded with commendable speed.

"One hundred credits, then," the disappointed official

announced from the platform. "Do I hear any more?" Naturally, she would not, but she played out the game for appearance's sake. A moment passed in silence. She shrugged, glanced over to where Mother Mastiff still stood on the stairway. "He's yours, old woman." Not "madam" any longer, Mother Mastiff thought sardonically. "Pay up, and mind the regulations, now."

"I've been dealing with the regulations of this government since long before ye were born, woman." She mounted the last few steps and, ignoring the official and the boy, strode back toward the Processing Office.

Inside, a bored clerk glanced up at her, noted the transaction-complete record as it was passed to his desk-top computer terminal, and asked matter-of-factly, "Name?"

"Mastiff," the visitor replied, leaning on her cane.

"That the last name?"

"First and last."

"Mastiff Mastiff?" The clerk gave her a sour look.

"Just *Mastiff*," the old woman said.

"The government prefers multiple names."

"Ye know what the government can do with its preferences."

The clerk sighed. He tapped the terminal's keys. "Age?"

"None of your business." She gave it a moment's thought and added, "Put down *old*."

The clerk did so, shaking his head dolefully. "Income?"

"Sufficient."

"Now look here, you," the clerk began exasperated, "in such matters as the acquisition of responsibility for welfared individuals, the city government requires certain specifics."

"The city government can shove its specifics in after its preferences." Mother Mastiff gestured toward the platform with her cane, a wide, sweeping gesture that the clerk had the presence of mind to duck. "The bidding is over. The other bidder has taken his leave. Hastily. Now I can take my money and go home, or I can contribute to the government's balance of payments and to your salary. Which is it to be?"

"Oh, all right," the clerk agreed petulantly. He completed his entries and punched a key. A seemingly endless form spat from the printout slot. Folded, it was about half a centimeter thick. "Read these."

Mother Mastiff hefted the sheaf of forms. "What are they?"

"Regulations regarding your new charge. The boy is yours to raise, not to mistreat. Should you ever be detected in violation of the instructions and laws therein stated"—he gestured at the wad—"he can be recovered from you with forfeiture of the acquisition fee. In addition, you must familiarize yourself with—" He broke off the lecture as the boy in question was escorted into the room by another official.

The youngster glanced at the clerk, then up at Mother Mastiff. Then, as if he'd performed similar rituals on previous occasions, he walked quietly up to her, took her left hand, and put his right hand in it. The wide, seemingly guileless eyes of a child gazed up at her face. They were bright green, she noted absently.

The clerk was about to continue, then found something unexpected lodged in his throat and turned his attention instead back to his desk top. "That's all. The two of you can go."

Mother Mastiff harrumphed as if she had won a victory and led the boy out onto the streets of Drallar. They had supplied him with that one vital piece of clothing, a small blue slickertic of his own. He pulled the cheap plastic tighter over his head as they reached the first intersection.

"Well, boy, 'tis done. Devil come take me and tell me if I know why I did it, but I expect that I'm stuck with ye now. And ye with me, of course. Do you have anything at the dorm we should go to recover?"

He shook his head slowly. Quiet sort, she thought. That was all to the good. Maybe he wouldn't be a quick squaller. She still wondered what had prompted her sudden and uncharacteristic outburst of generosity. The boy's hand was warm in her gnarled old palm. That palm usually enfolded a credcard for processing other people's money or artwork to be studied with an eye toward purchase and even, on occasion, a knife employed for something more radical than the preparation of food, but never before the hand of a small child. It was a peculiar sensation.

They worked their way through crowds hurrying to beat the onset of night, avoiding the drainage channels that ran down the center of each street. Thick aromas drifted from the dozens of food stalls and restaurants that fringed the avenue they were walking. Still the boy said not a word. Finally, tired of the way his face would turn toward any place from which steam and smells rose, Mother Mastiff halted before one establishment with which she was familiar. They were nearly home, anyway.

"You hungry, boy?"

He nodded slowly, just once.

"Stupid of me. I can go all day without food and not give it a second thought. I forget sometimes that others have not that tolerance in their bellies." She nodded toward the doorway. "Well, what are ye waiting for?"

She followed him into the restaurant, then led the way to a quiet booth set against the wall. A circular console rose from the center of the table. She studied the menu imprinted on its flank, compared it with the stature of the child seated expectantly next to her, then punched several buttons set alongside the menu.

Before too long, the console sank into the table, then reappeared a moment later stacked with food; a thick, pungent stew dimpled with vegetables, long stalks of some beige tuber, and a mass of multistriped bread.

"Go ahead," she said when the boy hesitated, admiring his reserve and table manners. "I'm not too hungry, and I never eat very much."

She watched him while he devoured the food, sometimes picking at the colorful bread to assuage what little hunger she felt herself, barely acknowledging the occasional greeting from a passing acquaintance or friend. When the bottom of the stew bowl had been licked to a fine polish and the last scrap of bread had vanished, she asked, "Still hungry?"

He hesitated, measuring her, then gave her a half nod. "I'm not surprised," she replied, "but I don't want ye to have any more tonight. You've just downed enough to fill a grown man. Any more on top of what you've already had and you'd end up wasting it all. Tomorrow morning, okay?" He nodded slowly, understanding.

"And one more thing, boy. Can ye talk?"

"Yes." His voice was lower than anticipated, unafraid and, she thought, tinged with thankfulness.

"I can talk pretty good," he added without further prompting, surprising her. "I've been told that for my age I'm a very good talker."

"That's nice. I was starting to worry." She slid from her seat, using her cane to help her stand, and took his hand once again. "It's not too far now."

"Not too far to where?"

"To where I live. To where ye will live from now on." They exited the restaurant and were enveloped by the wet night.

"What's your name?" He spoke without looking up at her, preferring instead to study the dim storefronts and isolated, illuminated shops. The intensity of his inspection seemed unnatural.

"Mastiff," she told him, then grinned. " 'Tis not my real name, boy, but one that someone laid upon me many years ago. For better or worse, it's stuck longer with me than any man. 'Tis the name of a dog of exceptional ferocity and ugliness."

"I don't think you're ugly," the boy replied. "I think you're beautiful."

She studied his open, little-boy expression. Dim-witted, dim-sighted, or maybe just very smart, she thought.

"Can I call you Mother?" he asked hopefully, further confusing her. "You are my mother now, aren't you?"

"Sort of, I expect. Don't ask me why."

"I won't cause you any trouble." His voice was suddenly concerned, almost frightened. "I've never caused anyone any trouble, honest. I just want to be left alone."

Now what would prompt a desperate confession like that? she wondered. She decided not to pursue the matter. "I've no demands to make on ye," she assured him. "I'm a simple old woman, and I live a simple life. It pleases me. It had best please ye as well."

"It sounds nice," he admitted agreeably. "I'll do my best to help you any way I can."

"Devil knows there's plenty to do in the shop. I'm not quite as flexible as I used to be." She chuckled aloud. "Get tired before midnight now. You know, I actually need a full four hours' sleep? Yes, I think ye can be of service. You'd best be. Ye cost enough."

"I'm sorry," he said, abruptly downcast.

"Stop that. I'll have none of that in my home."

"I mean, I'm sorry that I upset you."

She let out a wheeze of frustration, knelt and supported herself with both hands locked to the shaft of the cane. It brought her down to his eye level. He stood there and gazed solemnly back at her.

"Now ye listen to me, boy. I'm no government agent. I don't have the vaguest notion what possessed me to take charge of ye, but 'tis done. I will not beat you unless you deserve it. I'll see to it that you're well fed and reasonably warm. In return, I demand that ye don't go about braying stupid things like 'I'm sorry.' Be that a deal?"

He didn't have to think it over very long. "It's a deal—Mother."

"That's settled, then." She shook his hand. The gesture brought forth a new phenomenon: his first smile. It made his tiny, lightly freckled face seem to glow, and suddenly the night seemed less chilly.

"Let's hurry," she said, struggling erect again. "I don't like being out this late, and you're not much the bodyguard. Never will be, by the looks of ye, though that's no fault of yours."

"Why is it so important to be home when it's dark?" he asked, and then added uncertainly, "Is that a stupid question?"

"No, boy." She smiled down at him as she hobbled up the street. "That's a smart question. It's important to be safe at home after dark because the dead tend to multiply in direct ratio to the absence of light. Though if you're cautious and never grow overconfident and learn the ways of it, you'll find that the darkness can be your friend as well as your enemy."

"I thought so," he said firmly. "I've thought so for"—his face screwed up as he concentrated hard on something—"for as long as I can remember."

"Oh?" She was still smiling at him. "And what makes you think that it's so besides the fact I just told it to ye?"

"Because," he replied, "most of the times I can ever remember being happy were in the dark."

She pondered that as they turned the corner. The rain had lessened considerably, giving way to the mist that passed for normal air in the city. It didn't trouble her lungs, but she worried about the boy. The one thing she didn't need was a sick child. He had cost her enough already.

Her stall-home was one of many scattered through the seemingly endless marketplace. Stout shutters protected the nondescript façade, which occupied ten meters at the far end of a side street. She pressed her palm to the door lock. The sensitized plastic glowed brightly for an instant, beeped twice, and then the door opened for them.

Once inside, she shoved the door shut behind them, then automatically turned to inspect her stock to make certain nothing had disappeared in her absence. There were racks of copper and silver wares, rare carved hardwoods for which Moth was justly renowned, well-crafted eating and drinking utensils, including many clearly designed for non-humans, cheap models of Moth itself with interrupted rings of flashy floatglitter, and various items of uncertain purpose.

Through this farrago of color and shape, the boy wandered. His eyes drank in everything, but he asked no questions, which she thought unusual.

It was in the nature of children to inquire about everything. But then, this was no ordinary child.

Toward the rear of the shop front a silver box stood on a dais. Its touch-sensitive controls connected the shop directly to the central bank of Drallar and enabled Mother Mastiff to process financial transactions for all customers, whether they came from up the street or halfway across the Commonwealth. A universal credcard allowed access to its owner's total wealth. Banks stored information; all hard currency was in general circulation.

Past the dais and the door it fronted were four rooms: a small storage chamber, a bathroom, a kitchen-dining area, and a bedroom. Mother Mastiff studied the arrangement for several minutes, then set about clearing the storage room. Ancient and long-unsold items were shoveled out onto the floor, together with cleaning equipment, clothing, canned goods, and other items. Somehow she would find room for them elsewhere.

Propped up against the far wall was a sturdy old cot. She touched a button on its side, and the device sprang to life, skittering about as it arranged itself on springy legs. Further excavation revealed a bag of support oil, which she plugged into the mattress. It was full and warm in minutes. Finally, she covered the cot with a thin thermosensitive blanket.

"This'll be your room," she told him. " 'Tis no palace, but 'tis yours. I know the importance of having something ye can call your own. Ye can fix up this bower however ye like."

The boy eyed her as if she had just bestowed all the treasures of Terra on him. "Thank you, Mother," he said softly. "It's wonderful."

"I sell things," she said, turning away from that radiant face. She gestured toward the storeroom out front. "The things ye saw on our way in."

"I guessed that. Do you make much money?"

"Now *ye* sound like the government agent back there at the platform." She smiled to show him she was teasing. "I get by. I'd much like to have a larger place than this, but at this point in my life"—she leaned her cane up against her bed as she strolled into the larger room—"it seems not likely I ever will. It does not bother me. I've had a good, full life and am content. You'll soon discover that my growls and barks are mostly show. Though not always." She patted him on the head and pointed toward the compact kitchen.

"Would ye like something hot to drink before we retire?"

"Yes, very much." Carefully, he took off his slickertic, which was dry by then. He hung it on a wall hook in his bedroom.

"We'll have to get ye some new clothes," she comment-ed, watching him from the kitchen.

"These are okay."

"Maybe they are for ye, but they're not for me." She pinched her nose by way of explanation.

"Oh. I understand."

"Now what would ye like to drink?"

His face brightened once again. "Tea. What kinds of tea do you have?"

"What kinds of tea do ye like?"

"All kinds."

"Then I'll choose ye one." She found the cylinder and depressed the main switch on its side as she filled it with water from the tap. Then she searched her store of food-stuffs.

"This is Anar Black," she told him, "all the way from Rhyinpine. Quite a journey for dead leaves to make. I think 'tis milder than Anar White, which comes from the same world but grows further down the mountain sides. I have some local honey if ye like your drink sweet. Expen-sive, it is. Moth's flowers are scarce save where they're grown in hothouses. This world belongs to the fungi and the trees; the bees, poor things, have a hard time of it, even those who've grown woolly coats thick enough to keep the damp and cold out. If honey's too thick for ye, I've other sweeteners."

Hearing no reply, she turned to find him lying still on the floor, a tawny, curled-up smudge of red hair and dirty old clothes. His hands were bunched beneath his cheek, cushioning his head.

She shook her head and pushed the cylinder's *off* but-ton. The pot sighed and ceased boiling. Bending, she got her wiry arms beneath him and lifted. Somehow she wrestled him onto the cot without waking him. Her hands pulled the thermal blanket up to his chin. It was pro-grammed and would warm him quickly.

She stood there awhile, amazed at how much pleasure could be gained from so simple an activity as watching a child sleep. Then, still wondering what had come over her, she left him and made her way across to her own room, slowly removing her clothes as she walked. Before long, the last light in the rear of the little shop winked out, joining its neighbors in nightfall. Then there was only the light wind and the hiss of moisture evaporating from warm walls to break the silence of the mist-shrouded dark.

Chapter Two

The boy ate as if the previous night's dinner had been no more substantial than a distant dream. She cooked him two full breakfasts and watched as he finished every bite. When the last pachnack was gone, and the final piece of bread wolfed down, she took him into the shop.

He watched intently as she entered the combination to the metal shutters. As they rose, they admitted a world entirely different from the empty night. One moment he was staring at the dully reflective line of metal strips. The next brought home to him all the noise, the confusion, and bustle and sights and smells of the great Drallarian marketplace; they flooded the stall, overwhelming him with their diversity and brilliance. Mother Mastiff was not a late sleeper—which was good, for the crowd would rise in tandem with the hidden sun. Not that the marketplace was ever completely deserted. There were always a few merchants whose wares benefited from the mask of night.

The boy could tell it was daytime because it had grown less dark. But the sun did not shine; it illuminated the raindrops. The morning had dawned warm, a good sign,

17

and the moisture was still more mist than rain. A good day for business.

Mother Mastiff showed the boy around the shop, describing various items and reciting their prices and the reasons behind such pricing. She hoped to someday entrust the operation of the business to him. That would be better than having to close up every time she needed to rest or travel elsewhere. The sooner he learned, the better, especially considering the way he ate.

"I'll do everything I can, Mother," he assured her when she had concluded the brief tour.

"I know ye will, boy." She plopped down into her favorite chair, an overupholstered monstrosity covered with gemmac fur. The skins were worn down next to nothing, and the chair retained little value, but it was too comfortable for her to part with. She watched as the boy turned to stare at the passing crowd. How quiet he is, she thought. Quiet and intense. She let him study the passersby for a while before beckoning him closer.

"We've overlooked several things in the rush of the night, boy. One in particular."

"What's that?" he asked.

"I can't keep calling ye 'boy'. Have ye a name?"

"They call me Flinx."

"Be that your last name or your first?"

He shook his head slowly, his expression unhappy. "Mother, I don't know. It's what they called me."

"What 'they' called ye. Who be 'they'? Your"—she hesitated—"mother? Your father?"

Again, the slow sad shake of the head, red curls dancing. "I don't have a mother or a father. It's what the people called me."

"What people?"

"The people who watched over me and the other children."

Now that was strange. She frowned. "Other children? Ye have brothers and sisters, then?"

"I don't"—he strained to remember—"I don't *think* so. Maybe they were. I don't know. They were just the other children. I remember them from the early time. It was a strange time."

"What was so strange about it?"

"I was happy."

She nodded once, as though she understood. "So. Ye remember an early time when you were happy and there were lots of other children living with you."

He nodded vigorously. "Boys and girls both. And we had everything we could want, everything we asked for. All kinds of good food and toys to play with and . . ."

A wealthy family brought to ruin, perhaps. She let him ramble on about the early time, the happy time, a while longer. What catastrophe had overtaken the boy in infancy?

"How big was this family?" she asked. "We'll call it your family for now. How many other boys and girls were there?"

"I don't remember exactly. Lots."

"Can you count?"

"Oh, sure," he said proudly. "Two, three, four, five, and lots more than that."

Sounded like more than just a family, though an extended family could not be ruled out, she knew. "Do ye remember what happened to them, and to you? Ye were all happy, and ye had lots of friends, and then something happened."

"The bad people came," he whispered, his expression turning down. "Very bad people. They broke into where we lived. The people who watched us and fed us and gave us toys fought the bad people. There was lots of noise and guns going off and—and people fell down all around me. Good people and bad people both. I stood and cried until somebody picked me up and carried me away. They carried me down lots of halls and dark places, and I remember getting into some kind of a—car?"

She nodded approvingly. "Probably. Go on, boy."

"I was moved around a lot. That was the end of the happy time."

"What happened after that?" she prompted him.

"I'm not sure," he said slowly. "It's so hard to remember."

"I know 'tis painful for ye, Flinx. I need to know all about ye that I can, so I can help ye as best as I'm able."

"If I tell you," he asked uncertainly, "you won't let the bad people come and take me away?"

"No," she said, her voice suddenly soft. "No, I won't let them come and take ye away, Flinx. I won't let *anyone* come and take ye away. Ever. I promise ye that."

He moved a little nearer and sat down on the extended leg support of the big chair. He had his eyes closed as he concentrated.

"I remember never staying in one place for very long at a time. The people, the good people who took care of me and fed me, they kept the bad people away. They were always upset about something, and they yelled at me a lot more than before."

"Were they mad at ye?"

"I don't think so. Not really." He licked his lips. "I think they were scared, Mother. I know I was, but I think they were, also. And then"—a look of confusion stole over his face—"I went to sleep. For a *long* time. Only, it wasn't really a sleep. It was like I was asleep and yet like I wasn't." He opened his eyes and looked up at her. "Do you understand that, Mother? I don't."

"No, I'm not sure I do, boy." Her mind worked. Now who, she wondered, would take the time and trouble to sedate a child for a long period of time? And why bother?

"Then some more bad people suddenly showed up, I think," he went on. "I didn't see them this time. But some of the people who watched me died or went away. Then there was just me and one man and one lady, and then they were gone, too."

"Your mother and father?"

"No, I don't think so," he told her. "Anyway, they never called themselves that. They were just two of the good people. Then some other people came and found me. People I'd never seen before. They took me away with them."

"Were they good people or bad people?"

"I don't think they were either," the boy replied carefully. "I think they were kind of in-between people. I think maybe they were sorry for me. They tried to be nice, but"—he shrugged—"they were just in-between people. They moved me around a lot again, and there were different places and lots of new children I didn't know, and then there was yesterday, and you bought me. Right?"

She put a hand to her mouth and coughed. "I didn't buy ye, actually. I agreed to take responsibility for ye."

"But you paid the government money for me, didn't you? I was told that was what was going to happen to me."

"It was only to pay off the debt the government incurred for taking care of ye," she explained to him. "I don't actually own ye. I would never do that."

"Oh," he said quietly. "That's nice. I'm glad." He waited a moment, watching her, then added, "That's everything I can remember."

"Ye did fine." She leaned forward and pointed to her right, up the street. The chair groaned. "If ye walk six stalls that way, ye'll find a very small shop run by a mur man. His name be Cheneth. Go up to him and tell him who ye be and where ye came from. And ye can buy from him"—she thought a moment, not wishing to overdo things—"a half credit's worth of whatever ye see in his shop."

"What kind of shop is it?" he asked excitedly.

"Candy," she said, enjoying the light that came into his face. "Ye remember what candy is, don't ye? I can see by the expression on your face that ye do." She could also tell by the speed with which he took off up the street. He was back before long, those deep emerald eyes shining from his dark face. "Thank you, Mother."

"Go on, go on, move to one side! You're blocking my—our—view of the customers. Wander about, learn the ins and outs of where ye live now."

He vanished like a ray of sunshine, his red hair disappearing into the crowd.

Expensive, she thought to herself. That boy's going to be expensive to raise. How by the ringaps did I ever let myself fall into this? She grumbled silently for another several minutes until a potential customer appeared.

Flinx learned rapidly. He was undemonstrative, highly adaptable, and so quiet she hardly knew when he was around. Soon he was amazing her with his knowledge of

the layout and workings of the marketplace and even the
greater city beyond. He worked constantly on expanding
his store of information, badgering shopkeepers with persistent questions, refusing to take "I don't know" for an
answer.

Mother Mastiff put no restrictions on him. No one had
ever told her it was improper to give an eight-year-old the
run of a city as wild as Drallar. Never having raised a
child before, she could always plead ignorance, and since
he returned dutifully every night, unscathed and unharmed,
she saw no reason to alter the practice despite the clucking
disapproval of some of her neighbors.

"That's no way to handle a boy of an age that tender,"
they admonished her. "If you're not careful, you'll lose
him. One night, he won't come home from these solo
forays."

"A boy he is, tender he's not," she would reply. "Sharp
he be, and not just for his age. I don't worry about him. I
haven't the time, for one thing. No matter what happens
to him, he's better off than he was under government
care."

"He won't be better off if he ends up lying dead in a
gutter somewhere," they warned her.

"He won't," she would reply confidently.

"You'll be sorry," they said. "You wait and see."

"I've been waiting and seeing going on ninety years"
was her standard reply, "and I haven't been surprised yet.
I don't expect this boy to break that record."

But she was wrong.

It was midafternoon. The morning mist had developed
into a heavy rain. She was debating whether or not to send
the boy out for some food or to wait. Half a dozen people
were wandering through the shop, waiting for the down-
pour to let up—an unusually large number for any day.

After a while, Flinx wandered over and tugged shyly at
her billowing skirt. "Mother Mastiff?"

"What is it, boy? Don't bother me now." She turned
back to the customer who was inspecting antique jewelry
that graced a locked display case near the rear of the stall.
It was rare that she sold a piece of the expensive stuff.
When she did, the profit was considerable.

The boy persisted, and she snapped at him. "I told ye, Flinx, not now!"

"It's very important, Mother."

She let out a sigh of exasperation and looked apologetically at the outworlder. "Excuse me a moment, good sir. Children, ye know."

The man smiled absently, thoroughly engrossed in a necklace that shone with odd pieces of metal and worn wood.

"What is it, Flinx?" she demanded, upset with him. "This better be important. You know how I don't like to be disturbed when I'm in the middle of—"

He interrupted her by pointing to the far end of the shop. "See that man over there?"

She looked up, past him. The man in question was bald and sported a well-trimmed beard and earrings. Instead of the light slickertic favored by the inhabitants of Moth, he wore a heavy offworld overcoat of black material. His features were slighter than his height warranted, and his mouth was almost delicate. Other than the earrings he showed no jewelry. His boots further marked him as an offworld visitor—they were relatively clean.

"I see him. What about him?"

"He's been stealing jewelry from the end case."

Mother Mastiff frowned. "Are you sure, boy?" Her tone was anxious. "He's an offworlder, and by the looks of him, a reasonably substantial one at that. If we accuse him falsely—"

"I'm positive, mother."

"You saw him steal?"

"No, I didn't exactly *see* him."

"Then what the devil"—she wondered in a low, accusatory voice—"are ye talking about?"

"Go look at the case," he urged her.

She hesitated, then shrugged mentally. "No harm in that, I expect." Now whatever had gotten into the boy? She strolled toward the case, affecting an air of unconcern. As she drew near, the outworlder turned and walked away, apparently unperturbed by her approach. He hardly acted like a nervous thief about to be caught in the act.

Then she was bending over the case. Sure enough, the

lock had been professionally picked. At least four rings, among the most valuable items in her modest stock, were missing. She hesitated only briefly before glancing down at Flinx.

"You're positive it was him, ye say?"

He nodded energetically.

Mother Mastiff put two fingers to her lips and let out a piercing whistle. Almost instantly, a half-dozen neighboring shopkeepers appeared. Still the bald man showed no hint of panic, simply stared curiously, along with the others in the store at the abrupt arrivals. The rain continued to pelt the street. Mother Mastiff raised a hand, pointed directly at the bald man, and said, "Restrain that thief!"

The man's eyes widened in surprise, but he made no move toward retreat. Immediately, several angry shopkeepers had him firmly by the arms. At least two of them were armed.

The bald man stood it for a moment or two, then angrily shook off his captors. His accent, when he spoke, marked him as a visitor from one of the softer worlds, like New Riviera or Centaurus B. "Now just a moment! What is going on here? I warn you, the next person who puts hands on me will suffer for it!"

"Don't threaten us, citizen," said Aljean, the accomplished clothier whose big shop dominated the far corner. "We'll settle this matter quick, and without the attention of police. We don't much like police on this street."

"I sympathize with you there," the man said, straightening his overcoat where he had been roughly handled. "I'm not especially fond of them myself." After a pause, he added in shock, "Surely that woman does not mean to imply that *I*—"

"That's what she's implyin', for sure," said one of the men flanking him. "If you've nothin' to fear, then you've no reason not to gift us a moment of your time."

"Certainly not. I don't see why—" The outworlder studied their expressions a moment, then shrugged. "Oh, well, if it will settle this foolishness."

"It'll settle it," another man said from behind a pistol.

"Very well. And I'll thank you to keep that weapon

pointed away from me, please. Surely you don't need the succor of technology in addition to superior numbers?"

The shopkeeper hesitated and then turned the muzzle of his gun downward. But he did not put it away.

Mother Mastiff stared at the man for a moment, then looked expectantly down at Flinx. "Well? Did ye see where he put the rings?"

Flinx was gazing steadily at the bald man, those green eyes unwinking. "No, I didn't, Mother. But he took them. I'm sure of it."

"Right, then." Her attention went back to the offworlder. "Sir, I must ask ye to consent to a brief body search."

"This is most undignified," he complained. "I shall lodge a complaint with my tourist office."

"I'm sorry," she told him, "but if you've nothing to hide, it's best that we're assured of it."

"Oh, very well. Please hurry and get it over with. I have other places to go today. I'm on holiday, you know."

Acting uncertainly now, two of the men who had responded to Mother Mastiff's whistle searched the visitor. They did a thorough job of it, working him over with the experience of those who had dealt with thieves before. They searched everything from the lining of his overcoat to the heels of his boots. When they had finished, they gazed helplessly over at Mother Mastiff and shook their heads.

"Empty he is," they assured her. "Nothing on him."

"What's missing, Mother?" Aljean asked gently.

"Kill rings," she explained. "The only four kill rings in my stock. Took me years to accumulate them, and I wouldn't know how to go about replacing them. Search him again." She nodded at the bald man. "They're not very big and would be easy enough to hide."

They complied, paying particular attention this time to the thick metal belt buckle the man wore. It revealed a hidden compartment containing the man's credcard and little else. No rings.

When the second search proved equally fruitless, Mother Mastiff gazed sternly down at her charge. "Well, Flinx, what have ye to say for yourself?"

"He *did* take them, he did," the boy insisted, almost crying. "I know he did." He was still staring at the bald man. Suddenly, his eyes widened. "He *swallowed* them."

"Swallowed—now just a minute," the visitor began. "This is getting ugly. Am I to wait here, accused by a mischievous child?" He shook an angry finger at Flinx, who did not flinch or break his cold, green stare.

"He took them," the boy repeated, "and swallowed them."

"Did you see me take these rings?" the bald man demanded.

"No," Flinx admitted, "I didn't. But you took them. You know you did. They're inside you."

"Charming, the experiences one has on the slumworlds," the man said sarcastically. "Really, though, this exercise has ceased to be entertaining. I must go. My tour allots me only two days in this *wonderful* city, and I wouldn't want to waste any more time observing quaint local customs. Out of the kindness of my nature, I will not call upon the gendarmes to arrest you all. One side, please." He shoved past the uncertain shopkeepers and walked easily out into the rain.

Mother Mastiff eyed the man's retreating back. Her friends and fellow merchants watched her expectantly, helplessly. She looked down at the boy. Flinx had stopped crying. His voice was calm and unemotional as he gazed back up at her.

"He took them, mother, and he's walking away with them *right now*."

She could not explain what motivated her as she calmly told Aljean, "Call a gendarme, then."

The bald man heard that, stopped, and turned back to face them through the now gentle rain. "Really, old woman, if you think I'm going to wait—"

"Aljean," Mother Mastiff said, "Cheneth?" The two shopkeepers exchanged a glance, then jogged out to bring the bald man back—if false restraint charges were filed, they would be against Mother Mastiff and not them.

"I'm sorry, sir," Cheneth, the candy man, said as he gestured with his pistol, "but we're going to have to ask you to wait until the authorities arrive."

"And then what? Are they going to haul a free citizen to the magistrate because a child demands it?"

"A simple body scan should be sufficient," Mother Mastiff said as the three re-entered the shop. "Surely you've no reason to object to that?"

"Of course I'd object to it!" the visitor responded. "They have no reason or right to—"

"My, but you're suddenly arguing a lot for someone with nothing to worry about," Aljean, the clothier, observed. She was forty-two years old and had run her way through four husbands. She was very adept at spotting lies, and she was suddenly less convinced of this visitor's innocence. "Of course, if perhaps you realize now that you've somehow made a bit of mistake and that we quaint locals aren't quite the simpletons you believe us to be, and if you'd rather avoid the inconvenience of a scan, not to mention official attention, you'll learn that we're agreeably forgiving here if you'll just return to Mother Mastiff what you've taken."

"I haven't taken a damn—" the bald man started to say.

"The jails of Drallar are very, very uncomfortable," Aljean continued briskly. "Our government resents spending money on public needs. They especially scrimp when it comes to the comfort of wrongdoers. You being an offworlder now, I don't think you'd take well to half a year of unfiltered underground dampness. Mold will sprout in your lungs, and your eyelids will mildew."

All of a sudden, the man seemed to slump in on himself. He glared down at Flinx, who stared quietly back at him.

"I don't know how the hell you saw me, boy. I swear, no one saw me! No one!"

"I'll be blessed over," Cheneth murmured, his jaw dropping as he looked from the thief to the boy who had caught him. "Then you did take the rings!"

"Ay. Call off the authorities," he said to Aljean "You've said it would be enough if I gave back the rings. I agree."

Mother Mastiff nodded slowly. "I agree, also, provided that ye promise never to show your reflective crown in this part of this marketplace ever again."

"My word on it, as a professional," the man promised

quickly. "I did not lie when I said that I was on holiday." He gave them a twisted smile. "I like to make my holidays self-supporting."

Mother Mastiff did not smile back. She held out a hand. "My kill rings, if ye please."

The man's smile twisted even further. "Soon enough. But first I will need certain edibles. There are several fruits which will suffice, or certain standard medications. I will also need clean cloths and disinfectant. The boy is right, you see. I did swallow them. Provide what I need and in an hour or so you will have your cursed rings back."

And forty minutes later she did.

After the thief and the little group of admiring shopkeepers had gone their respective ways, Mother Mastiff took her charge aside and confronted him with the question no one else had thought to ask.

"Now, boy, ye say ye didn't see him swallow the rings?"

"No, I didn't, Mother." Now that the crowd had dispersed and he had been vindicated, his shyness returned.

"Then how the ringap did ye know?"

Flinx hesitated.

"Come now, boy, out with it. Ye can tell me," she said in a coaxing tone. "I'm your mother now, remember. The only one you've got. I've been fair and straightforward with ye. Now 'tis your turn to do the same with me."

"You're sure?" He was fighting with himself, she saw. "You're sure you're not just being nice to me to fool me? You're not one of the bad people?"

That was a funny thing for him to bring up, she thought. "Of course I'm not one of them. Do I look like a bad people?"

"N-n-no," he admitted. "But it's hard to tell, sometimes."

"You've lived with me for some time now, boy. Ye know me better than that." Her voice became gentle again. "Come now. Fair is fair. So stop lying to me by insisting you didn't see him swallow those rings."

"I didn't," he said belligerently, "and I'm not lying. The man was—he was starting to walk away from the case, and he was uncomfortable. He was, he felt—what's the word? He felt guilty."

"Now how do ye know that?"

"Because," he murmured, not looking at her but staring out at the street where strange people scurried back and forth in the returning mist, "because I felt it." He put his small hand to his forehead and rubbed gently. "Here."

Great Ganwrath of the Flood, Mother Mastiff thought sharply. The boy's a Talent. "You mean," she asked again, "you read his mind?"

"No," he corrected her. "It's not like that. It's just—it's a feeling I get sometimes."

"Do ye get this feeling whenever ye look at someone who's been guilty?"

"It's not only guilty," he explained, "it's all kinds of feelings. People—it's like a fire. You can feel heat from a fire." She nodded slowly. "Well, I can feel certain things from people's heads. Happiness or fear or hate and lots of other things I'm not sure about. Like when a man and a woman are together."

"Can ye do this whenever ye wish?" she asked.

"No. Hardly ever. Lots of times I can't feel a thing. It's clean then and doesn't jump in on me, and I can relax. Then there's other times when the feeling will just be there—in here," he added, tapping his forehead again. "I was looking toward that man, and the guilt and worry poured out of him like a fire, especially whenever he looked at the jewel case. He was worried, too, about being discovered somehow and being caught, and a lot of other things, too. He was thinking, was throwing out thoughts of lots of quick money. Money he was going to get unfairly."

"Emotions," she mused aloud, "all emotions." She began to chuckle softly. She had heard of such things before. The boy was an empathic telepath, though a crude one. He could read other people's emotions, though not their actual thoughts.

"It's all right, Flinx," she assured him. She put out a hand and gave his hair a playful tousle. "Ye did right well. Ye saved me, saved us both, a lot of money." She looked over at the small leatherine purse that now held the four recovered and cleansed rings. They still smelled of disinfectant.

"No wonder that thief couldn't figure out how you'd spotted him. Ye really didn't see him take the rings."

"No, mother. I wasn't even sure what he'd taken."

"Ye just felt the reaction in his mind?"

"I guess," he said. "I—I don't know how it happens, but I know that most people can't do it, can they?"

"No," she said gently, "most other people can't. And sometimes they become very upset if they think there's someone around like ye who can."

Flinx nodded solemnly. "Like the bad people?"

"Maybe," she said, considering that possibility. "Maybe like the bad people, yes. Ye can't control the power, you're sure?"

"I'm sure. I've tried. Sometimes it's just there, a burning inside my head. But most of the time it's not."

She nodded. "That's too bad, too bad. Ye have what's called a Talent, Flinx."

"A Talent." He considered that a moment, then asked uncertainly, "Is it a good thing?"

"It can be. It can also be a dangerous thing, Flinx. We must make a secret of it, your secret and mine. Don't ever tell anyone else about it."

"I won't," he murmured, then added energetically, "I promise. Then you're not mad at me?"

"Mad?" She let out a long, rolling cackle. "Now how could I be mad with ye, boy? I've regained my jewelry, and you've gained quite a bit of respect among our neighbors. In the marketplace, that can be a tradable commodity, as ye may discover someday. They think you've a sharp eye and a sharper tongue. The reality be something more, though I wouldn't argue ye can cut words with the best of them. Keep your Talent to yourself. Remember, our secret."

"Our secret," he repeated solemnly.

"Can ye do anything else?" she asked him, trying not to sound eager. "Anything besides feeling what others be feeling?"

"I don't think so. Though sometimes it feels like—I don't know. It burns, and it makes me afraid. I don't know how it happens to me, or why."

"Don't trouble yourself about it, boy." She didn't press

the matter when she saw how it upset him. "There's nothing to be afraid of." She drew him close, held him next to her thin, warm frame.

"Ye utilize your mind and everything else ye own. That's what it all's been given to ye for. A Talent be no different from any other ability. If there be anything else ye want to try with yourself, ye go ahead and try it. 'Tis your body and brain and none other's."

Chapter Three

The couple came from Burley. Mother Mastiff could tell that by their rough accents and by the inordinate amount of gleaming metal jewelry they wore. They were handicraft hunting. The intricately worked burl of black caulderwood in Mother Mastiff's shop caught their attention immediately. It had been finely carved to show a panoramic view of a thoruped colony, one of many that infested Moth's northern-hemisphere continents. The carving ran the entire width of the burl, nearly two meters from end to end. It was a half meter thick and had been polished to a fine ebony glow.

It was a spectacular piece of work. Ordinarily, Mother Mastiff would not have considered parting with it, for it was the kind of showpiece that brought passers-by into the stall. But this couple wanted it desperately, and only the impossibly high price seemed to be holding them back.

Flinx wandered in off the street, picked at a pile of small bracelets, and watched while the man and woman argued. Quite suddenly, they reached a decision: they had to have the piece. It would complete their recreation room, and they would be the envy of all their friends. Hang the shipping cost, the insurance, and the price! They'd take it. And they did, though the amount on their credcard barely covered it. Two men came later that afternoon to pick up the object and deliver it to the hotel where the visitors were staying.

Later that night, after the shop had closed, after supper, Mother Mastiff said casually, "You know, boy, that couple who bought the caulderwood carving today?"

"Yes, Mother?"

"They must have been in and out of the shop half a dozen times before they made up their minds."

"That's interesting," Flinx said absently. He was seated in a corner studying a chip on his portable viewer. He was very diligent about that. She never thought of sending him to a formal school—rental chips had been good enough for her as a child, and they'd damn well be good enough for him.

"Yes," she continued. "They barely had the money for it. I pressed them, I backed off, I did everything I could think of to convince them of its worth once I saw that they were really serious about buying the thing. Every time, no matter what I said, they left the shop and went off arguing between themselves.

"Then ye put in an appearance and stood there and watched them, and lo-de-do-de, sudden-like, their sales resistance just crumpled up and went aflight. Be that not interesting?"

"Not really," he replied. "Doesn't that happen lots of times?"

"Not with an item as expensive as the caulderwood, it doesn't. It hardly ever happens that way. Now I don't suppose ye had anything to do with the sudden change of heart on the part of those two? 'Tis not likely ye sensed their hesitation and maybe did something to help them along?"

"Of course not, Mother." He looked away from his viewer in surprise. "I can't do anything like that."

"Oh," she murmured, disappointed. "Ye wouldn't be lying to me now, would ye, boy?"

He shook his head violently. "Why would I do a thing

like that? I'm just happy you made so much money on the sale. I'm always glad when you make money."

"Well, that be one thing we have in common, anyway," she said gruffly. "That's enough viewing for one night. You'll strain your young eyes. Be to bed, Flinx."

"All right, Mother." He walked over and bestowed the obligatory peck on her cheek before scurrying off to his own room. "G'night."

"Good night, boy."

She stayed awake in her own bedroom for a while, watching one of the rented entertainment chips on her own viewer. The show had been recorded on Evoria and benefited from the exotic location and the presence of thranx performers. It was late when she finally shut it off and readied herself for sleep. A quick shower, half an hour brushing out her hair, and she was able to slide with a sigh beneath the thermal blanket.

As she lay in the dark, waiting for sleep, a sudden disquieting thought stole into her mind. Why *would* the boy lie to her about such a possible ability?

He might do it, she thought, because if he could convince one couple to make an unwanted purchase, he probably could do it to others. And if he could do it to others, what about this past autumn when she had been hurrying past the government auction platform on her way across town, and something had brought her to a puzzling halt. Wasn't it possible that the purchase she had made then— the unwanted, inexplicable-to-this-day purchase that she had never looked at too closely—had been helped along its way by the mental nudging of the purchased? Why had she bought him? None of her friends could quite understand it either.

Disturbed, she slipped out of the bed and walked across the resting and eating space to the boy's room. A glance inside revealed him sleeping soundly beneath his cover, as innocent-looking a child as one could hope to set eyes upon. But now something else was there, too, something unseen and unpredictable that she could never be certain about. Never again would she be able to relax completely in the boy's presence.

Already she had forgotten her initial regrets and had begun to extend to him the love she had never before been able to give to his like. He was an endearing little twit and had been more than helpful around the shop. It was good to have such company in her old age. But for a while now, just for a while, she would pat and reassure him with one hand and keep the other close by a weapon. At least until she could be sure in her own mind that it still was her own mind she could be sure of.

Silly old fool, she thought as she turned back toward her own room. You've praised him for having a Talent, and now you're worried about it. You can't have it both ways. Besides, what need to fear a Talent its owner could not control? That confession of the boy's seemed truthful enough, to judge by his distress and bewilderment.

She was feeling easier by the time she slipped into her bed the second time. No, there was no reason to worry. It was interesting, his Talent, but if he couldn't control it, well, no need to be concerned.

Clearly, anyone unable to master such an ability would never amount to much, anyway.

"Haithness, Cruachan, come here!"

The woman seated before the computer screen had spent still another morning poring through reams of abstract data. She was trying to put together a chemical puzzle of considerable complexity. But that morning, as happens on rare occasions, an especially vital piece of the puzzle had unexpectedly fallen into place. Instead of a morass of figures and undisciplined graphics, the screen now beamed out an image of perfect symmetry.

The man who hurried over from the center of the room to glance over her shoulder was tall, the lines striping his face impressive. The dark-haired woman who joined him in staring at the screen was equally imposing.

The chamber in which the three of them worked was situated in a small, nondescript office building located in an unimportant city on a backwater world. For all that the equipment they hovered over had a cobbled-together appearance, most of it was still of a type requiring enormous expertise to operate and great expense to fund.

Both the knowledge and the money came from scattered,

seemingly unrelated locations throughout the Commonwealth. To the men and women who practically lived in the room, isolation was their honored burden, obscurity their most potent weapon. For they were members of a uniquely despised and persecuted minority, at war with the tenets of civilized society. Truly were their hearts pure and their purposes of noble mien—it was just their methodology that the rest of civilization questioned.

The three staring intently at the computer screen certainly did not look like candidates for such special attention. The tall man, Cruachan, had the look of a kindly grandfather; the oriental lady seated before the console would have seemed more at home in an ancient era, clad in flowing silks and wooden shoes. Only the tall black woman standing opposite Cruachan showed some of her inner hardness in her face.

That hardness and cold resolve lived in each of them, however, fostered and intensified by two decades of persecution. They saw themselves as men and women apart from the common herd. Their aim was nothing less than the improvement of mankind in spite of itself. That their methods might result in damage to the innocent was something they had known from the beginning. They had put that and other conventionally moral beliefs aside, believing that such sacrifices were necessary that the majority might benefit. They called their group the Meliorare Society, an innocent-sounding name drawn to mask the intention of improving humanity via the artificial manipulation of genetic material.

Their troubles began when several of their less successful experiments came to light, whereupon the outcry over the revelations had been enormous. Now they were compelled to work in scattered outposts instead of in a single research installation, always barely a jump ahead of pursuing government authorities. They were looked down upon and viewed with horror by the general populace.

Many of their associates had already vanished, having been discovered and taken into custody by the relentless minions of an ignorant officialdom: martyrs to science, the survivors knew—inhuman monsters, according to the media reports.

Of course, the aims of the Meliorare Society were dangerous! Improvement—change—was always viewed as dangerous by the shortsighted. The members had steeled themselves to that way of thinking, and it no longer affected them. What mattered were results, not the opinions of the ignorant masses.

So they did not fear dying, did not fear the even more horrible punishment of selective mindwipe, because they believed in the rightness of their cause. If only one of their experiments turned out successfully, it would vindicate the work propounded on Terra some forty years earlier by the Society's founder. Then they would be able to re-emerge into the scientific community that had disowned them. They would be able to point with pride to a mature, noticeably improved human being.

The air of excitement that pervaded the room was restrained but clearly felt as they gathered around the computer screen.

"This had better live up to its readout, Nyassa-lee," Cruachan warned. "I have half a volume of information to process from the Cannachanna system, and as you know, we're likely going to have to abandon this place and move on within the month. That means reset, breakdown of equipment, and all the difficulties moving entails."

"You know me better than that, Cruachan," said the woman seated in the chair. There was no feeling of triumph in what she had just done; they had progressed beyond such trivialities. "I've been feeding and cross-correlating records on dispersal and individual subject characteristics for months now. It's finally paid off. I've located Number Twelve."

The tall black woman leaned closer to the screen. "Number Twelve—that sticks in the mind. Male, wasn't it?"

Nyassa-lee nodded and indicated the screen. "Here, I'll run the relevants back for you."

They refamiliarized themselves with the details of the case in question. It had been eight years since case interdiction. In the eight years since, they had encountered a number of other subjects. Most of them had grown into normal childhood. A few had even displayed tiny flashes of promise, but nothing worth a full-scale follow-up.

Then there had been those whose minds and bodies had been horribly distorted and twisted by the original surgical manipulations, for which they each shared the blame. Unfortunate failures such as those had been made public by the government and had raised such an emotional outcry among the scientifically unsophisticated public that the government had been able to legalize its witch hunt against the Society.

Most of the subject children had been recovered by the government, raised in special homes, and restored to normality. Where possible, the genetic alterations performed by the Society's surgeons had been corrected to enable all the children to live a normal life.

If we cannot improve upon the normal, thought Haithness, then we do not deserve to explore and master the universe. Nature helps those who help themselves. Why should we not employ our learning and knowledge to give evolution a boost?

From the far corner of the darkened room, a man called out. "Brora reports that a government shuttle has landed at Calaroom shuttleport."

"Could be the usual load of agricultural specialists," Cruachan said thoughtfully.

"Possible," agreed the individual manning the communications console, "but can we afford that risk?"

"I hate to order evacuation on such slim evidence. Any word on how many passengers?"

"Hard to say," the man ventured, listening intently to his receiver. "Brora says at least a dozen he doesn't recognize."

"That's a lot of agricultural specialists, Cruachan," Haithness pointed out.

"It is." He called across to the communications specialist. "Tell Brora to pull back and prepare for departure. We can't take chances. Push evac time from a month to tonight."

"Tonight?" The voice of the communicator had a dubious ring. "I won't have half the equipment broken down by then."

"New communications equipment we can buy," Cruachan reminded him. "Replacements for ourselves are not available."

The man at the com console nodded and turned back to his station, speaking softly and hurriedly into the pickup. Cruachan returned his attention to the computer screen.

Information emerged. NUMBER TWELVE. MALE. PHYSICALLY UNDISTINGUISHED AS A CHILD. Next were descriptions of cerebral index and figures for cortical energy displacement.

Oh, yes; Cruachan remembered now. Unpredictable, that Number Twelve. Patterns in brain activity suggesting paranormal activity but nothing concrete. Particularly fascinating had been the amount of activity emerging from the left side of the cerebrum, usually detected only in females. That by itself was not reason enough for excitement, but there was also continuous signs of functioning in at least two sections of brain that were not normally active, the "dead" areas of the mind. That activity, like the child himself, had also been unpredictable.

And yet, despite such encouraging evidence, the case history of Number Twelve was devoid of the usual promising developments. No hint of telepathy, psychokinesis, pyrokinesis, dual displacement, or any of the other multitude of abilities the Society had hoped to bring to full flower in its experimental children.

Still, Number Twelve at least exhibited a possible something.

"Well, this one certainly shows more promise than the last dozen or so," Haithness had to admit. "It's been so long since we had contact with him, I'd nearly forgotten those activity readings. We need to get to this one as quickly as possible. Where's he situated?"

Nyassa-lee tapped keys below the readout, bringing forth answers. "Where in the Commonwealth is that?" Haithness grumbled.

"Trading world," Cruachan put in, thinking hard. "Centrally located but unimportant in and of itself. A stopover world, low in native population."

"You won't mind going there once you've seen this," Nyassa-lee assured them both. Her fingers moved delicately over the keyboard a second time, and fresh information glowed on screen. "This is recent, from the local operative who relocated the subject. It appears that the child has definitely displayed one Talent, possibly two. Furthermore, he has done so in public and apparently without any specialized training."

"Without training," Cruachan whispered. "Remarkable, if true."

Nyassa-lee tapped the screen. "This operative has been reliable in the past and particularly noteworthy for the accuracy of his observations. The Talent in question is a telepathic variant of some sort. The operative is not a scientifically trained observer, of course, and he is even less certain of the second one, though its potential value may be even greater."

"What is it?" Haithness asked.

"I've been hard put to find a name for it. Basically, it seems that the child may be an emolterator."

The other woman looked confused. "I don't remember that on the list of possible Talents."

"It wasn't there. It's an original. Original with this child, it seems," Cruachan said. Nyassa-lee nodded. "It means that he may be able to influence the actions of others. Not mind control, nothing as strong as that. It would be more subtle. One possessing such an ability would have to utilize it very carefully. If this report is true . . ." His voice and thoughts drifted for a moment as he studied the readout.

"It seems the child's Talents have gone unnoticed by the authorities and that he has developed naturally. All without even the most rudimentary training. The signs certainly point to powerful potentials waiting to be unlocked."

"Either the child has grown up unaware of these Talents," Nyassa-lee said, studying new information as it appeared on the screen, "or else he is precociously clever."

"It may be just natural caution," Haithness put in. "It will be interesting to find out which is the case."

"Which we will do," Cruachan said firmly. "It's been a long time since we've had a subject as promising as this one come back to us. He could be the one we've searched for all these years."

"It had better not be a repeat of the last time we located a subject with these figures," Haithness cautioned, then indicated the new figures materializing on the screen. "Look at those neurological potentials. Remember the only other child who showed numbers like that?"

"Of course, I remember," Cruachan said irritably. "We won't lose this one the way we lost that girl—what the devil was the little monster's name?"

"Mahnahmi," Nyassa-lee reminded him. "Yes, if this boy's anything like that one, we're going to have to be extremely careful. I couldn't take a repeat of that experience."

"Neither could I, frankly," Cruachan admitted. "Our mistake was in trying to regain control over her directly. End result: the girl vanishes again, and two more of the society go to a premature end. And we're still not sure how she accomplished it."

"We'll run across her again someday, when our methods are improved," Haithness said coolly. "Then we'll deal with her properly."

"I'm not sure I'd want to chance it." Nyassa-lee looked back at the screen. "Meanwhile, it would be good to keep in mind the fact that the potential of this Number Twelve theoretically exceeds even that of the girl."

"True," Cruachan admitted, studying the figures, "but it's clear that his development has been much slower. We should have plenty of time to cope with any maturing Talent and make certain it is safely contained, for the child's benefit as well as our own, of course."

"Of course," Haithness agreed calmly. "I am curious to know how you propose to accomplish that. You know how volatile a Talent can become if stressed."

"Yes, the girl gave us an impressive demonstration of that, didn't she?" Nyassa-lee's fingers brought forth fresh information from the console.

Another call sounded from across the room. "Brora says he's now convinced that the new arrivals at the port have nothing to do with the agricultural station. They have not stopped by the Agri section of government house; they are gathering instead in the subterranean quarter."

"Tell Brora to speed things up," Cruachan replied. "I definitely want the installation broken down by midnight."

"Yes, sir," the communicator responded briskly.

"You didn't answer my question," Haithness reminded the tall man. "How are we going to handle this one? If we try direct control as we did with the girl, we risk the same consequences. There is no way of predicting how a subject may react."

"Remember that the girl was still in infancy when we encountered her. We wrongly mistook her age for harmlessness. There was no reason to appeal to in her case— she was too young. I never expected that to work against us."

"It doesn't matter. The important thing is that he is still unskilled in the use of his Talent. That is also what makes him dangerous." Haithness indicated the figures on the screen. "Look at those. Undisciplined or not, we must handle this Number Twelve with extreme caution. We need a check of some kind, something strong enough to mute any juvenile emotional reactions."

Nyassa-lee glanced back and up at her colleague. "But we cannot wait."

"I agree with you there. This may be our last chance to gain control and direction over a subject with such potential. We don't want to waste our chance."

"I am aware of the considerations and risks," Cruachan assured them both. "I do not intend that we should try, as we did with the girl, to gain control directly. Instead, we will try to obtain control over someone who exercises control over the subject. Is there anyone who fits the requisite pattern?"

Nyassa-lee turned back to her keyboard. There was a pause before she replied, "One. It appears that the subject was purchased from government control by an elderly woman. She has raised the boy as her own."

"Surrogate mother," Haithness murmured. "That's good. It is virtually made to order. We could not hope for a stronger emotional bond."

There was no warmth in the voice of Haithness. Only one thing mattered to her: the success of the experiment.

Time was running out for the Society, she knew; they had no way of knowing when the authorities might close in on them forever. They needed a success *now,* and this boy might be their last chance.

"I see one possible drawback," Cruachan said while pondering the information glowing on the screen. "The woman in question, the surrogate mother, is of an advanced age, though apparently healthy." He nudged Nyassa-lee, who obediently made room for him on the edge of the chair.

Cruachan fingered controls and frowned when the information he sought did not appear on the screen. "No detailed medical information on her. It could be difficult."

Haithness shrugged indifferently. "It does not matter what her condition is. We have to proceed regardless."

"I know, I know," Cruachan replied impatiently. "Our course is set, then. We will not go from here to Loser's World in hopes of relocating subject Number Fifty-six. Instead, we will establish standard mobile operations aboard the ship. Once we are certain we have escaped pursuit, we will plot course for this Moth. Then we should have enough time to proceed as planned."

"It will be necessary to isolate the subject from the mother." Haithness was thinking out loud. "Given the nature of the subject's observed Talents, if our information is accurate, it may be that within a limited geographical area he might be able to trace our activities. We will naturally need an uninterrupted period with the surrogate," she hesitated only briefly, "to persuade her to cooperate with us." A thin smile did little to alter her expression.

Cruachan nodded. "That should not be difficult to arrange. Fortunately for us, Moth is lightly populated. Technology is not unknown, but the level varies widely according to location. We should be able to establish ourselves and the necessary equipment at a sufficient distance from the metropolis where the subject and his parent are living to ensure our privacy and standard security."

The communicator turned from his instrumentation and interrupted them without hesitation. "Brora reports that at least half of the newly arrived agricultural experts are armed."

"That's that, then," Cruachan murmured with a resigned sigh. Another hurried move, another dash to still another strange world.

"Nyassa-lee, make certain that this information is transferred to ship storage. Haithness, you—"

"I know what needs to be done, Cruachan." She turned from him and calmly began transferring data from main storage to a portacube.

The communicator leaned back in his chair and frowned at his instruments. "I won't have time to break down much and move it out to the shuttle."

"It doesn't matter, Osteen," Cruachan assured him. "We have some duplicate equipment already aboard. I don't like abandoning more than we have to any more than you do." He indicated the expensive electronics with which the room had been paneled. "But we don't have a choice now. Regardless, something promising, truly promising, has come to our notice. After all these years, it appears that we have relocated one of the most promising of all the subject children."

"That's good news indeed, sir." Osteen was one of the few young men in the Meliorare Society. Cruachan would have prefered a man with more vision as prime communicator, but such individuals were scarce. Osteen at least was loyal and efficient. It was not his fault that he was intellectually inferior to the Society's original membership. But then, such a collection of visionary minds was not likely to join together again in Cruachan's lifetime, he knew.

Unless . . . unless the Society could put forth a shining testament to their noble ideals in the person of a single successful subject. This boy, perhaps, might be their vindication. They had to get to him quickly. During the past several years, they had had less and less time in which to work as the Commonwealth closed in on the remnants of the Society. Their survival rate did not bode well for the future: natural attrition was beginning to damage the cause as much as government interference.

The three of them, along with the sharp-eyed Brora, who had sounded the latest warning, represented the largest surviving group from the original membership. The trust of all who had perished devolved upon them, Cruachan thought. They must not fail with this boy.

And he must not fail them.

Chapter Four

Loneliness had never bothered Flinx before. He knew what it was, of course—the condition had been with him all his short life. In the past, he'd always been able to distance himself from its pain, but this feeling—this empty aloneness—was different from any loneliness he'd ever experienced before. It was a physical reality, stabbing at him, creating an ache in a mysterious, new part of his brain. It was different not only from his own loneliness but from the aloneness he'd occasionally sensed in others via his unpredictable Talent.

In fact, the experience was so radically new that he had nothing to compare it with. Yet it *was* loneliness; of that he was certain. Loneliness and something else equally intense and recognizable: hunger. A gnawing, persistent desire for food.

The feelings were so bright and uncomplicated that Flinx couldn't help but wonder at their source. They beat insistently on his mind, refusing to fade away. Never before had such emotions been so open to him, so clear and strong. Normally, they would begin to fade, but these grew not weaker but stronger—and he did not have to strain to hold them at bay. They kept hammering at him until his mind finally gave in and woke him up.

Flinx rubbed at his eyes. It was pouring outside the shop, and the narrow window over the bed admitted the dim light of Moth's multiple moons, which somehow seeped through the nearly unbroken cloud cover. Flinx had rarely seen the bright rust-red moon called Flame or its smaller companions, but he'd spent his years of study well, and he knew where the light came from.

Slipping silently from the bed, he stood up and pulled on pants and shirt. A glow light bathed the kitchen and dining area in soft yellow. Across the way, ragged snores came from the vicinity of Mother Mastiff's bedroom. The loneliness he sensed was not hers.

The feeling persisted into wakefulness. Not a dream, then, which had been his first thought. The back of his head hurt with the strength of it, but though the actual pain was beginning to fade, the emotion was still as strong as it had been in sleep.

He did not wake Mother Mastiff as he inspected the rest of the kitchen area, the bathroom, and the single narrow closet. Quietly, he opened the front door and slipped out into the stall. The shutters were locked tight, keeping out weather and intruders alike. The familiar snoring provided a comforting background to his prowling.

Flinx had grown into a lithe young man of slightly less than average height and mildly attractive appearance. His hair was red as ever, but his dark skin now hid any suggestion of freckles. He moved with a gracefulness and silence that many of the older, more experienced marketplace thieves might have envied. Indeed, he could walk across a room paved with broken glass and metal without making a sound. It was a technique he had picked up from some of Drallar's less reputable citizens, much to Mother Mastiff's chagrin. All a part of his education, he had assured her. The thieves had a word for it: "skeoding," meaning to walk like a shadow. Only Flinx's brighter than normal hair made the professional purloiners cluck their tongues in disapproval. They would have welcomed him into their company, had he been of a mind to make thievery his profession. But Flinx would steal only if absolutely necessary, and then only from those who could afford it.

"I only want to use my ability to supplement my income," he had told the old master who had inquired about his future intentions, "and Mother Mastiff's, of course."

The master had laughed, showing broken teeth. "I understand, boy. I've been supplementin' my income in that manner goin' on fifty years now." He and his colleagues could not believe that one who showed such skill at relieving others of their possessions would not desire to make a career of it, especially since the youth's other prospects appeared dim.

"Yer goin' into the Church, I suppose?" one of the other thieves had taunted him, "t'become a Counselor First?"

"I don't think the spiritual life is for me," Flinx had replied. They all had a good laugh at that.

As he quietly opened the lock on the outside door, he thought back to what he had learned those past few years. A wise man did not move around Drallar late at night, particularly on so wet and dark a one. But he couldn't go back to sleep without locating the source of the feelings that battered at him. Loneliness and hunger, hunger and loneliness, filled his mind with restlessness. Who could possibly be broadcasting twin deprivations of such power?

The open doorway revealed a wall of rain. The angled street carried the water away to Drallar's efficient underground drainage system. Flinx stood in the gap for a long moment, watching. Suddenly an intense burst of emptiness made him wince. That decided him. He could no more ignore that hot pleading than he could leave an unstamped credcard lying orphaned in the street.

"That curiosity of yours will get ye into real trouble someday, boy," Mother Mastiff had told him on more than one occasion. "Mark me word."

Well, he had marked her word. Marked it and filed it. He turned away from the door and skeoded back to his little room. It was early summer, and the rain outside was relatively warm. Disdaining an underjacket, he took a slickertic from its wall hook and donned it; thus suitably shielded from the rain, he made his way back to the stall, out into the street, and closed the main door softly behind him.

A few lights like hibernating will-o'-the-wisps glowed faintly from behind unshuttered shop fronts on the main avenue where the idling wealthy night-cavorted in relative safety. On the side street where Mother Mastiff plied her trade, only a rare flicker of illumination emerged from behind locked shutters and windows.

As water cascaded off his shoulders, Flinx stood there and searched his mind. Something sent him off to his right. There was a narrow gap between Mother Mastiff's shop and that of old lady Marquin, who was on vacation in the south, and by turning sideways, he could just squeeze through.

Then he was standing in the service alleyway that ran behind the shops and a large office building. His eyes roved over a lunar landscape of uncollected garbage and refuse: old plastic packing crates, metal storage barrels, honeycomb containers for breakables, and other indifferently disposed of detritus. A couple of fleurms scurried away from his boots. Flinx watched them warily. He was not squeamish where the omnipresent fleurms were concerned, but he had a healthy respect for them. The critters were covered in a thick, silvery fur, and their little mouths were full of fine teeth. Each animal was as big around as Flinx's thumb and as long as his forearm. They were not really worms but legless mammals that did very well in the refuse piles and composting garbage that filled the alleys of Drallar to overflowing. He had heard horror stories of old men and women who had fallen into a drunken stupor in such places—only their exposed bones remained for the finding.

Flinx, however, was not drunk. The fleurms could inflict nasty bites, but they were shy creatures, nearly blind, and greatly preferred to relinquish the right of way when given the choice.

If it was dark on the street in front of the shop, it was positively stygian in the alley. To the east, far up the straightaway, he could make out a light and hear intermittent laughter. An odd night for a party. But the glow gave him a reference point, even if it was too far off to shed any light on his search.

The continuing surge of loneliness that he felt did not come from that distant celebration, nor did it rise from the heavily shuttered and barred doorways that opened onto the alley. The emotions Flinx was absorbing came from somewhere very near.

He moved forward, picking his way between the piles of debris, taking his time so as to give the fleurms and the red-blue carrion bugs time to scurry from his path.

All at once something struck with unexpected force at his receptive mind. The mental blow sent him to his knees. Somewhere a man was beating his wife. No unique circumstance, that, but Flinx felt it from the other side of the city. The woman was frightened and angry. She was reaching for the tiny dart gun she kept hidden in her bedroom dresser and was pointing its minuscule barrel at the man. Then it was the husband's turn to be frightened. He was pleading with her, not in words that Flinx could hear but via an emotional avalanche that ended in an abrupt, nonverbal scream of shock. Then came the emptiness that Flinx had grown to recognize as death.

He heard laughter, not from the party up the alley but from one of the lofty crystal towers that reared above the wealthy inurbs where the traders and transspatial merchants made their homes. And there was plotting afoot; someone was going to be cheated.

Far beyond the city boundaries in the forest to the west: happiness and rejoicing, accompanied by a new liquid sensation of emergence. A baby was born.

Very near, perhaps in one of the shops on Mother Mastiff's own street, an argument was raging. It involved accounts and falsification, waves of acrimonious resentment passing between short-term partners. Then the private grumblings of someone unknown and far away across the city center, someone plotting to kill, and kill more than one time, but plotting only—the kind of fantasizing that fills spare moments of every human brain, be it healthy or sick.

Then all the sensations were gone, all of them, the joyful and the doomed, the debaters and lovers and ineffectual dreamers. There was only the rain.

Blinking, he staggered to his feet and stood swaying unsteadily on the slope of the alley. Rain spattered off his slickertic, wove its way down the walls of the shops and the office building, to gurgle down the central drains. Flinx found himself staring blankly up the alley toward the distant point of light that marked the location of the party. Abruptly, the emotions of everyone at the party were sharp in his mind; only now he felt no pain. There was only a calm clarity and assurance.

He could see this woman anxiously yet uncertainly trying to tempt that man, see another criticizing the furniture, still another wondering how he could possibly live through the next day, feel laughter, fear, pleasure, lust, admiration, envy: the whole gamut of human emotions. They began to surge toward him like the storm he had just weathered, threatening the pain again, threatening to overwhelm him—

STOP IT, he ordered himself. Stop it—easy.

By careful manipulation of a piece of his mind he hadn't even been aware existed before, he discovered he was able to control the intensity of the emotions that threatened to drown him—not all of which had been human, either. He had felt at least two that were bizarre, yet recognizable enough for him to identify. They were the feelings of a mated pair of ornithorpes. It was the first time he had sensed anything from a nonhuman.

Slowly, he found he was able to regulate the assault, to damp it down to where he could manage it, sort out the individual feelings, choose, analyze—and then they were gone as suddenly as they had struck, along with all the rest of the blaze of emotion he had sucked in from around the city.

Hesitantly, he tried to focus his mind and bring back the sensations. It was as before. Try as he might, his mind stayed empty of any feelings save his own. His own—and one other. The loneliness was still there, nagging at him. The feeling was less demanding now, almost hesitant. The hunger was there, too.

Flinx took a step forward, another, a third—and something alive quickly scuttled out of his path, shoving aside empty containers and cans, plastic and metal clinking in the damp alley. He strained to see through the dimness, wishing now that he had had the presence of mind to bring a portable light from the shop. He took a cautious step toward the pile, ready to jump up and clear should the fleurms or whatever prove unexpectedly aggressive.

It was not a fleurm. For one thing, it was too long: nearly a meter. It was thicker, too, though not by much. He thought of the snakelike creatures that roamed the temperate forests to the south of Drallar. Some of them were poisonous. Occasionally, they and other forest predators made their way into the city under cover of rain and darkness to hunt out the small creatures that infested the urban trash heaps. It was rare, but not unheard of, that a citizen encountered such an intruder.

Flinx leaned close to the pile, and as he did so the hunger faded. Simultaneously, the feeling of loneliness intensified; the strength of it almost sent him reeling back against the shop wall. He was certain it came from the snakelike unknown.

The bump of curiosity—which Mother Mastiff was at such pains to warn him about—quickly overcame his natural caution. All he felt was amazement that such powerful mental projections could arise from so lowly a creature. Furthermore, there was no anger in the animal, no rudimentary danger signals. Only that persistent loneliness and the fleeting sense of hunger.

The creature moved again. He could see the bright, flashing red eyes even in the alley's faint light. Not a true reptile, he was sure. A cold-blooded creature would have been reduced to lethargy by the cool night air. This thing moved too rapidly.

Flinx took a step back, away from the pile. The creature was emerging. It slithered onto the wet pavement and then did something he did not expect. Snakes were not supposed to fly.

The pleated wings were blue and pink, bright enough for him to identify even in the darkness. No, the snake-thing certainly was not lethargic, for its wings moved in a blur, giving the creature the sound and appearance of a gigantic bee. It found a place on his shoulder in a single, darting movement. Flinx felt thin, muscular coils settle almost familiarly around his shoulder. The whole thing had happened too fast for him to dodge.

But the creature's intent was not to harm. It simply sat, resting against his warmth, and made no move to attack. The speed of the approach had paralyzed Flinx, but only for a moment. For as soon as it had settled against him, all that vast loneliness, every iota of that burning need had fled from the snake. At the same time, Flinx experienced a clarity within his own mind that he had never felt before. Whatever the creature was, wherever it had come from, it not only had the ability to make itself at home, it seemed to make its new host feel comfortable as well.

A new sensation entered Flinx's mind, rising from the snake. It was the first time he had ever experienced a mental purr. He sensed no intelligence in the creature, but there *was* something else. In its own way, the empathic communication was as clear as speech, the emotional equivalent of an ancient Chinese ideograph—a whole series of complex thoughts expressed as a single projection. Simple, yet efficient.

The small arrowhead-shaped head lifted from Flinx's shoulder, its bright little eyes regarding him intently. The pleated wings were folded flat against the side of the body, giving the creature a normal snakelike appearance. Flinx stared back, letting his own feelings pour from him.

Slowly, the creature relaxed. The single long coiled muscle of itself, which had been squeezing Flinx's shoulder with instinctive strength, relaxed, too, until it was only maintaining a gentle grip, just enough to hold its position. Pins and needles started to run down Flinx's arm. He ignored them. The animal's head lowered until it moved up against Flinx's neck.

The snake was sound asleep.

Flinx stood there for what felt like an eternity, though surely it was not even half that long. The strange apparition that the night had brought slept on his shoulder, its small head nestled in the hollow of shoulder bone and neck tendon. The animal shivered once. Flinx knew it could not be drawing full warmth from his body because the slickertic formed a layer between them. Better to get the poor thing inside, he thought, suddenly aware of how long he had been standing there in the rain. His new companion needed rest as well as warmth. How he knew that, he could not have explained; but he knew it as clearly as he recognized his own exhaustion.

Flinx did not for a moment debate the snake's future. Its presence on his shoulder as well as in his mind was too natural for him to consider parting with it—unless, of course, some owner appeared to claim it. Clearly, this was no wild animal. Also, Flinx was well-read, and if this creature was native to the Drallarian vicinity, it was news to him. He had never seen or heard of such an animal before. If it was some kind of valuable pet, its owner would surely come looking for it, and soon. For now, though, the snake was clearly as much an orphan as Flinx himself had once been. Flinx had experienced too much suffering in his own life to ignore it in anything else, even in a lowly snake. For a while, it was his charge, much as he was Mother Mastiff's.

She had wanted to know his name on that first day long ago. "What do I call you?" he wondered aloud. The sleeping snake did not respond.

There were thousands of books available to Flinx via the library chips he rented from Central Education. He had only read a comparative few, but among them was one with which he had particularly identified. It was pre-Commonwealth—precivilization, really—but that hadn't mitigated its impact on him. Those characters with the funny names; one of them was called—what? Pip, he remembered. He glanced back down at the sleeping snake. That'll be your name unless we learn otherwise one day.

As he started back for the shop, he tried to tell himself that he would worry about that proverbial "one day" if and when it presented itself, but he could not. He was already worried about it, because although he had only had contact with the creature for less than an hour, it seemed a part of him. The thought of returning the snake to some indifferent, offworld owner was suddenly more than he could bear. Since he had been an infant, he couldn't recall becoming so deeply attached to another living creature. Not even Mother Mastiff had such a lock on his feelings.

Feelings. This creature, this snake-thing, it *understood* what he was feeling, understood what it meant to have the emotions of strangers flood unbidden into one's mind, interrupting one's life and making every waking moment a potential abnormality. That was what made it special. He knew it, and the snake knew it, too. No longer were they individuals; they had become two components of a larger whole.

I will not give you up, he decided then and there in the cold morning rain. Not even if some wealthy, fatuous offworlder appears to lay claim to you. You belong with me. The snake dozed on, seemingly oblivious to any decisions the human might make.

The street fronting the shop was still deserted. The lock yielded to his palm, and he slipped inside, glad to be out of the weather. Carefully, he relocked the door. Then he was back in the dining area where the glow light still shone softly. Using both hands, he unraveled the snake. It did not resist as he slid the coils from his shoulder. From the bedroom to his right came Mother Mastiff's steady snores, a drone that matched the patter of rain on the roof.

Gently, he set the snake down on the single table. In the glow lamp's brighter light he could see its true colors for the first time. A bright pink and blue diamondback pattern ran the length of the snake's body, matching the pleated wings. The belly was a dull golden hue and the head emerald green.

"Exquisite," he murmured to the snake. "You're exquisite."

The creature's eyes—no, he corrected himself, Pip's eyes—opened in lazy half sleep. It seemed to smile at him. Mental projection, Flinx thought as he slipped out of the slickertic and hung it on its hook.

"Now where can I keep you?" he whispered to himself as he glanced around the small living area. The stall out front was out of the question. Mother Mastiff surely had customers suffering from snake phobias, and they might not take kindly to Pip's presence—besides, the stall was unheated. By the same token, he didn't think Mother Mastiff would react with understanding if the snake playfully sprang out at her from one of the kitchen storage cabinets while she was trying to prepare a meal.

His own room was spartan: There was only the small computer terminal and chip readout, the single clothes closet he had rigged himself, and the bed. The closet would have to do. Carrying the snake into his room, Flinx set it down on the foot of the bed. Then he made a pile of some dirty clothes on the closet floor. Pip looked clean enough; most scaled creatures were dirt-shedders, not collectors. He lifted the snake and set it down gently in the clothes, careful not to bruise the delicate wings. It recoiled itself there, seemingly content. Flinx smiled at it. He didn't smile often.

"Now you stay there, Pip," he whispered, "and in the morning we'll see about scrounging something for you to eat." He watched the snake for several minutes before fatigue returned with a rush. Yawning, he pushed his own clothes off the bed, set his boots on the drypad, and climbed back into bed. A few droplets of water had crawled under the edge of the slickertic. He brushed them from his hair, sighed deeply, and lapsed into a rich, undisturbed sleep.

Once the flow of mental energy from the human in the bed had smoothed out and the snake was certain its new symbiote was not about to enter a disturbing REM period, it quietly uncoiled itself and slithered out of the closet. Silently, it worked its way up one of the bed legs, emerging next to the single battered pillow.

The animal rested there for a long moment, gazing through double lidded eyes at the unconscious biped. Inside itself, the snake was warm and comfortable. The hunger was still there, but it had received an indication of sorts that it would soon be fed.

The bed was very warm, both the thermal blanket and the symbiote's mass exuding comfortable, dry heat. The snake slithered across the pillow until it was resting against the back of the human's head. It stretched itself once, the wings flexing and retracting. Then it coiled itself tightly into the convenient pocket formed by the symbiote's neck and shoulder. Soon its own brain waves matched those of the human as it drifted into its own variety of sleep.

Chapter Five

Mother Mastiff was careful not to wake the boy as she slowly began backing out of his room. Her eyes, alert and fearful, remained fixed on the alien thing curled up against his head. There was no telling what it might do if startled into wakefulness.

How the invader had penetrated her tight little home, she had no idea. No time to worry about that now. Her thoughts went to the little gun, the delicate, ladylike needler she kept under her pillow. No, too chancy—the snake was much too close to the boy's head, and she was not as good a shot as she had been twenty years ago.

There was also the possibility the invader might not even be dangerous. She certainly did not recognize it. In the ninety plus years she had spent on Moth, she had seen nothing like it. For one thing, there was no hint of fur anywhere on its body. Only scales. That immediately identified it as a non-native. Well, maybe. Moth was home to a few creatures—deep-digging burrowers—that did not sport fur. This didn't look like a burrower to her, but she was no zoologist, nor had she ever traveled far outside the city limits.

Yet she felt certain it came from offworld. Something she couldn't put a mental finger on marked the beast as alien, but that didn't matter. What did was that it had somehow penetrated to the boy's room, and she had better do something about it before it woke up and decided the matter for her.

Get it away from him, she told herself. Away from his head, at least. Get it away, keep it occupied, then wake the boy and have him make a run for the gun under her pillow.

The broom she hefted had a light metal handle and wire bristles. Taking it out of storage, she re-entered Flinx's room and reached past his head with the broom's business end. The metal bristles prodded the invader.

The snake stirred at the touch, opened its eyes, and stared at her. She jabbed at it again, harder this time, trying to work the bristles between the snake's head and the boy's exposed neck. It opened its mouth, and she instinctively jerked back, but it was only a yawn. Still sleepy, then, she thought. Good, its reactions would be slowed. Leaning forward again, she reached down and shoved hard on the broom. Several of the snake's coils went rolling over to the side of the bed, and for the first time she had a glimpse of its brilliant coloring.

Again, she shoved with the broom, but the snake was no longer on the bed. It hovered in midair, its wings moving so rapidly they were no more than a blue-pink blur. They generated a rich, vibrant humming sound in the small room. Aghast and uncertain how to attack this new threat, Mother Mastiff backed away, holding the broom defensively in front of her. Awakened by the last shove of the broom, the boy blinked sleepily at her. "Mother? What is it?"

"Hush, be quiet!" she warned him. "I don't know how this thing got into your room, but—"

Flinx sat up quickly. He glanced up at the hovering snake, admiring it for the first time in daylight, and bestowed a reassuring grin on Mother Mastiff.

"Oh, that. That's just Pip."

The broom dipped slightly, and she stared narrowly at her charge. "Ye mean, ye know what it be?"

"Sure," he said cheerfully. "I, uh, heard something last night, so I went outside to investigate." He gestured with a thumb at the snake. "It was back in the garbage, cold and hungry. Hey, I bet he's still hungry, and—"

"I'll bet it is, too," she snapped, "and I'll not have some scaly, gluttonous carrion eater crawling about my house. Get out!" she yelled at it. "Shoo!" She swung the broom at the snake once, twice, a third time, forcing Flinx to duck the flying bristles. Each time, the snake dodged nimbly in the air, displaying unexpected aerial agility. Once it darted straight to its left, then backward, then toward the ceiling.

"Don't!" Flinx shouted, suddenly alarmed. "It might think you're trying to hurt me."

"A guardian angel with beady eyes and scales? Mockmush, boy, it knows well what I'm swinging at!"

In fact, the snake was well aware the new human had no intention of harming its symbiote, for it could feel the honest affection and warmth flowing between them. It did not worry on that score. Conversely, no love flowed toward it from the new person, and the shiny thing that was being thrust at it was hard to avoid in the small, enclosed space.

"Please, Mother," Flinx pleaded anxiously, scrambling out of bed and dragging the blanket with him, "stop it. I don't know how it'll react."

"We're going to find out, boy," she told him grimly. The broom struck, missed, bounced off the far wall. She cocked her arms for another swing.

The snake had been patient, very patient. It understood the bond between the two humans. But the broom had backed it into a corner, and the hard bristles promised danger if they connected solidly with the snake's wings. It opened its mouth. There was a barely perceptible squirting sound. A thin, tight stream of clear liquid shot forward. It sparkled in the light and impacted on the broom as it was swinging forward. As Mother Mastiff recovered and brought the broom back for yet another strike, she heard a faint but definite hissing that did not come from the snake. She hesitated, frowning, then realized the noise was coming from the broom. A glance showed that approximately half of the metal bristles had melted away. Something was foaming and sizzling as it methodically ate its way down the broom.

She dropped the weapon as if the metal handle had abruptly become red hot, her expression fearful. The liquid continued to sputter and hiss as it ate away the metal. Soon it had worked its way through the last stubble and was beginning to eat holes in the metal handle itself.

"Boy, get out of the room while ye have the chance," she called huskily, staring wide-eyed at the snake while continuing to back toward her own bedroom. "If it can do that to metal, there's no telling what——"

Flinx laughed, then hurriedly put a hand to his mouth and forced himself to be understanding. "I'm sorry, Mother," he said apologetically. "It's just that Pip would never hurt me. And he's just proved that he wouldn't hurt anyone close to me, either."

"How do ye know that?" she sputtered.

"You *know*," he replied, sounding puzzled, "I don't know how I know it. But it's true. Here, see?" He extended his left arm.

Still keeping a wary eye on the woman, who continued to block the exit, the snake zipped down to land on the proffered perch. In an instant, it had multiple coils wrapped around the human's shoulder. Then the snake relaxed, the pleated wings folding up to lie flat against the gleaming body.

"See?" Flinx lowered his arm and gently rubbed the back of the snake's head. "He's just naturally friendly."

"Naturally ugly, ye mean," Mother Mastiff snorted. Bending, she picked up the remnant of the broom and inspected it. All the bristles were gone, along with several centimeters of handle. A weak crackling still came from the raw edges of the tube where the metal had dissolved, though the extraordinarily corrosive liquid seemed to have largely spent itself.

She showed the remains of the broom to Flinx, still nervous about getting too near the thing wrapped around his shoulder. "See that? Imagine what it would do to your skin."

"Oh, Mother, can't you see?" Flinx spoke with all the exasperation of the young for the aged. "He was protecting himself, but because he senses that you're important to me, he was careful not to spit any of it on you."

"Lucky thing for it," she said, some of her normal bravado returning. "Well, it can't stay here."

"Yes, it can," Flinx argued.

"No, it can't. I can't have some lethal varmint like that fluttering and crawling all over the place, frightening off the customers."

"He'll stay with me all the time," Flinx assured her soothingly. His hand continued to caress the snake's head. Its eyes closed contentedly. "See? He's just like any other house pet. He responds to warmth and affection." Flinx brought forth his most mournful, pleading expression. It had the intended affect.

"Well, it won't get any warmth or affection from me," Mother Mastiff grumbled, "but if you're determined to keep it . . ."

"I think," Flinx added, throwing fuel on the fire, "he would become very upset if someone tried to separate us."

Mother Mastiff threw up her hands, simultaneously signifying acquiescence and acceptance. "Oh, Deity, why couldn't ye stumble over a normal pet, like a cat or a saniff? What does the little monster eat, anyways?"

"I don't know," Flinx admitted, remembering the hunger he had sensed the night before and resolving to do something about it soon. He had been hungry himself and knew more of the meaning of that word than most people. "Aren't most snakes carnivorous?"

"This one certainly looks like it," she said.

Reaching down, Flinx gently ran a forefinger along the edge of the snake's mouth until he could pry it open. The snake opened one eye and looked at him curiously but did not raise any objection to the intrusion. Mother Mastiff held her breath.

Flinx leaned close, inspecting. "The teeth are so small I can't tell for sure."

"Probably swallows its food whole," Mother Mastiff told him. "I hear that's the way of it with snakes, though this

be no normal snake and I wouldn't care to make no pre-
dictions about it, much less about its diet."

"I'll find out," Flinx assured her. "If you don't need me
to help in the shop today——"

"Help, hah! No, go where ye will. Just make sure that
creature goes with ye."

"I'm going to take him around the marketplace," Flinx
said excitedly, "and see if anyone recognizes him. There's
sure to be someone who will."

"Don't bet your blood on it, boy," she warned him. "It's
likely an offworld visitor."

"I thought so, too," he told her. "Wouldn't that be interesting? I wonder how it got here?"

"Someone with a grudge against me brought it, probably," she muttered softly. Then, louder, she said, "There
be no telling. If 'tis an escaped pet and a rare one, ye can
be sure its owner will be stumbling about here soonest in
search of it."

"We'll see." Flinx knew the snake belonged right where
it was, riding his shoulder. It felt right. He could all but
feel the wave of contentment it was generating.

"And while I'm finding out what he is," he added
briskly, "I'll find out what he eats, too."

"Ye do that," she told him. "Fact be, why not spend the
night at it? I've some important buyers coming around
suppertime. They were referred to me through the
Shopkeeper's Association and seem especial interested in
some of the larger items we have, like the muriwood table.
So ye take that awful whatever-it-be," and she threw a
shaky finger in the direction of the snake, "and stay ye out
'til well after tenth hour. Then I'll *think* about letting the
both of ye back into my house."

"Yes, Mother, thank you." He ran up to give her a kiss.
She backed off.

"Don't come near me, boy. Not with that monster sleeping on your arm."

"He wouldn't hurt you, Mother. Really."

"I'd feel more confident if I had the snake's word on it
as well as yours, boy. Now go on, get out, be off with the
both of ye. If we're fortunate, perhaps it will have some
homing instinct and fly off when you're not looking."

But Pip did not fly off. It gave no sign of wishing to be anywhere in the Commonwealth save on the shoulder of a certain redheaded young man.

As Flinx strolled through the marketplace, he was startled to discover that his ability to receive the emotions and feelings of others had intensified, though none of the isolated bursts of reception matched in fury that first overpowering deluge of the night before. His receptivity had increased in frequency and lucidity, though it still seemed as unpredictable as ever. Flinx suspected that his new pet might have something to do with his intensified abilities, but he had no idea how that worked, anymore than he knew how his Talent operated at the best of times.

If only he could find someone to identify the snake! He could always work through his terminal back home, but requests for information were automatically monitored at Central, and he was afraid that a query for information on so rare a creature might trigger alarm on the part of curious authorities. Flinx preferred not to go through official channels. He had acquired Mother Mastiff's opinion of governmental bueaucracy, which placed it somewhere between slime mold and the fleurms that infested the alleys.

By now, he knew a great many inhabitants of the marketplace. Wherever he stopped, he inquired about the identity and origin of his pet. Some regarded the snake with curiosity, some with fear, a few with indifference. But none recognized it.

"Why don't you ask Makepeace?" one of the vendors eventually suggested. "He's traveled offworld. Maybe he'd know."

Flinx found the old soldier sitting on a street corner with several equally ancient cronies. All of them were pensioneers. Most were immigrants who had chosen Moth for their final resting place out of love for its moist climate and because it was a comparatively cheap world to live on, not to mention the laxity of its police force. On Moth, no one was likely to question the source of one's pension money. For several of Makepeace's comrades, this was the prime consideration.

The other aged men and women studied the snake with

nothing more than casual interest, but Makepeace reacted far more enthusiastically. "Bless my remaining soul," he muttered as he leaned close—but not too close, Flinx noted—for a better look. Pip raised his head curiously, as if sensing something beyond the norm in this withered biped.

"You know what he is?" Flinx asked hopefully.

"Aye, boy. Those are wings bulging its flanks, are they not?" Flinx nodded. "Then it's surely an Alaspinian miniature dragon."

Flinx grinned at the old man, then down at Pip. "So that's what you are." The snake looked up at him as if to say, I'm well aware of what I am, and do you always find the obvious so remarkable?

"I thought dragons were mythical creatures," he said to Makepeace.

"So they are. It's only a name given from resemblance, Flinx."

"I suppose you know," Flinx went on, "that he spits out a corrosive fluid."

"Corrosive!" The old man leaned back and roared with laughter, slapping his legs and glancing knowingly at his attentive cronies. "Corrosive, he says!" He looked back at Flinx.

"The minidrag's toxin is, my boy, a venomous acid known by a long string of chemical syllables which this old head can't remember. I was a soldier-engineer. Biochemistry was never one of my favorite subjects. I'm more comfortable with mathematical terms than biological ones. But I can tell you this much, though I never visited Alaspin myself." He pointed at the snake, which drew its head back uncertainly. "If that there thing was to spit in your eye, you'd be a kicking, quivering mess on the ground inside a minute—and dead in not much more than that.

"I also remember that there's no known antidote for several of the Alaspinian toxins, of which that minidrag of yours wields the most potent. A corrosive, neurological poison—aye, who wouldn't remember hearing about that? You say you know it's corrosive?"

Flinx had an image of the dissolved end of the broomstick, the metal melted away like cheese before a hot blade. He nodded.

"Just make sure you never get to know of it personally, lad. I've heard tell of such creatures being kept as pets, but it's a rare thing. See, the associational decision's all made by the snake. The would-be owner has no choice in the matter. You can't tame 'em. They pick and choose for themselves." He gestured toward Flinx's shoulder. "Looks like that one's sure settled on you."

"He's more than welcome," Flinx said affectionately. "He feels natural there."

"Each to his own," an elderly woman observed with a slight shudder. Affirmative nods came from others in the group.

"And there's something else, too." The old soldier was frowning, struggling to remember long-dormant knowledge. "What you just said about it feeling 'natural' there reminded me. They say those flying snakes have funny mental quirks all their own. Now me, I wouldn't be able to say for certain if that's so—I'm only relating hearsay, didn't read it off no chip. But the stories persist."

"What kind of stories?" Flinx asked, trying not to appear overanxious.

"Oh, that the snakes are empathic. You know, telepathic on the emotional level." He scratched his head. "There's more to it than that, but I'm damned if I can remember the rest of it."

"That's certainly interesting," Flinx said evenly, "but pretty unlikely."

"Yeah, I always thought so myself," Makepeace agreed. "You wouldn't have noticed anything like that since being around this one, of course."

"Not a thing." Flinx was an expert at projecting an aura of innocence; in this case, it glowed from his face, not his mind. "Thanks a lot for your time, Mr. Makepeace, sir."

"You're more than welcome to it, boy. Old knowledge dies unless somebody makes use of it. You watch yourself around that thing. It's no saniff, and it might could turn on you."

"I'll be careful," Flinx assured him brightly. He turned and hurried away from the gaggle of attentive oldsters.

Makepeace was rubbing his chin and staring after the youngster as he vanished into the swirling crowd. "Funny. Wonder where the little flying devil came from? This is one hell of a long way from Alaspin. That reminds me of the time . . ."

Flinx glanced down at his shoulder. "So you're poisonous, huh? Well, anyone could have guessed that from the little demonstration you gave with Mother's broom this morning. If you spit in my eye, I'll spit in yours."

The snake did not take him up on the offer. It stared at him a moment, then turned its head away and studied the street ahead, evidently more interested in its surroundings than in its master's indecipherable words.

Maybe miniature dragons don't have much of a sense of humor, Flinx mused. Probably he would have ample opportunity to find out. But at least he knew what his pet was. Glancing up beyond the fringe of the slickertic hood, he wondered where the snake's home world lay. Alaspin, old Makepeace had called it, and said it was far away.

The morning mist moistened his upturned face. The cloud cover seemed lighter than usual. If he was lucky, the gloom would part sometime that night and he would have a view of Moth's fragmented ice rings, of the moon Flame, and beyond that, of the stars.

Someday, he thought, someday I'll travel to far places as Makepeace and the others have. Someday I'll get off this minor wet world and go vagabonding. I'll be a free adult, with nothing to tie me down and no responsibilities. I'll lead a relaxed, uncomplicated life of simple pleasures. He glanced down at his new-found companion. Maybe someday they would even travel to the snake's home world of Alaspin, wherever it might be.

Sure you will, he thought bitterly. Better be realistic, like Mother Mastiff says. You're stuck here forever. Moth's your home, and Moth's where you'll spend the rest of your days. Count yourself fortunate. You've a concerned mother, a warm home, food . . . .

Food. Surely the flying snake was hungrier than ever. "We'd better get you something to eat," he told Pip, who gazed up at him with fresh interest.

He checked his credcard. Not much money there. Not that there ever was. Well, he could manage. Trouble was, he had no idea what Alaspinian minidrags liked to eat. "I wonder what you'd settle for," he murmured. The snake did not respond. "If it's live food only, then I don't think there's much I can do to help you. Not on a regular basis, anyway. Let's try here, first."

They entered a stall well known to Flinx. Most of the booths and tables were unoccupied, since it was between mealtimes. As it developed, finding suitable food for the minidrag turned out to be less of a problem than he had feared. Much to Flinx's surprise, the flying snake was omnivorous. It would eat almost anything he set in front of it, but raw meat seemed to be a special favorite. Flinx cut the meat into small chunks, which the snake gulped down whole. Flinx helped himself to an occasional bite. When times were bad, he and Mother Mastiff had existed on far less savory items.

Pip was fond of any kind of fruit or berry, though it shied away from vegetables. Something else they had in common. Flinx thought. Oddly enough, the snake would even lap up milk. Flinx was sure he could supply enough variety to keep his pet both happy and alive. Maybe it would even eat table scraps. Perhaps *that* would weaken Mother Mastiff's antagonism. As he experimented further, he discovered that the snake was particularly fond of anything with a high iron content, such as raisins or flakes of guarfish. Had he been a biochemist equipped with a field laboratory, he might have learned that the minidrag's blood contained an extraordinary amount of hemoglobin, vital to transport the oxygen necessary to sustain the snake's hummingbirdlike flight.

When Pip had swollen to twice his normal diameter, Flinx stopped trying new foods on his pet. He relaxed in the booth, sipping mulled wine and watching the lights of the city wink to life. It wouldn't be too bad to live out his life on Moth, he admitted to himself. Drallar was never dull, and now he had a special companion with whom to share its excitement.

Yes, the flying snake had filled a definite void in his life as well as in some mysterious, deeper part of himself. But he still longed for the stars and the magical, unvisited worlds that circled them.

Be realistic, he ordered himself.

He waved to some acquaintances as they strolled past the restaurant. Older men and women. Sometimes Mother Mastiff worried that he preferred the company of adults to youngsters his own age. He couldn't help it. It wasn't that he was antisocial, merely that he chose his friends carefully. It was the immaturity of those his own age that drove him into the company of adults.

A fleeting emotion from one of those to whom he had waved reached back to him as the group rounded a corner, laughing and joking in easy camaraderie. Flinx snatched at it, but it was gone. He sat back in his booth, the wine making him moody. Better to have no Talent at all, he thought, than an unmanageable one that only teases.

He paid the modest bill, slipping his card into the table's central pylon. Outside, the evening rain had begun. Pip rode comfortably on his shoulder beneath the slickertic, only its head exposed. It was sated, content. Ought to be after all you ate, Flinx thought as he gazed fondly down at his pet.

Rain transformed the brilliant scales of the snake's head into tiny jewels. The moisture did not seem to bother the snake. I wonder, Flinx thought. Is Alaspin a wet world, also? I should have asked old Makepeace. He'd probably have known. People lucky enough to travel learn everything sooner or later.

Suddenly a stinging, serrated burst of emotion—hammer blow, unexpected, raw—doubled him over with its force. It was like a soundless screaming inside his head. Flinx was feeling the naked emotion behind a scream instead of hearing the scream itself. He had never experienced anything like it before, and despite that, it felt sickeningly familiar.

A bundled-up passer-by halted and bent solicitously over the crumpled youngster. "Are you all right, son? You—" He noticed something and quickly backed off.

"I—I'm okay, I think," Flinx managed to gasp. He saw

what had made the man flinch. Pip had been all but asleep on his master's shoulder only a moment before. Now the snake was wide awake, head and neck protruding like a scaly periscope as it seemed to search the night air for something unseen.

Then the last vestiges of that desperate, wailing cry vanished, leaving Flinx's head aching and infuriatingly empty. Yet it had lingered long enough for him to sort it out, to identify it.

"Listen, son, if you need help, I can—" the stranger started to say, but Flinx did not wait to listen to the kind offer. He was already halfway down the street, running at full speed over the pavement. His slickertic fanned out like a cape behind him, and his boots sent water flying over shop fronts and pedestrians alike. He did not pause to apologize, the curses sliding off him as unnoticed as the rain.

Then he was skidding into a familiar side street. His heart pounded, and his lungs heaved. The street appeared untouched, unaltered, yet something here had been violated, and the moment of it had touched Flinx's mind. Most of the shops were already shuttered against the night. There was no sign of human beings in that damp stone canyon.

"Mother!" he shouted. "Mother Mastiff!" He pounded on the lock plate with his palm. The door hummed but did not open—it was locked from inside.

"Mother Mastiff, open up. It's me, Flinx!" No reply from the other side.

Pip danced on his shoulder, half airborne and half coiled tight to its master. Flinx moved a dozen steps away from the door, then charged it, throwing himself into the air sideways and kicking with one leg as Makepeace had once shown him. The door gave, flying inward. It had only been bolted, not locksealed.

He crouched there, his eyes darting quickly around the stall. Pip settled back onto his shoulder, but its head moved agitatedly from side to side, as if it shared its master's nervousness and concern.

The stall looked undisturbed. Flinx moved forward and

tried the inner door. It opened at a touch. The interior of the living area was a shambles. Pots and pans and food had been overturned in the kitchen. Clothing and other personal articles lay strewn across floor and furniture. He moved from the kitchen-dining area to his own room, lastly to Mother Mastiff's, knowing but dreading what he would find.

The destruction was worse in her room. The bed looked as if it had been the scene of attempted murder or an uncontrolled orgy. Across the bed, hidden from casual view, a small curved door blended neatly into the wall paneling. Few visitors would be sharp-eyed enough to notice it. It was just wide enough for a man to crawl through.

It stood ajar. A cold breeze drifted in from outside.

Flinx dropped to his knees and started through, not caring what he might encounter on the other side. He emerged from the slip-me-out into the alley and climbed to his feet. The rain had turned to mist. There was no hint that anything unusual had occurred here. All the chaos was behind him, inside.

Turning, he ran two or three steps to the north, then stopped himself. He stood there, panting. He had run long and hard from the street where the scream had struck him, but he was too late. There was no sign that anyone had even been in the alley.

Slowly, dejectedly, he returned to the shop. Why? he cried to himself. Why has this happened to me? Who would want to kidnap a harmless old woman like Mother Mastiff? The longer he thought about it, the less sense it made.

He forced himself to take an inventory out front. There was no sign of anything missing. The shop's stock seemed to be intact. Not thieves, then, surprised in the act of burglary. Then what? If not for the ample evidence that there had been a struggle, he would not even have suspected that anything was amiss.

No, he reminded himself, not quite true. The lockseal on the front door was dead. It would have taken half the thieves in Drallar to drag Mother Mastiff from her shop while it stood unsealed. He thought of thieves a second time, knowing he would not be staying here long. His mind full of dark and conflicting thoughts, he set about repairing the lock.

Chapter Six

"*Pssst!* Boy! Flinx-boy!"

Flinx moved the door aside slightly and gazed out into the darkness. The man speaking from the shadows operated a little shop two stalls up the side street from Mother Mastiff's, where he made household items from the hardwoods that Moth grew in abundance. Flinx knew him well, and stepped out to confront him.

"Hello, Arrapkha." He tried to search the man's face, but it was mostly hidden by the overhanging rim of his slickertic. He could feel nothing from the other man's mind. A fine and wondrous Talent, he thought sarcastically to himself.

"What happened here? Did you see anything?"

"I shouldn't be out like this." Arrapkha turned to glance worriedly up the street to where it intersected the busy main avenue. "You know what people say in Drallar, Flinx-boy. The best business is minding one's own."

"No homilies now, friend," Flinx said impatiently. "You've been neighbor to my mother for many years, and you've watched me grow up. Where is she?"

"I don't know." Arrapkha paused to gather his thoughts.

Flinx held back his anxiety and tried to be patient with the man—Arrapkha was a little slow upstairs but a good soul.

"I was working at my lathe, feeling good with myself. I'd only just sold a pair of stools to a programmer from the Welter Inurb and was counting my good fortune when I thought I heard noises from your house." He smiled faintly. "At first, I thought nothing of it, You know your mother. She can fly into a rage at any time over nothing in particular and make enough noise to bring complaints from the avenue stores.

"Anyhow, I finished turning a broya post—it will be a fine one, Flinx-boy, fashioned of number-six harpberry wood—"

"Yes, I'm sure," Flinx said impatiently. "I'm sure it will be a fine display stand, as all your work is, but what about Mother Mastiff?"

"I'm getting to that, Flinx-boy," Arrapkha said petulantly. "As I said, I finished the post, and since the noise continued, I grew curious. It seemed to be going on a long time even for your mother. So I put down my work for a moment and thought to come see what was going on. I mediate for your mother sometimes.

"When I was about halfway from my shop to yours, the noise stopped almost entirely. I was about to return home when I saw something. At least, I think I did." He gestured toward the narrow gap that separated Mother Mastiff's shop from the vacant shop adjoining hers.

"Through there I thought I saw figures moving quickly up the alley behind your home. I couldn't be certain. The opening is small, it was raining at the time, and it's dark back there. But I'm pretty sure I saw several figures."

"How many?" Flinx demanded. "Two, three?"

"For sure, I couldn't say," Arrapkha confessed sadly. "I couldn't even for certain tell if they were human or not. More than two, surely. Yet not a great number, though I could have missed seeing them all.

"Well, I came up to the door quickly then and buzzed. There was no answer, and it was quiet inside, and the door was locked, so I thought little more of it. There was no reason to connect shapes in the alleyway with your mother's arguing. Remember, I only heard noise from the shop.

"As it grew dark I started to worry, and still the shop stayed closed. It's not like Mother Mastiff to stay closed up all day. Still, her digestion is not what it used to be, and sometimes her liver gives her trouble. Too much bile. She could have been cursing her own insides."

"I know," Flinx said. "I've had to listen to her complaints lots of times."

"So I thought best not to interfere. But I *have* known both of you for a long time, Flinx-boy, just as you say, so I thought, when I saw you moving about, that I ought to come and tell you what I'd seen. It's clear to me now that I should have probed deeper." He struck his own head. "I'm sorry. You know that I'm not the cleverest man in the marketplace."

"It's all right, Arrapkha. There's no blame for you in this matter." Flinx stood there in the mist for a long moment, silent and thinking hard.

Arrapkha hesitantly broke in on his contemplation. "So sorry I am, Flinx-boy. If there's anything I can do to help, if you need a place to sleep tonight, ay, even with the devil thing on your shoulder, you are welcome to share my home."

"I've spent many a night out on my own, sir," Flinx told him, "but the offer's appreciated. Thank you for your help. At least now I have a better idea of what happened, though not for the life of me *why*. Could you see if Mother Mastiff was among those running down the alley? She's not here."

"So I guessed from your look and words. No, I cannot say she was one of them. I saw only shapes that seemed to be human, or at least upright. But they seemed to run with difficulty."

"Maybe they were carrying her."

"It may be, Flinx-boy, it may be. Surely she would not go off on her own with strangers without leaving you so much as a message."

"No, she wouldn't," Flinx agreed, "and if she went with the people you saw, it wasn't because they were her friends. The inside of the house is all torn up. She didn't go with them quietly."

"Then surely for some reason she's been kidnaped," Arrapkha concurred. "Fifty years ago, I might could give a reason for such a thing. She was a beauty then, Mother Mastiff, though she has not aged gracefully. Grace was not a part of her, not even then. A hard woman always, but attractive. But for this to happen now——" He shook his head. "A true puzzle. Did she have access to much money?"

Flinx shook his head rapidly.

"Um. I thought not. Well, then, did she owe anyone any dangerous amounts?"

"She owed a lot of people, but no great sums," Flinx replied. "At least, nothing that she ever spoke to me about and nothing I ever overheard talk of."

"I do not understand it, then," Arrapkha said solemnly.

"Nor do I, friend."

"Perhaps," Arrapkha suggested, "someone wished a private conversation with her and will bring her back in the morning?"

Flinx shook his head a second time. "I think that since she didn't go with them voluntarily, she won't be allowed to come back voluntarily. Regardless, one thing she always told me was not to sit around and stare blankly at the inexplicable but always to try and find answers. If she does come walking freely home tomorrow, then I can at least try to meet her coming."

"Then you're determined to go out after her?" Arrapkha lifted bushy black eyebrows.

"What else can I do?"

"You could wait. You're a nice young fellow, Flinx-boy." He waved toward the distant avenue. "Most everyone in the marketplace who knows you thinks so, also. You won't lack for a place to stay or food to eat if you decide to wait for her. Your problem is that you're too young, and the young are always overanxious."

"Sorry, Arrapkha. I know you mean well for me, but I just can't sit around here and wait. I think I'd be wasting my time and, worse, maybe hers as well. Mother Mastiff doesn't have much time left to her."

"And what if her time, excuse me, has already fled?" Arrapkha asked forcefully. Subtlety was not a strong trait of the marketplace's inhabitants. "Will you involve yourself then in something dangerous which has chosen to spare you?"

"I have to know. I have to go after her and see if I can help."

"I don't understand," Arrapkha said sadly. "You're a smart young man, much smarter than I. Why risk yourself? She wouldn't want you to, you know. She's not really your mother."

"Mother or mother-not," Flinx replied, "she's the only mother I've ever known. There's more to it than simple biology, Arrapkha. The years have taught me that much."

The older man nodded. "I thought you might say something like that, Flinx-boy. Well, I can at least wish you luck. It's all I have to give you. Do you have credit?"

"A little, on my card."

"If you need more, I can transfer." Arrapkha started to pull out his own card.

"No, not now, anyway. I may need such help later." He broke into a broad smile. "You're a good friend, Arrapkha. Your friendship is as solid as your woodwork." He turned. "Did you see which direction these figures took?"

"That's little to start on." He pointed to the north. "That way, up the alley. They could have turned off any time. And in the weather"—he indicated the clouds hanging limply overhead—"they'll have left no trail for you to follow."

"Perhaps not," Flinx admitted. "We'll see."

"I expect you will, Flinx-boy, since you feel so strongly about this. All I can do, then, is wish luck to you." He turned and strode back up the street toward his shop, keeping the slickertic tight around his head and neck.

Flinx waited until the rain had swallowed up the older man before going back inside and closing the door behind him. He wandered morosely around the living area, salvaging this or that from the mess and returning things to their proper places. Before long, he found himself in

Mother Mastiff's room. He sat down on the bed and stared at the ajar slip-me-out that led to the alley.

"What do you think, Pip? Where did she go, and who took her, and why? And how am I going to find her? I don't even know how to start."

He shut his eyes, strained, tried to sense the kinds of emotions he knew she must be generating, wherever she had been taken. There was nothing. Nothing from Mother Mastiff, nothing from anyone else. His Talent mocked him. He started fixing up the bedroom, hoping that contact with familiar objects might trigger some kind of reaction in his mind. Something, anything, that would give him a start on tracking her down. Pip slipped off his shoulder and slithered across the bed, playing with covers and pillows.

There were gaps—missing clothing—in the single closet, Flinx noted. Whoever had abducted her had evidently intended to keep her for a while. The sight cheered him because they would not have troubled to take along clothing for someone they intended to kill immediately.

Pip had worked its way across the bed to the night table and was winding its sinuous way among the bottles and containers there. "Back off that, Pip, before you break something. There's been enough damage done here today." The irritation in his voice arose more out of personal upset than any real concern. The minidrag had yet to knock over anything.

Pip reacted, though not to his master's admonition. The snake spread luminous wings and fluttered from the tabletop to the slip-me-out. It hovered there, watching him. While Flinx gaped at his pet, it flew back to the night table, hummed over a bottle, then darted back to the opening.

Flinx's momentary paralysis left him, and he rushed to the end table. The thin plasticine bottle that had attracted Pip was uncapped. It normally held a tenth liter of a particularly powerful cheap perfume of which Mother Mastiff was inordinately fond. Now he saw that the bottle was empty.

If Mother Mastiff had retained enough presence of mind to remember that the Drallarian gendarmery occasionally employed the services of tracking animals—for the first time hope crowded despair from Flinx's thoughts.

Those animals could track odors even through Moth's perpetual dampness.

If an Alaspinian minidrag possessed the same ability . . . Was he completely misinterpreting the flying snake's actions? "Pip?"

The flying snake seemed to accept the mention of its name as significant, for it promptly spun in midair and darted through the slip-me-out. Flinx dropped to his hands and knees and crawled after. In seconds, he was in the alley again. As he climbed to his feet, he searched for his pet. It was moving eastward, almost out of sight.

"Pip, wait!" The snake obediently halted, hovering in place until its master had caught up. Then it took off up the alley again.

Flinx settled into a steady run. He was an excellent runner and in superb condition, on which he had always prided himself. He resolved to follow the flying snake until one or the other of them dropped.

Any moment he expected the snake to pause outside one of the innumerable faceless structures that peppered the commercial sections of Drallar. But while the minidrag twisted and whirled down alleys and up streets, not once did it hesitate in its steady flight. Soon Flinx found his wind beginning to fail him. Each time he stopped, the snake would wait impatiently until its master caught up again.

Drallar was the largest city on Moth, but it was a village compared to the great cities of Terra or the underground complexes of Hivehom and Evoria, so Flinx was not surprised that when Pip finally began to slow, they had reached the northwestern outskirts of the metropolis. Here the buildings no longer had to be built close to one another. Small storage structures were scattered about, and individual homes of blocked wood and plastic began to blend into the first phalanx of evergreen forest. Pip hesitated before the trees, zooming in anxious circles, soaring to scan the treetops. It ignored Flinx's entreaties and calls until finally satisfied, whereupon the snake turned and dropped down to settle once again on the familiar perch of his master's shoulder.

Turning a slow circle, Flinx fought to pick up even a

fragment of lingering emotion. Once again, his efforts met with failure. It seemed clear that whoever had carried off Mother Mastiff had taken her into the forest and that the olfactory trail that had led Pip so far had finally dissipated in the steady onslaught of mist and rain. On a drier world or in one of Moth's few deserts, things might have been different, but here Pip had come to a dead end.

After a moment's thought, Flinx started away from the trees. In addition to the storage buildings and homes, several small industrial complexes were visible nearby, including two of the ubiquitous sawmills that ringed the city and processed Moth's most prolific crop. Flinx wandered among them until he located a public com station on a service street. He stepped inside and slid the spanda-wood door shut behind him. Even after curing, spanda retained a significant coefficient of expansion. When he closed the door, it sealed itself against the elements, and only the ventilation membranes would keep him from suffocating. He took out his battered credcard and slid it into the receptacle on the unit, then punched the keyboard. A pleasant-looking middle-aged woman appeared on the small viewscreen. "Yes, sir. What can I do for you?"

"Is there a Missing Persons Bureau in the Drallar Municipal Strata?"

"Just a moment, please." There was a pause while she glanced at something out of range of the pickup. "Human or alien?"

"Human, please."

"Native or visitor?"

"Native."

"You wish connection?"

"Thank you, yes." The woman continued to stare at him for a moment, and Flinx decided she was fascinated by the coiled shape riding his shoulder. The screen finally flashed once and then cleared.

This time, the individual staring back at him was male, bald, and bored. His age was indeterminate, his attitude barely civil. Flinx had never liked bureaucrats. "Yes, what is it?

"Last night," he declared, "or early this morning"—in his rush through the city streets he'd completely lost track of the time—"I—my mother disappeared. A neighbor saw some people running away down an alley, and our house was all torn apart. I don't know how to start looking for her. I think she's been taken out of the city via the northwest quadrant, but I can't be sure."

The man perked up slightly, though his voice sounded doubtful. "I see. This sounds more like a matter for the police than for Missing Persons."

"Not necessarily," Flinx said, "if you follow my meaning."

"Oh." The man smiled understandingly. "Just a moment. I'll check for you." He worked a keyboard out of Flinx's view. "Yes, there was a number of arrests made last night, several of them including women. How old is your mother?"

"Close to a hundred," Flinx said, "but quite lively."

"Not lively enough to be in with the group I was thinking of," the clerk responded. "Name?"

Flinx hesitated. "I always just called her Mother Mastiff."

The man frowned, then studied his unseen readout. "Is Mastiff a first name or last name? I'm assuming the 'Mother' is an honorific."

Flinx found himself staring dumbly at the clerk. Suddenly, he was aware of the enormous gaps that made up much of his life. "I—I don't know, for sure."

The bureaucrat's attitude turned stony. "Is this some kind of joke, young man?"

"No, sir," Flinx hastened to assure him, "it's no joke. I'm telling you the truth when I say that I don't know. See, she's not my natural mother."

"Ah," the clerk murmured discreetly. "Well, then, what's your last name?"

"I—" To his great amazement, Flinx discovered that he was starting to cry. It was a unique phenomenon that he had avoided for some time; now, when he least needed it, it afflicted him.

The tears did have an effect on the clerk, though. "Look, young man, I didn't mean to upset you. All I can tell you is that no woman of that advanced an age is on last night's arrest recording. For that matter, no one that old has been reported in custody by any other official source. Does that help you at all?"

Flinx nodded slowly. It helped, but not in the way he'd hoped. "Th-thank you very much, sir."

"Wait, young man! If you'll give me your name, maybe I can have a gendarme sent out with—" The image died as Flinx flicked the disconnect button. His credcard popped from its slot. Slowly, wiping at his eyes, he put it back inside his shirt. Would the clerk bother to trace the call? Flinx decided not. For an instant, the bureaucrat had thought the call was from some kid pulling a joke on him. After a moment's reflection, he would probably think so again.

No one of Mother Mastiff's age arrested or reported in. Not at Missing Persons, which was bad, but also not at the morgue, which was good because that reinforced his first thoughts: Mother Mastiff had been carried off by unknown persons whose motives remained as mysterious as did their identity. He gazed out the little booth's window at the looming, alien forest into which it seemed she and her captors had vanished, and exhaustion washed over him. It was toasty warm in the com booth.

The booth's chair was purposely uncomfortable, but the floor was heated and no harder. For a change, he relished his modest size as he worked himself into a halfway comfortable position on the floor. There was little room for Pip in the cramped space, so the flying snake reluctantly found itself a perch on the com unit. Anyone entering the booth to make a call would be in for a nasty shock.

It was well into morning when Flinx finally awoke, stiff and cramped but mentally rested. Rising and stretching, he pushed aside the door and left the com booth. To the north lay the first ranks of the seemingly endless forest, which ran from Moth's lower temperate zone to its arctic. To the south lay the city, friendly, familiar. It would be hard to turn his back on it.

Pip fluttered above him, did a slow circle in the air, then rose and started northwestward. In minutes, the mini-drag was back. In its wordless way, it was reaffirming its feelings of the night before: Mother Mastiff had passed that way. Flinx thought a moment. Perhaps her captors, in order to confuse even the most unlikely pursuit, had carried her out into the forest, only to circle back into the city again.

How was he to know for certain? The government couldn't help him further. All right, then. He had always been good at prying information from strangers. They seemed to trust him instinctively, seeing in him a physically unimposing, seemingly not-too-bright youngster. He could probe as facilely here as in the markeplace.

Leaving the booth and the sawmill block, he began his investigation by questioning the occupants of the smaller businesses and homes. He found most houses deserted, their inhabitants having long since gone off to work, but the industrial sites and businesses were coming alive as the city's commercial bloodstream began to circulate. Flinx confronted the workers as they entered through doors and gates, as they parked their occasional individual transports, and as they stepped off public vehicles.

Outside the entrance to a small firm that manufactured wooden fittings for kitchen units, he encountered someone not going to work but leaving. "Excuse me, sir," he said for what seemed like the hundred thousandth time, "did you by any chance see a group of people pass through this part of town last night? They would have had an upset old lady with them, perhaps restrained somehow."

"Now that's funny of you to mention," the man said unexpectedly. "See, I'm the night guard at Koyunlu over there." He gestured at the small building that was filling up with workers. "I didn't see no old woman, but there was something of a commotion late last night over that way." He pointed at the road which came to a dead end against the nearby trees.

"There was a lot of shouting and yelling and cursing. I took a look with my nightsight—that's my job, you know—and I saw a bunch of people getting out of a rented city transport. They were switching over to a mudder."

The watchman appeared sympathetic. "They weren't potential thieves or young vandals, so I didn't watch them for long. I don't know if they were the people you're looking for."

Flinx thought a moment, then asked, "You say that you

heard cursing. Could you tell if any of it was from a woman?"

The man grinned. "I see what you thinking, son. No, they were too far away. But I tell you this: someone in that bunch could swear like any dozen sewer riders."

Flinx could barely contain his excitement. "That's them; that's her! That's *got* to be her!"

"In fact," the watchman continued, "that's really what made it stick in me mind. Not that you don't see people switching transports at night—you do, even way out here. It's just a bad time to go mudding into the woods, and when it is done, it's usually done quietly. No need that I can see for all that yelling and shouting."

"It was them, all right," Flinx murmured decisively. "It was her swearing—or her kidnappers swearing at her."

"Kidnap—" The man seemed to notice Flinx's youth for the first time. "Say, son, maybe you'd better come along with me."

"No, I can't." Flinx started to back up, smiling apologetically. "I have to go after them. I have to find her."

"Just hold on a second there, son," the watchman said. "I'll give a call to the police. We can use the company coms. You want to do this right and proper so's—"

"They won't do anything," Flinx said angrily. "I know them." On an intimate basis, he could have added, since he'd been arrested for petty theft on more than one occasion. He was probably on their question-list right now. They would hold him and keep him from going after Mother Mastiff.

"You wait, son," the watchman insisted. "I'm not going to be part of something—" As he spoke, he reached out a big hand. Something bright blue-green-pink hissed threateningly. A triangular head darted menacingly at the clutching hand. The man hastily drew it back.

"Damn," he said, "that's alive!"

"Very alive," Flinx said, continuing to back away. "Thanks for your help, sir." He turned and dashed toward the city.

"Boy, just a minute!" The watchman stared after the retreating figure. Then he shrugged. He was tired. It had been a long, dull night save for that one noisy bunch he'd seen, and he was anxious to be home and asleep. He sure as hell didn't need trouble himself with the antics of some kid. Pushing the entire incident from his thoughts, he headed toward the company transport stop.

Once he was sure he was out of sight of the watchman, Flinx paused to catch his breath. At least he knew with some certainty that Mother Mastiff had been kidnapped and taken out of the city. Why she had been carried off into the great northern forest he could not imagine

In addition to the hurt at the back of his mind, a new ache had begun to make itself felt. He had had nothing to eat since the previous night. He could hardly go charging off into Moth's vast evergreen wilderness on an empty stomach.

Prepare yourself properly, then proceed. That's what Mother Mastiff had always taught him. I'll go home, he told himself. Back to the shop, back to the marketplace. The kidnapers had switched to a mudder. Such a vehicle was out of Flinx's financial reach, but he knew where he could rent a stupava running bird. That would give him flexibility as well as speed.

His legs still throbbed from the seemingly endless run across the city the previous day, so he used public transport to return home. Time was more important than credits. The transport chose a main spoke avenue and in minutes deposited him in the marketplace.

From the drop-off, it was but a short sprint to the shop. He found himself half expecting to see Mother Mastiff standing in the entrance, mopping the stoop and waiting to bawl him out for being gone for so long. But the shop was quiet, the living space still disarranged and forlorn. Nonetheless, Flinx checked it carefully. There were several items whose positions he had memorized before leaving; they were undisturbed.

He began to collect a small pile of things to take with him. Some hasty trading in the market produced a small backpack and as much concentrated food as he could cram into it. Despite the speed of his bargaining, he received full value for those items he traded off from Mother Mastiff's stock. With Pip riding his shoulder, few thought to cheat him. When anyone tried, the minidrag's reactions instantly alerted its master and Flinx simply took his trade elsewhere.

Flinx switched his city boots for less gaudy but more durable forest models. His slickertic would serve just as well among the trees as among the city's towers. The outright sale of several items gave his credcard balance a healthy boost. Then it was back to the shop for a last look around. Empty. So empty without her. He made certain the shutters were locked, then did the same to the front door. Before leaving, he stopped at a stall up the street.

"You're out of your mind, Flinx-boy." Arrapkha said from the entrance to his stall, shaking his head dolefully. The shop smelled of wood dust and varnish. "Do you know what the forest is like? It runs from here to the North Pole. Three thousand, four thousand kilometers as the tarpac flies and not a decent-sized city to be found.

"There's mud up there so deep it could swallow all of Drallar, not to mention things that eat and things that poison. Nobody goes into the north forest except explorers and herders, hunters and sportsmen—crazy folk from offworld who like that sort of nowhere land. Biologists and botanists—not normal folk like you and me."

"Normal folk didn't carry off my mother," Flinx replied.

Since he couldn't discourage the youngster, Arrapkha tried to make light of the situation. "Worse for them that they did. I don't think they know what they've gotten themselves into."

Flinx smiled politely. "Thanks, Arrapkha. If it wasn't for your help, I wouldn't have known where to begin."

"Almost I wish I'd said nothing last night," he muttered sadly. "Well, luck to you, Flinx-boy. I'll remember you."

"You'll see me again," Flinx assured him with more confidence than he truly felt. "Both of us."

"I hope so. Without your Mother Mastiff, the marketplace will be a duller place."

"Duller and emptier," Flinx agreed. "I have to go after her, friend Arrapkha. I really have no choice."

"If you insist. Go, then."

Flinx favored the woodworker with a last smile, then spun and marched rapidly toward the main avenue. Arrapkha watched until the youngster was swallowed up by the crowd, then retreated to his own stall. He had business to attend to, and that, after all, was the first rule of life in the marketplace.

Flinx hadn't gone far before the smells of the market were replaced by the odors, heavy and musky, of locally popular native transport animals. They were usually slower and less efficient then mechanized transport, but they had other advantages: they could not be traced via their emissions, and they were cheap to rent and to use.

In a licensed barn, Flinx picked out a healthy-looking stupava. The tall running bird was a good forager and could live off the land. It stood two and a half meters at its bright orange crest and closely resembled its far more intelligent cousins, the ornithorpes, who did not object to the use of ignorant relatives as beasts of burden. Flinx haggled with the barn manager for a while, finally settling on a fair price. The woman brought the bird out of its stall and saddled it for the youngster. "You're not going to do anything funny with this bird, now?"

"Just going for a little vacation," Flinx answered her blithely. "I've finished my studies for the year and owe myself the time off."

"Well, Garuyle here will take you anywhere you might want to go. He's a fine, strong bird." She stroked the tall bird's feathers.

"I know." Flinx put his right foot in the first stirrup, his left in the second, and threw his body into the saddle. "I can see that from his legs."

The woman nodded, feeling a little more relaxed. Evidently, her youthful customer knew what he was doing. She handed him the reins.

"All right, then. Have a pleasant journey."

Flinx had indeed ridden such birds before, but only within the city limits and not for any length of time. He snapped the reins, then gave the bird a serious whistle. It hooted back and started off, its long legs moving easily. Guiding it with gentle tugs of the reins and sharp whistles, Flinx soon had the stupava moving at a respectable rate up the first spoke avenue, jostling aside irritated pedestrians and avoiding faster public vehicles. The stupava seemed undisturbed by Pip's presence, a good sign. It would not do to head into the great forest on an easily spooked mount.

In a gratifyingly short time, Flinx found they had retraced his frenzied marathon of the night before. A sawmill passed by on his left, the com booth that had sheltered him somewhere behind it. Then only the forest loomed ahead. Trees, a hundred meters tall and higher soared above scattered smaller trees and bushes. Where the pavement vanished there was only a muddy trail. The stupava wouldn't mind that—its splayed, partially webbed feet would carry them over the bogs and sumps with ease.

"Heigh there!" he shouted softly at the bird, following the command with a crisp whistle. The stupava cawed once, jerked its head sharply against the bridle, and dashed off into the woods. The regular *flap-flap* from beneath its feet gave away to an irregular *whacking* sound broken by occasional splashes as it spanned a deeper puddle. Sometimes they touched thick moss or fungi and there was no sound at all. In no time, the immense trees formed a solid wall of bark and green behind Flinx, and the city that was his home was for the first time completely out of his sight.

Chapter Seven

Joppe the Thief thought sure he had found himself a couple of fleurms. The man and woman he was stalking so intently looked to be in their midthirties. Their dress was casual, so casual that one not interested in it might not have identified them as offworlders. Their presence in that part of Drallar's marketplace late at night proved one of two things to Joppe: either they had a great deal of confidence in their ability to pass unnoticed, or they were simply ignorant. Joppe guessed they were searching for a little excitement.

That was fine with Joppe. He would happily provide them with some excitement, something really memorable to relate to the neighbors back home on some softer world like Terra or New Riviera. They did not look like the kind who would be awkward about it. If they were, then they might have more than merely an interesting encounter to talk about.

Joppe was hungry. He had not made a strike in over a week. He regarded the strolling, chatting couple with the eye of a covetous farmer examining a pair of his prize meat animals.

As it was still comparatively early, not all the lights had been extinguished in that part of the marketplace, but enough of the shops had closed to give Joppe hope. The nature of his work required privacy. He did not rush himself. Joppe had an instinctive feel for his work. He had to balance waiting for more shopkeepers to retire against the possibility of the couple's realizing their error and turning back toward the more brightly lit sections of the market.

The couple did not seem inclined to do that. Joppe's hopes continued to rise. He could hear them clearly, talking about some sight seen earlier in the day. Joppe's hand closed around the handle of the little needler in his pocket, and he started forward, closing the distance between himself and his prey.

By now the couple had reached the end of the cul-de-sac and had stopped in front of the last shop, which was shuttered and dark. They seemed to be debating something. Then the man bent to the shop's door and took several objects from his pockets. He started manipulating something out of Joppe's view.

The thief slowed, the needler only halfway out of his holster pocket, and stared in confusion. What were they up to? He moved a little nearer, still clinging to the shadows. He was close enough to see that the door was sealed with a palm lock, which required the imprint of all five of the shop owner's fingers, in proper sequence, to release. The little black disk that the tourist had attached to the palm lock was a very expensive, sophisticated device for decoding and solving such locks. The man's fingers roved over the keys, and he examined the readout with the attitude of someone who not only knew exactly what he was doing but who had done it frequently.

While the man worked at the door, his companion stood watching him, hands on hips, obviously intent on what he was doing. Abruptly, she glanced away from her husband, and Joppe found himself staring straight at her.

The matronly giggle she had affected all evening was abruptly gone from her voice. Suddenly, nothing about her seemed soft. The unexpected transformation, accomplished solely by a change in posture and tone, was shocking. "I'm sorry we had to waste your evening, friend, but we needed a good screen to keep away the rest of the rabble. Thanks for that. Now turn around, call it a bad day, and look elsewhere. We don't have time for you right now. Oh, and leave that gun where it won't do you or anyone else any harm, okay?" Then she smiled pleasantly.

Too startled to react, Joppe just stood there, his hand still clutching the needler. He could take this one, he thought momentarily. However, something in her stance held him back. The proximity of a weapon was clearly implied, as was the intent to use it. Her companion had paused in his work and crouched before the doorway in a waiting position.

This was all very wrong, Joppe thought. He was not an especially imaginative individual, but he was an intent observer, and he was good at putting things together.

Here stood an offworld couple dressed for an evening out, calmly working a lock decoder on an unprepossessing stall doorway at the end of a side street on a dark and damp night. That, plus the way the woman had spoken to him, did not add up.

Joppe let go the needler and took his hand from his pocket. Slowly, his fingers spread so that they could see he held nothing in them. He nodded once, smiled a twisted, fleeting smile at the woman, and backed away. She returned his smile. He backed away until the shadows engulfed him once again and he stood behind a protective stone wall. He sucked in a deep breath and let it out. His pulse was racing. Unable to restrain his curiosity, he turned and just peeked around the edge of the wall. The woman had not budged, and was still staring after him. The man had returned to his work.

Joppe was well out of his depth, and he knew it. Without another backward glance, he turned and jogged off toward the main avenue, disappointed with his luck and still hungry for a strike. As to the purpose of the peculiar couple, he gave it not another thought. Such folk operated on a level far above that of Joppe and his ilk and were better forgotten.

"Sensible, that one," the woman said thoughtfully. She turned her attention from the distant street to her companion's work. "I thought he might give us trouble."

"Better that he didn't," her companion agreed. "We don't need to fool with such silliness. Not now." His fingertips danced lightly over the keys set into the black disk.

"How you coming?" the woman asked, peering over his shoulder.

"How does it look like I'm coming?"

"No need to be sarcastic," she said easily.

"It's an updated twenty-six," he informed her. "I didn't expect anyone in this slum would take the trouble and expense to keep updating something like this. Someone sure likes his privacy."

"Don't you?"

"Very funny." Suddenly, the disk emitted a soft beep, and the numbers on the readout froze. "That's got it." The man's tone was relaxed, methodical. There was no pleasure in his announcement, only a cool, professional satisfaction. He touched buttons set at five points spaced evenly around the black disk. It beeped again, twice. The illuminated numbers vanished from the readout. Unsealing the disk, he slid it back inside his coat. There were a number of pockets inside that coat, all filled with the kinds of things that would raise the hackles of any police chief. The man put a hand on the door and pushed. It moved aside easily. After a last, cursory glance up the narrow street, the two of them stepped inside.

The center section of the man's ornate belt buckle promptly came to life, throwing a narrow but powerful beam of light. It was matched a moment later by a similar beam projected from his companion's brooch. They wandered around the stall, noting the goods on display and occasionally sniffing disdainfully at various overpriced items. Inspection led them to an inner door and its simpler locking mechanism.

Both stood just inside the second doorway and gazed around the living area. "Someone put up a hell of fight," the man commented softly.

"The boy—or his adoptive mother, do you think?" The woman moved in, stooping to examine an overturned end table and the little silver vase that had tumbled from it. The vase was empty. She carefully replaced it where it had fallen.

"Maybe both of them." Her companion was already inspecting the larger of the two bedrooms. They went through the area methodically: kitchen, bedrooms, even the hygiene facilities.

When they had finished—and it did not take them very long—and when fingerprinted samples of air and dust and tiny bits of hopefully significant detritus had been relegated to the safety of tiny storage vials, the man asked his companion, "What do you think? Wait for them here?"

The woman shook her head as she glanced around the kitchen-dining area. "They obviously left under duress—and you know what that suggests."

"Sure, that's occurred to me. No way it couldn't. But there's no guarantee."

She laughed, once. "Yeah, there's no guarantee, but what do you *think*?"

"The same as you. I'm just saying we shouldn't jump to conclusions."

"I know, I know. Isn't it odd, though, that both of them are missing? That surely suggests something other than a common break-in."

"I said I concurred." The man's tone was a mite testy. "What now?"

"The shopkeeper up the street who watched us break in," she said. He nodded agreement.

They retraced their steps, leaving nothing disturbed save the air and the dust. The palm lock snapped tight behind them as they stepped back out into the street, giving no hint that it had been foiled. The couple strolled back up the little side street until they stood before Arrapkha's doorway. They thumbed the buzzer several times.

After the third try, the man leaned close to the little speaker set above the buzzer. "It's been a long, hard day for us, sir, and we're both very tired. We mean you no harm, but we are empowered to take whatever steps we think advisable to carry out our assignment. Those steps will include making our own entrance if you don't let us in.

"We saw you watching us as we let ourselves into the old woman's shop. I promise you we can let ourselves into your place just as easily. You might also like to know that we have an automon trained on the alley behind your shop. If you have a slip-me-out in your back wall, it won't do you a bit of good. So why not be pleasant about this"—he smiled in case the shopkeeper had a video pickup hidden somewhere—"and come on out? If you prefer, we can chat here on the street, in full view of your other neighbors."

They waited a suitable time. The woman looked at her companion, shrugged, and withdrew a small, thimble-shaped object from an inside breast pocket. The door opened immediately. The man nodded, then smiled. The woman put the thimble-thing away and moved back.

Arrapkha stepped outside, closing the door behind him, and looked hesitantly from one visitor to the other. "What can I do for you, lady and sir, this night? Your insistence moved me to concern despite the fact that I am closed now for more than—"

"Skip the banter," the man said crisply. "We know you were watching us. You know that we're not here to buy"—he glanced at the sign above the doorway—"woodwork. Or do you deny having watched us?"

"Well, no," Arrapkha began, "but I—"

"And you didn't call the police," the man continued easily, "because the police often ask questions you'd rather not answer, right?"

"Sir, I assure you that I—"

"We're looking for the old woman and the boy who live in that shop." The man glanced briefly back toward Mother Mastiff's stall. "You wouldn't happen to know where they are, would you?"

Arrapkha shook his head, his expression blank. "No, sir, I would not."

"There are signs of a struggle inside. This is a small street. You didn't hear anything, see anything?"

"A struggle? Dear me," Arraphka muttered, showing signs of distress. "Well, you know, even though this is a small street, it can still be very noisy here, even at night. We don't always pay close attention."

"I'll bet," the woman muttered. "Just like you didn't pay attention to all the noise we weren't making while we were letting ourselves into your neighbor's shop?"

Arrapkha favored her with a wan smile.

"We haven't time for these games," the man said impatiently, reaching into his pants pocket.

"Please, sir and lady." A look of genuine concern came over Arrapkha's face. "You said that you wouldn't do anything—"

"We won't." The man's hand paused a moment as he saw the shopkeeper's nervous stare. "Even if we have to, we probably won't." He slowly withdrew his hand to bring out a small folder. Arrapkha let out a relieved sigh, and studied the contents of the folder. His eyes widened.

The visitor slipped the little case back into his pocket. "Now, then," he said pleasantly, "I tell you again that we mean you no harm, nor have we any intention of harming the old woman and her boy. Quite the contrary. If they've been the victims of violence, as seems probable, we need to know everything you know, so that if they're still alive, we can help them. Regardless of what you may think of *us* personally and what we stand for, you must realize that if they've met with ill fortune, they're bound to be better off in our care than in the hands of whoever carried them away. You can see that, surely."

"Besides," his companion added matter-of-factly, "if you don't tell us what you know, we'll escort you to a place in city center where you'll be strapped into a machine, and you'll end up telling us, anyway. It won't hurt you, but it will waste our time. I don't like wasted time." She stared into his eyes. "Understand?"

Arrapkha nodded slowly.

"The old woman you seek—Mother Mastiff?" The man nodded encouragingly. "I think I saw her carried off by several figures. I couldn't even tell you if they were human or alien. It was dark and misty."

"Isn't it always here?" the man muttered. "Go on."

"That's all I know, all I saw." Arrapkha shrugged. "Truly." He pointed down the street toward the gap that separated Mother Mastiff's shop from the one next to hers. "Through there I saw struggling shapes in the alley. It still confuses me. She is a very old woman, quite harmless."

"How long ago was this?" the man asked him. Arrapkha told him. "And the boy? What of the boy?"

"He returned home that same night. He often goes off by himself until quite late. At least he's been doing so for as long as I've known him, which is most of his life."

"Long solo walks through this city? At his age?" the woman asked. Arrapkha tried not to show his surprise at the woman's seemingly casual remark. These people knew a great deal in spite of how far they had come from.

"He's not your average youth," Arrapkha informed them, seeing no harm in doing so. "He's grown up largely on his own here." He waved toward the brighter lights and the noise that drifted in from the main avenue. "If you let it, Drallar will mature you quickly."

"I'm sure." The man nodded. "You were saying about the boy?"

"He came back that night, saw what had happened, and was very upset. He's an emotional type, though he fights not to show it, I think. Mother Mastiff is all he has."

Still the couple did not respond, remaining maddeningly uninformative. Arrapkha went on. "He vowed to find her. I don't think he has much chance."

"He went after her, then?" the woman asked eagerly. "How long ago?"

Arrapkha told her. She muttered in some language that Arrapkha did not recognize, then added in the more familiar Commonwealth lingua franca to her companion, "Only a couple of days. We missed them by a lousy couple of days."

"It's happened before," the man reminded her, seeming unperturbed. His attention returned to Arrapkha. "Which way did the boy intend to go?"

"I have no idea," the shopkeeper said.

"You know," the man said pleasantly, "maybe we just ought to all take that little jaunt downtown and visit the machine."

"Please, sir, I tell you truly everything. You have believed my words until now. Why should it be different because the facts no longer please you? That is not my fault. What reason would I have for suddenly lying to you?"

"I don't know," the man said in a more conversational tone. "What reason would you?"

"No reason." Arrapkha felt his few wits deserting him.

"Please, I don't understand what's happening here. It's all very confusing to me. What is all this interest suddenly in poor old Mother Mastiff and this Flinx-boy?"

"We'd only confuse you further by telling you, wouldn't we?" the man said. "So you have no idea how the boy intended to begin his search?"

"None at all because that is all that he told me," Arrapkha confessed. "He said only that he was determined to find her. Then he left."

"Well, that's wonderful. That's just wonderful," the man declared sardonically. "All that work, all that research, and we get them narrowed down to one modest-size city. Now we get to start all over again with a whole damn world to cover."

"It's not that bad," the woman soothed. "The native population is thin outside the city."

"It's not that which worries me." The man sounded tired. "It's our happy competitors."

"I think we'll run into them simultaneously." The woman gestured at Arrapkha as if he weren't there. "We've learned all we can from this one."

"Yes. One more thing, though." He turned to Arrapkha and handed him a small blue metal box. A single button marred its otherwise smooth, vitreous surface. "This is a sealed-beam, high-intensity, low-power transmitter," he explained to the shopkeeper. "If either the woman or the boy should return here, all you have to do is push that button once. That will summon help, both for them and for you. Do you understand?"

"Yes," Arrapkha said slowly. He accepted the metal box, then turned it over in his hand and inspected it.

"There is a reward—a considerable reward," the woman added, "for anyone who assists us in bringing this matter to a speedy and successful resolution." She looked past him, into the little woodworking shop. "I don't know what kind of a life you make for yourself here, but it can't be much. This isn't exactly the high-rent district. The reward would amount to more, much more, than you're likely to clear in an entire year."

"It sounds nice," Arrapkha admitted slowly. "It would be very nice to make a lot of money."

"All right, then," the man said. "Remember, the people who'll show up here in response to a signal from the cube won't necessarily include us, but they'll be people familiar with our mission. We'll follow as quickly as we're able. You're certain you understand all this, now?"

"I understand."

"Fine." The man did not offer to shake Arrapkha's hand. "Your help is appreciated, and I'm sorry if we upset you."

Arrapkha shrugged. "Life is full of tiny upsets."

"So it is," the man agreed. He turned to his companion. "Let's go." They ran back toward the main avenue, leaving Arrapkha standing in front of his shop.

After several hours, Arrapkha put away his woodworking tools, cleaned himself, and prepared to retire. The blue metal cube sat on the stand next to his bed. Arrapkha studied it for a moment. Then he picked it up and walked into the bathroom. Without ceremony or hesitation, he dropped it into the waste-disposal unit and thumbed the "flush" control. He wondered how it would affect the cube, if it would send any kind of signal, and if those on the receiving end of such a signal would interpret it properly.

Feeling much better, he slipped into bed and went to sleep.

Chapter Eight

The forest was full of revelations for the thoroughly urbanized Flinx. The first few nights were hard. The silence hit him with unexpected force, and he found sleeping difficult. Pip spent those nights in uneasy rest, sensing its master's discomfort. Only the stupava, its head bobbing methodically with its soft snores, was content.

By the fourth night, Flinx slept soundly, and by the fifth, he was actually enjoying the silence. I've been deceived by circumstances and fate, he thought. This is much better than city life. True, he missed the color, the excitement, the ever-shifting landscape of beings from dozens of worlds parading through the marketplace and the wealthy inurbs, the smells of different foods and the sounds of sinister bargains being consummated. Nor did the forest offer him any opportunity to practice his skills: there wasn't anything to steal. The woods gave freely of their bounty. It was all too easy, somehow.

He had almost relaxed when the squook surprised him. It shot out of its hole in the ground, startling the stupava and nearly causing it to buck Flinx off. The squook was, like its near-relative the canish, a hyperactive ground-dwelling carnivore. It was somewhat larger, boasting claws the length of Flinx's own fingers. The slim, brown-and-black-striped body was built low to the ground. It spent the majority of its life burrowing, searching out other, herbivorous burrowers, but it occasionally would erupt from its hole in an attempt to snag and drag down some larger prey.

The critter had evidently mistaken the comparatively light footsteps of the stupava for those of a much smaller animal. The bird squawked and wrenched at its reins while Flinx fought to bring it under control. At its master's surge of alarm, Pip had instantly leaped clear and now hovered menacingly over the occupied burrow.

The squook favored the minidrag with an impressive snarl but could only glare at its airborne nemesis. Though the riding bird was clearly afraid of it, the squook still had a healthy respect for the bird's long, powerfully muscled legs. Still, if it could just get its teeth around one of those legs, it could bring the large meal to the ground.

But it wasn't so sure about the human perched on the bird's back. Though uncommon thereabouts, humans were not unknown to the inhabitants of that part of the great forest. A squook could kill a human, but the reverse was also true. And then there was that peculiar and utterly unfamiliar humming thing that darted through the air overhead. That made three opponents, one alien and unpredictable, the other two potentially dangerous. Letting out a last, disgruntled snarl, the squook backed into its burrow and expanded to fill the opening. With only its muzzle showing, it sat there and set up a steady warning bark.

Flinx finally got the stupava back under control and urged it forward. The angry calls of the squook receded slowly behind him.

There had been no real danger, he thought. On the other hand, if he had lost his saddle and fallen off—he recalled clearly the long, toothy snout of the carnivore and watched the forest with more respect.

Nothing else emerged to menace them. They encountered nothing larger than the many soaring rodents which inhabited that part of the forest. Pip amused itself by flying circles around them, for they were natural gliders rather than true fliers. They could do nothing but squeak angrily at the intruder as it executed intricate aerial maneuvers in their midst. Those that chattered and complained the loudest, the flying snake selected for lunch.

"That's enough, Pip," Flinx called out to the gallivanting minidrag one day. "Leave them alone and get down here." Responding to the urgency of its master's mind, the flying snake stopped tormenting the flying rodents and zipped down to wrap itself gently around Flinx's neck.

The inn they were approaching was one of hundreds that formed an informal backwoods network in the uninhabited parts of the vast forests. Such establishments provided temporary home to hardwood merchants and cutters, sightseers, fishermen and hunters, prospectors, and other nomadic types. There were more inns than a casual observer might expect to find because there were more nomads. They liked the endless forest. The trees concealed many people and a comparable quantity of sin.

Flinx tethered the stupava in the animal compound, next to a pair of muccax. The inn door sensed his presence and slid aside, admitting him. Smoke rose from a central chimney, but the stone fireplace was more for atmosphere than for heating. The latter was handled by thermal coils running beneath the inn floors. Many of the structures dotting the forest were rustic only in appearance, their innards as modern in design and construction as the shuttleport outside Drallar. The offworlder tourists who came to Moth to sample the delights of its wilderness generally liked their rough accommodations the same as their liquor: neat.

"Hello." The innkeeper was only a few years older than Flinx. "You're out by yourself?" He glanced at Pip. "That's an interesting pet you have."

"Thanks," Flinx said absently, ignoring the first comment. "What time do you serve midday meal?" He looked longingly toward the nearby dining room, calculating what remained on his credcard. At the present rate, he would starve before he could catch up to his quarry.

"You don't want a room, then?"

"No, thanks." He would sleep in a tube tent in the

forest, as usual. Exhaustion made him sleep as soundly these days as any soft bed.

"What about your animal?" The innkeeper gestured toward the animal compound outside.

"He'll be all right."

The young innkeeper looked indifferent. A pleasant-enough sort, Flinx thought, but sheltered—like so many of his potential friends back in Drallar.

"You can get a meal here anytime. We're all autoserve here. This isn't a fancy place. We can't afford a live kitchen."

"The machines will be fine for me," Flinx told him. He walked through the entry area and on into the dining room. Other people were already seated about, enjoying their food. There was a young touring couple and one solitary man far back in a corner. After the usual curious glance at Pip, they ignored the newcomer.

Flinx walked over to the autochef, his mouth watering. Living off the land was fine for the stupava, but occasionally he needed something neither stale nor dehydrated. He made his selections from the extensive list, inserted his card, and waited while it processed the request. Two minutes later he picked up his meal, chose a table, and dug into the roast, fried tuber, and crisp green vegetable. Two tall cups of domestic coffee-substitute washed it down.

The innkeeper strolled in. He chatted a moment with the couple, then sauntered over to Flinx's table. Despite his desire for solitude, Flinx didn't feel much like arguing, so he said nothing when the 'keeper pulled over a chair and sat down nearby.

"Excuse me," the young man said cheerfully. "I don't see many people my own age here, let alone anyone younger traveling on his own—certainly never with so interesting a companion." He pointed to Pip.

The flying snake had slithered down from Flinx's neck and was sprawled across the table, gulping down green seeds. They complemented a steady diet of arboreal rodents. The seeds really weren't necessary, but the minidrag was not one to pass up a meal that couldn't fight back.

"What are you doing out here all by yourself?"

A real diplomat, this one, Flinx thought to himself. "I'm looking for a friend," he explained, chewing another chunk of roast.

"No one's left any messages for you here if that's what you're wondering," the innkeeper said.

"The friends I'm looking for don't like to leave messages," Flinx said between mouthfuls. "Maybe you've seen them," he asked without much hope. "A very old woman is traveling with them."

"We don't get many very old people out this way," the innkeeper confessed. "They stay closer to the city. That's what's so funny." Flinx stopped in midchew. "There was a group in here just recently that might be the friends you're looking for."

Flinx swallowed carefully. "This old woman is short, a good deal shorter than me. She's close to a hundred."

"Except for her mouth, which is a lot younger?"

"You've seen her!" The meal was suddenly forgotten.

"Five days ago," the innkeeper said. Flinx's heart sank. The distance between them was increasing, not growing shorter.

"Did you happen to see which way they went?"

"Their mudder took off almost due north. I thought that was odd, too, because the line of inns most tourists follow runs pretty much northwest from here, not north. There are a few lodges due north, of course, up in the Lakes District, but not many. They were a funny bunch, and not just because the old woman was with them. They didn't look like sightseers or fishermen."

Trying not to show too much anxiety, Flinx forced himself to finish the rest of his meal. It wasn't that he didn't appreciate the help, but the talkative youth seemed just the type to blab to anyone who might be curious about a visiting stranger, including the forest patrol. Flinx did not want anyone slowing his pursuit with awkward questions—especially since he intended to increase his speed as soon as feasible and like as not by methods the police would frown upon. Nor had he forgotten the watchman in Drallar whose helpfulness had nearly turned to interference.

"You've been a big help," he told the other.

"What's all this about?" the innkeeper persisted as Flinx finished the last of his food and let Pip slide up his proffered arm and onto his shoulder. "What's going on?"

Flinx thought frantically. What could he say to keep this loudmouthed innocent from calling up the patrol? "They're on vacation—my great-grandmother and some other relatives. They argue a lot." The innkeeper nodded knowingly. "I wasn't supposed to be able to go along," Flinx continued with a wink. "But I slipped away from my studies, and I've sort of been playing at trailing them. You know. When they get to the lodge where they'll be spending the rest of the month, I'm going to pop in and surprise them. Once I land in their laps, they can hardly send me home, can they?"

"I get it." The innkeeper smiled. "I won't tell anyone."

"Thanks." Flinx rose. "Food's good." He gathered up Pip and headed for the door.

"Hey," the innkeeper called out at a sudden thought, "what lodge are your relatives headed for?" But Flinx was already gone.

Outside, he hurriedly mounted his stupava and turned it into the woods. Five days, he thought worriedly. Two more at this pace and they would be ten ahead of him. The stupava was doing its best, but that was not going to be good enough. Somehow he had to increase his speed. He reined in and let the bird catch its breath as he extracted a ten-centimeter-square sheet of plastic from his backpack. It was half a centimeter thick and had cost him plenty back in the marketplace, but he could hardly have risked this journey without it. A series of contact switches ran down the left side of the plastic. He touched the uppermost one, and the sheet promptly lit up. Additional manipulation of the controls produced a map of the forest, and further adjustments zoomed in on a blowup of his immediate surroundings.

He entered the name of the inn where he had had his hasty meal. Instantly, the map shifted position. It was as if he were flying above an abstract landscape. When the image settled, he widened the field of view, expanding the map until it included several other inns and a small town that he had unknowingly skirted the previous day. He touched controls, and the map zoomed in on the town. On its fringe was a small wood-processing plant, several minor commercial structures, a forest service station, and a communications supply-and-repair terminal. He thought about trying the forest service station first, then decided that of all the structures it was the one most likely to be manned around the clock. That left the communications depot. He turned off the map, replaced it carefully in his pack, and chucked the reins. The bird whistled and started forward.

Night was falling, and soon the sun would have settled completely behind the shielding clouds. One thing he could count on was the absence of moon—even Flame's maroon glow could not penetrate the cloud cover that night.

Though he had completely missed the town, it was not far off. The buildings were scattered across a little knoll—the driest land around—and remained hidden by trees until he was right on top of them. Most of the homes and apartments were located across the knoll. To his left was a low, rambling structure in which a few lights shone behind double-glazed windows: the forest station. The communications depot was directly ahead of him. He slid easily off the back of the stupava, tied it to a nearby log, and waited for midnight.

A single, three-meter-high fence ran around the depot, enclosing the servicing yard. Flinx could make out the silhouettes of several large vehicles designed for traveling through the dense forest with a full complement of crew and equipment. Flinx wasn't interested in them. They were too big, too awkward for his needs. Surely there had to be something better suited to his purpose parked inside the machine-shed beyond. There had better be. He doubted that the sawmill or smaller commercial buildings would have anything better to offer.

He made certain the stupava's bonds were loose. If he failed, he would need the riding bird in a hurry, and if he succeeded, the stupava would grow restless before too long and would break free to find its way back to Drallar and its barn. That was another reason Flinx had chosen the riding bird over the toadlike muccax: a muccax had no homing instinct.

With Pip coiled firmly around his left shoulder, he made

his way down through the night mist. The yard was not paved, but the ground there had been packed to a comparative dryness and he was able to move silently along the fence. He carefully made a complete circuit of both yard and buildings. No lights were visible, nor did he see any suggestion of alarm beams. Though he had circumvented antitheft equipment before, this would be the first time he had tried to break into a government-owned facility.

The fence arched outward at the top, a design that would make climbing over it difficult, and he could clearly see transmitter points positioned atop each post, ready to set off the alarm if anything interrupted their circuit. Flinx lowered his gaze to the back gate. The catch there appeared to be purely mechanical, almost too simple. He could open it without any special tools. The catch to the catch was a duplicate of the units that ran along the crest of the fence. He could not open the latch without interrupting the beam and setting off the alarm.

Cutting through the mesh of the fence itself was out of the question. The meal was sensitized: any nonprogrammed disruption of its structure would sound the alarm as surely as if he had tried to knock a section over with a dozer.

Nudging Pip aside, Flinx slipped off his backpack and hunted through it. In addition to the concentrated foods and basic medical supplies, he carried equipment that would have shocked the innkeeper who had chatted with him earlier that day. He didn't need long to find what he was looking for. From the pack he extracted one of several odd lengths of wire. A single contact switch was spliced to its center. Making certain the switch was open, he looped one end of the wire carefully around the tiny transmitter point on the left side of the gate latch. Gently, he formed the wire into an arch and brought it across the long latch to loop it over the transmitter on the opposite side. A minuscule LED on the wire's switch glowed a satisfying green.

Then out of the backpack Flinx took a small, oddly formed piece of dull metal, inserted it into the gate lock, and turned it a couple of times. In the heat from his hand, the metal softened and flowed obediently. The latch *click*ed. Holding the metal tool with only two fingers, Flinx lowered the heat it was absorbing until it resolidified, and then turned it. He heard a second, softer click from the latch. He pulled it free, put a hand on the gate, and pushed. It moved two meters inward, swaying slightly on its supports. He hesitated. No audible alarm ran through the night. He hoped that a rural cummunity would have no need of silent alarms. Still, he gathered up his tools and backpack and retreated hastily to the forest.

He waited until half an hour had passed without anyone's appearing to check the gate or the yard, then he crept back to the fence. The gate still sat ajar. The glass fiber, looped from terminal to terminal, permitted the alarm beam to flow uninterrupted, but there would be a problem when he had to open the gate farther than the length of the wire allowed.

He slipped easily into the maintenance yard. Pip flew over the fence and hovered just above its master's tousled hair.

Flinx searched the yard. There was still no hint that his intrusion had been detected. The machine shed lay directly in front of him, doorless and open to the night. He used the huge repair vehicles for cover as he made his way into the shed. Among the equipment and supplies were a pair of two-passenger mudders. His heart beat a little faster. The compact vehicles had flared undersides and enclosed cabs to protect pilot and passenger in side-by-side comfort.

He tried them both. Jumping the simple electric engines was easy enough. He grew anxious when the fuel gauge on the first machine didn't react, indicating an empty storage cell, but the second mudder showed a ninety-five-percent charge. That was better than good; it was critical, because he doubted he would have access to recharge stations where he was going.

Since the depot remained peaceful, Flinx gambled his success thus far to resolve one additional difficulty: the mudder's government markings. In a storage cabinet, he found dozens of cans of catalytic bonding paint. He chose a couple of cans of brown. After a moment's thought, he went back to the cabinet and selected an additional canister of red. He had never had a personal transport of his own—as long as he was going to add a little art, he might as well put some flash into it. Besides, that would be more in keeping with the character of a sixteen-year old boy. The trees would still conceal it well.

When he had finished spraying the mudder, he climbed into the pilot's seat. Pip settled into the empty one alongside. The controls were simple and straightforward, as he'd expected. His right hand went to the little steering wheel, his left to the jump he had installed beneath the dash. The engine came to life, its steady hum little louder than Pip's. A nudge on the accelerator sent the mudder forward. The single, wide-beam searchlight mounted on its nose remained dark. It would stay that way until he was sure he was safe.

He drove into the yard, and still there was no sign of concern from the nearby buildings. At the gate, he left the craft on hover and jumped out. Patching his remaining passfibers onto the first, he was able to open the gate wide enough for the mudder to pass through. He was so fearful of being spotted that he nearly forgot to duck as he drove through the gap—the fibers that served to fool the alarm system almost decapitated him.

Then he was out through the gate, on the smooth surface bordering the depot. In moments, he was concealed by the forest. A touch on a dash control locked the transparent plastic dome over his head, shutting out the mist. Another control set the craft's heater to thrumming. For the first time since he had left Drallar, he was warm.

He held the mudder's speed down until he was well away from the town. Then he felt safe in turning on the searchlight. The high-power beam pierced the darkness and revealed paths between the trees. Now he was able to accelerate, and soon the mudder was skipping along over the moist earth. Too fast, perhaps, for night-driving, but Flinx wanted to make up time on his quarry. And he was a little drunk with success.

It wouldn't have been that easy in Drallar, he told himself. Out here, where there wasn't much to steal, he had succeeded because thieves were scarce.

The underside of the mudder was coated with a special hydrophobic polyresin that allowed it to slide across a moist but solid surface with almost no friction, propelled by the single electric jet located in the vehicle's stern. It also made very little noise; not that he could detect any sign of pursuit. The mudder's compass control kept him headed north.

It was midmorning before Flinx finally felt the need to stop. He used daylight and the canister of red paint to decorate the brown vehicle, adding decorative stripes to side and front. It took his mind off his problems for a little while. Then he was traveling again, in a craft no casual observer would ever have mistaken for a sober government vehicle.

The night before there had been a touch of a mental tingle of almost painful familiarity. As usual, it vanished the instant he sought to concentrate on it, but he felt sure that that touch had reached out to him from somewhere to the north.

Confident and comfortable, he soared along with the dome retracted. Suddenly, the air turned gray with thousands of furry bodies no bigger than his little finger. They swarmed about him on tiny membranous wings, and he swatted at them with his free hand as he slowed the car to a crawl. They were so dense he couldn't see clearly.

Pip was delighted, both with the opportunities for play and for dining. Soon the storm of miniature fliers became so thick that Flinx had to bring the mudder to a complete halt for fear of running into something ahead. At least now he could use both hands to beat at them.

He hesitated to close the protective dome for fear of panicking the dozens that would inevitably be trapped inside. Besides, except for blocking his view, they weren't bothering him. Their square little teeth were designed for cracking the hulls of nuts and seeds, and they showed no interest in live flesh. They had large bright-yellow eyes, and two thin legs suitable for grasping branches. Flinx wondered at them, as well as how long it would be before they moved on and he could resume his journey.

Suddenly, the air was full of *whooshing* sounds. The earth erupted head-sized round shapes. Flinx saw long thin snouts full of needlelike teeth and multiple arms projecting from narrow bodies. The *whooshing* noise was composed of a long series of explosive popping sounds.

He squinted through the mass of fliers and saw one creature after another emerge from vertical burrows. The poppers were black-bodied with yellow and orange variolitic colorings. They became airborne by inflating a pair of sausage-shaped air sacs attached to their spines—by regulating the amount of air in the sacs, the animals could control not only their altitude but their direction. They lit into the swarm of fliers, utilizing long, thin snouts to snatch one after another from the air. Once a popper had made several catches, it would deflate its air sacs and settle parachutelike to the ground. They always seemed to land directly above their respective burrows, down which they would promptly vanish.

When neither the cloud of fliers nor attacking poppers showed any signs of thinning, Flinx made the decision to move forward. He traveled slowly, picking his way through the trees. He had traveled nearly a kilometer before the swarms started to disperse, and eventually he passed into open forest once again. A backward glance showed a solid wall of gray, black, and yellow-orange shifting like smoke among the trees. It took a moment before he realized something was missing from the mudder.

"Pip?" The minidrag was not coiled on the passenger seat, nor was it drifting on the air currents above the mudder.

It took Flinx several worried minutes before he located his pet lying on its belly in the storage compartment behind the seats, swollen to three times its usual diameter. It had thoroughly gorged itself on the tasty little gray fliers. Flinx was convinced that his currently immobile companion did not look at all well.

"That'll teach you to make a durq of yourself," he told his pet. The minidrag moved once, slowly, before giving up totally on the effort. It would be a while before it flew again, even to its master's shoulder.

Flinx continued northward, hardly pausing to sleep. Two days had passed since he had appropriated the mudder. Given the likely laxity of rural bureaucratic types, it might be some time before its absence was remarked upon. By the time someone figured out that a real theft had been pulled off, Flinx would be two hundred kilometers away, and the local authorities would have no way of knowing which direction he had taken. Skimming along just above the surface, a mudder left no trail. Its simple electric jet emitted practically no waste heat to be detected from the air. But Flinx did not expect any kind of elaborate pursuit, not for a single, small, comparatively inexpensive vehicle.

He continued to wonder about all the effort and expense someone was going through to abduct a harmless old woman. The implausibility of the whole situation served only to heighten his anxiety and did nothing to dampen his anger or determination.

Several days went by before he detected the change in the air. It was an alien feeling, something he couldn't place. The omnipresent dampness remained, but it had become sharper, more direct in his nostrils. "Now what do you suppose that is, Pip?" he murmured aloud. The flying snake would not have answered had it been able. All its efforts and energies were still directed to the task of digesting fur, meat, and bone.

The mudder moved up a slight hill. At its crest a gap in the trees revealed a scene that took Flinx's breath away. At first, he thought he had somehow stumbled onto the ocean. No, he knew that couldn't be. No ocean lay north from Drallar, not until one reached the frozen pole or unless one traveled east or west for thousands of kilometers.

Though the body of water looked like an ocean, he recognized it for what it was: a lake, one of the hundreds that occupied the territory from his present position northward to the arctic. No sunlight shone directly on it, for the clouds were as thick here as they were in distant Drallar, but enough light filtered through to create a glare—a glare that exploded off that vast sheet of water to reflect from the cloud cover overhead and bounced again from the water.

The-Blue-That-Blinded, Flinx thought. He knew enough of Moth's geography to recognize the first of the lakes which bore that collective description. The lake itself he could not put a name to, not without his map. It was only one of hundreds of similarly impressive bodies of fresh water whose names he had had no need to memorize during his readings, for he had never expected to visit that part of the world.

The glare imprisoned between surface and clouds brought tears to his eyes as he headed the mudder toward the water's edge. The lake blocked his path northward. He needed to know whether to skirt it to the east or the west or to attempt a crossing. He had no way of figuring out what his quarry had done.

The weather was calm. Only a modest chop broke the otherwise smooth expanse before him. A mudder could travel over water as well as land, provided its charge held out; if not, the vehicle would sink quickly.

Flinx decided that the first thing he needed was some advice. So he turned to his map, which showed a single, isolated lodge just to the east. He headed for it.

The building came into view ten minutes later, a large rambling structure of native stone and wood. Boats were tied up to the single pier out back. Several land vehicles were parked near the front. Flinx tensed momentarily, then relaxed. None of the craft displayed government markings. Surely his theft had been discovered by now, but it was likely that the search would tend more in the direction of populated areas to the south—toward Drallar—rather than into the trackless north.

Nevertheless, he took a moment to inspect the assembled vehicles carefully. All four were deserted. Two of them were tracked—strictly land transportation. The others were mudders, larger and fancier than his own, boasting thickly upholstered lounges and self-darkening protective domes. Private transport, he knew. More comfortable than his own craft but certainly no more durable. There was no sign of riding animals. Probably anyone who could afford to travel this far north could afford mechanized transportation.

Flinx brought the mudder to a stop alongside the other vehicles and took the precaution of disconnecting the ignition jumper. It wouldn't do to have a curious passer-by spy the obviously illegal modification. The mudder settled to the ground, and he stepped out over the mudguard onto the surface.

The parking area had not been pounded hard and smooth, and his boots picked up plenty of muck as he walked up to the wooden steps leading inside. Suction hoses cleaned off most of the mud. The steps led onto a covered porch populated by the kind of rustic wooden furniture so popular with tourists who liked to feel they were roughing it. Beyond was a narrow hall paneled with peeled, glistening tree trunks, stained dark.

Flinx thought the inn a likely place to obtain information about lake conditions, but before that, something equally important demanded his attention. Food. He could smell it somewhere close by, and he owed himself a break from the concentrates that had been fueling him for many days. His credcard still showed a positive balance, and there was no telling when he would be fortunate enough to encounter honest cooking again. Nor would he have to worry about curious stares from other patrons—Pip, still unable to eat, would not be dining with him this time. He inhaled deeply. It almost smelled as if the food were being prepared by a live chef instead of a machine.

Flinx found his way to the broad, exposed-beam dining room. The far wall had a fire blazing in a rock fireplace. To the left lay the source of the wonderful aroma: a real kitchen. A couple of furry shapes snored peacefully nearby. An older couple sat near the entrance. They were absorbed in their meal and didn't even turn to look up at him. Two younger couples ate and chatted close by the fireplace. In the back corner was a group of oldsters, all clad in heavy north-country attire.

He started down the few steps into the dining room, intending to question someone in the kitchen about the possibility of a meal. Suddenly, something hit his mind so hard he had to lean against the nearby wall for support.

Two younger men had entered the dining room from a far, outside door. They were talking to the group of diners in the far corner. No one had looked toward Flinx; no one had said a word to him.

He tottered away from the wall, caught and balanced himself at the old couple's table. The man looked up from his plate at the uninvited visitor and frowned.

"You feeling poorly, son?"

Flinx didn't answer, but continued to stare across the room. Faces—he couldn't make out faces beneath all that heavy clothing. They remained hidden from his sight—but not from something else.

He spoke sharply, unthinkingly.

"Mother?"

Chapter Nine

One of the bundled figures spun in its chair to gape at him. Her eyes were wide with surprise as well as with a warning Flinx ignored. She started to rise from her seat.

The rest of the group gazed at the young man standing across the room. One of the younger men put a hand on Mother Mastiff's shoulder and forced her back into her chair. She promptly bit him. The man's companion pulled something out of a coat pocket and started toward Flinx. The group's stunned expressions, brought on by Flinx's unexpected appearance, had turned grim.

Flinx searched the floor and walls nearby, found the switch he was hunting for, and stabbed at it. The lights in the dining room went out, leaving only the dim daylight from the far windows to illuminate the room.

What a fantastic Talent he possessed, he thought as he dove for cover. It had reacted sharply to Mother Mastiff's presence—after he had all but tripped over her.

The room filled with screams from the regular guests, mixed with the curses of those Flinx had surprised. He did not try to make his way toward the table where Mother Mastiff was being held; he had been through too many street fights for that. Keeping the layout of the dining room in his mind, he retreated and dropped to a crawl, taking the long way around the room toward the table in an attempt to sneak behind her captors. Three had been seated at the table with her, plus the two who had arrived later. Five opponents.

"Where is he—somebody get some lights!" Very helpful of them, Flinx mused, to let him know their location. He would have to make use of the information quickly, he knew. Soon one of the guests, or a lodge employee, would have the lights back on, robbing him of his only advantage.

A sharp crackling richocheted around the room, accompanied by a brief flash of light. One of the other guests screamed a warning. Flinx smiled to himself. With everyone hugging the floor, that ought to keep the lights off a little longer.

A second bolt split the air at table level, passing close enough to set his skin twitching. Paralysis beam. Though Flinx took some comfort from this demonstration of his opponent's intent not to shoot to kill, he did not stop to think why they might take such care. The kidnappers continued to fire blindly through the darkness. With those nerve-petrifying beams filling the room, no employee was likely to take a stab at a light switch.

Grateful once more for his small size, Flinx kept moving on his belly until he reached the far wall. At the same time, the random firing ceased. Imagining one of his opponents feeling along the walls in search of a light switch, Flinx readied himself for a hurried crawl past the glow of the fireplace. Then someone let out a violent curse, and he heard the sound of chair and table going over very close by. Flinx's hand went to his boot. He rose to a crouching position, waiting.

Again, he heard the sound of stumbling, louder and just ahead. He put his hand on a nearby chair and shoved it into the darkness. A man appeared in the glow from the fireplace, and a flash enveloped the chair. Flinx darted in behind the man and used the stiletto as old Makepeace had instructed him. The man was twice Flinx's size, but his flesh was no tougher than anyone else's. He exhaled once, a sharp wheeze, before collapsing in a heap. Flinx darted forward, out of the illuminating glare of the fire.

"Erin," a voice called uncertainly, "you okay?" Several new flashes filled the air, striking the stone around the fireplace where Flinx had stood moments earlier. If the intent of those shots was to catch Flinx unaware, they failed; on the other hand, they did force him to hug the floor again.

Moments later, the lights winked back on, shockingly bright. Flinx tensed beneath the table that sheltered him, but he needn't have worried. The party of travelers had fled, along with the remaining paralysis-beam wielder and Mother Mastiff.

Flinx climbed to his feet. The other guests remained cowering on the floor. There was no hint of what had brought the lights back to life, and he had no time to think about it.

The door at the far end of the room was ajar. It led out onto a curving porch. He hurried to it but paused just inside to throw a chair out ahead of him. When no one fired on it, he took a deep breath and jumped out, rolling across the porch and springing out of the roll into a fighting crouch.

There was no enemy waiting to confront him—the porch was deserted. The beach off to the left was not. Two mudders were parked on the shore. As Flinx watched helplessly, the travelers he had sought for so long piled into the two crafts. Heedless now of his own safety, he charged down the steps onto the slight slope leading toward the lake shore. The first mudder was already cruising across the wave tops. By the time he reached the water's edge and sank exhausted to his knees, the useless knife held limply in his right hand, both craft were already well out on the lake surface itself.

Fighting for breath, Flinx forced himself erect and started back up the slope. He would have to go after them quickly. If he lost sight of them on the vast lake, he would have no way of knowing on which far shore they would emerge. He staggered around the front of the lodge and grabbed at the entrance to his mudder. A supine and unsettled shape stared back at him. Pip looked distinctly unhappy. It flittered once, then collapsed back onto the seat.

"Fine help you were," Flinx snapped at his pet. The minidrag, if possible, managed to look even more miserable. Clearly, it had sensed danger to Flinx and had tried to go to his aid, but simply couldn't manage to get airborne.

Flinx started to climb into the cab when a voice and a hand on his shoulder restrained him. "Just a minute." Flinx tensed, but a glance at Pip showed that the flying snake was not reacting defensively.

"I can't," he started to say as he turned. When he saw who was confronting him, he found himself able only to stare.

She seemed to tower over him, though in reality she was no more than a couple of centimeters taller. Black hair fell in tight ringlets to her shoulders. Her bush jacket was tucked into pants that were tucked into low boots. She was slim but not skinny. The mouth and nose were child-sized, the cheekbones high beneath huge, owl-like brown eyes. Her skin was nearly as dark as Flinx's, but it was a product of the glare from the nearby lake and not heredity. She was the most strikingly beautiful woman he had ever seen.

He tracked down his voice and mumbled, "I have to go after them." The hand remained on his shoulder. He might have thrown it off, and might not.

"My name's Lauren Walder," she said. "I'm the general manager at Granite Shallows." Her voice was full of barely controlled fury as she used her head to gesture toward the lake. Ringlets flew. "What have you to do with those idiots?"

"They've kidnapped my mother, the woman who adopted me," he explained. "I don't know why, and I don't much care right now. I just want to get her back."

"You're a little out-numbered, aren't you?"

"I'm used to that." He pointed toward the dining-room windows and the still-open porch doorway. "It's not me lying dead on your floor in there."

She frowned at him, drawing her brows together. "How do you know the man's dead?"

"Because I killed him."

"I see," she said, studying him in a new light. "With what?"

"My stiletto," he said.

"I don't see any stiletto." She looked him up and down.

"You're not supposed to. Look, I've got to go. If I get too far behind them—"

"Take it easy," she said, trying to soothe him. "I've got something I have to show you."

"You don't seem to understand," he said insistently. "I've no way to track them. I won't know where they touch land and—"

"Don't worry about it. You won't lose them."

"How do you know?"

"Because we'll run them down in a little while. Let them relax and think they've escaped." Her fingers tightened on his shoulder. "I promise you we'll catch them."

"Well . . ." He spared another glance for Pip. Maybe in a little while the flying snake would be ready to take to the air. That could make a significant difference in any fight to come. "If you're sure . . ."

She nodded once, appearing as competent as she was beautiful. Lodge manager, he thought. She ought to know what she was talking about. He could trust her for a few minutes, anyway.

"What's so important to show me?" he asked.

"Come with me." Her tone was still soaked with anger.

She led him back into the lodge, across the porch and back into the dining room. Several members of her staff were treating one of the women who had been dining when the lights had gone out and the guns had gone off. Her husband and companions were hovering anxiously over her; and she was panting heavily, holding one hand to her chest.

"Heart condition," Lauren explained tersely.

Flinx looked around. Tables and chairs were still overturned, but there was no other indication that a desperate fight had been fought in the room. Paralysis beams did not damage inanimate objects. The man he had slain had been moved by lodge personnel. He was glad of that.

Lauren led him toward the kitchen. Lying next to the

doorway were the pair of furry shapes he had noticed when he had first entered the room. Up close, he could see their round faces, twisted in agony. The short stubby legs were curled tightly beneath the fuzzy bodies. Their fur was a rust red except for yellow circles around the eyes, which were shut tight. Permanently.

"Sennar and Soba." Lauren spoke while gazing at the dead animals with a mixture of fury and hurt. "They're wervils—or were," she added bitterly. "I raised them from kittens. Found them abandoned in the woods. They liked to sleep here by the kitchen. Everybody liked to feed them. They must have moved at the wrong time. In the dark, one of those"—she used a word Flinx didn't recognize, which was unusual in itself—"must have mistaken them for you. They were firing at anything that moved, I've been told." She paused a moment, then added, "You must have the luck of a pregnant Yax'm. They hit just about everything in the room except you."

"I was down on the floor," Flinx explained. "I only stand up when I have to."

"Yes, as that one found out." She jerked a thumb in the direction of the main hall. Flinx could see attendants wrapping a body in lodge sheets. He was a little startled to see how big his opponent had actually been. In the dark, though, it's only the size of your knife that matters.

"They didn't have to do this," the manager was murmuring, staring at the dead animals. "They didn't have to be so damned indiscriminate. Four years I've coddled those two. Four years. They never showed anything but love to anyone who ever went near them." Flinx waited quietly.

After a while, she gestured for him to follow her. They walked out into the main hall, down a side corridor, and entered a storeroom. Lauren unlocked a transparent wall case and removed a large, complex-looking rifle and a couple of small, wheel-shaped plastic containers. She snapped one of them into the large slot set in the underside of the rifle. The weapon seemed too bulky for her, but she swung it easily across her back and set her right arm through the support strap. She added a pistol to her service belt, then led him back out into the corridor.

"I've never seen a gun like that before." Flinx indicated the rifle. "What do you hunt with it?"

"It's not for hunting," she told him. "Fishing gear. Each of those clips"—and she gestured at the wheel-shapes she had handed over to Flinx—"holds about a thousand darts. Each dart carries a few milliliters of an extremely potent neurotoxin. Prick your finger on one end . . ." She shrugged meaningfully.

"The darts are loaded into the clips at the factory in Drallar, and then the clips are sealed. You can't get a dart out unless you fire it through this." She patted the butt of the rifle, then turned a corner. They were back in the main hallway.

"You use a gun to kill fish?"

She smiled across at him. Not much of a smile but a first, he thought. "You've never been up to The-Blue-That-Blinded before, have you?"

"I've lived my whole life in Drallar," he said, which for all practical purposes was the truth.

"We don't use these to kill the fish," she explained. "Only to slow them up if they get too close to the boat."

Flinx nodded, trying to picture the weapon in use. He knew that the lakes of The-Blue-That-Blinded were home to some big fish, but apparently he had never realized just how big. Of course, if the fish were proportional to the size of the lakes . . . "How big is this lake?"

"Patra? Barely a couple of hundred kilometers across. A pond. The really *big* lakes are further off to the northwest, like Turquoise and Hanamar. Geographers are always arguing over whether they should be called lakes or inland seas. Geographers are damn fools."

They exited from the lodge. At least it wasn't raining, Flinx thought. That should make tracking the fleeing mudders a little easier.

Flinx jumped slightly when something landed heavily on his shoulder. He stared down at it with a disapproving look. "About time." The flying snake steadied himself on his master but did not meet his eyes.

"Now that's an interesting pet," Lauren Walder commented, not flinching from the minidrag, as most strangers did. Another point in her favor, Flinx thought. "Where on Moth do you find a creature like that?"

"In a garbage heap," Flinx said, "which is what he's turned himself into. He overate a few days ago and still hasn't digested it all."

"I was going to say that he looks more agile than that landing implied." She led him around the side of the main lodge building. There was a small inlet and a second pier stretching into the lake. Flinx had not been able to see it from where he had parked his mudder.

"I said that we'd catch up to them." She pointed toward the pier.

The boat was a single concave arch, each end of the arch spreading out to form a supportive hull. The cabin was located atop the arch and was excavated into it. Vents lined the flanks of the peculiar catamaran. Flinx wondered at their purpose. Some heavy equipment resembling construction cranes hung from the rear corners of the aft decking. A similar, smaller boat bobbed in the water nearby.

They mounted a curving ladder and Flinx found himself watching as Lauren shrugged off the rifle and settled herself into the pilot's chair. She spoke as she checked readouts and threw switches. "We'll catch them inside an hour," she assured Flinx. "A mudder's fast, but not nearly as fast over water as this." A deep rumble from the boat's stern; air whistled into the multiple intakes lining the side of the craft, and the rumbling intensified.

Lauren touched several additional controls whereupon the magnetic couplers disengaged from the pier. She then moved the switch set into the side of the steering wheel. Thunder filled the air, making Pip twitch slightly. The water astern began to bubble like a geyser as a powerful stream of water spurted from the subsurface nozzles hidden in the twin hulls. The boat leaped forward, cleaving the waves.

Flinx stood next to the pilot's chair and shouted over the roar of the wind assailing the open cabin. "How will we know which way they've gone?"

Lauren leaned to her right and flicked a couple of switches below a circular screen, which promptly came to life. Several bright yellow dots appeared on the transparency. "This shows the whole lake." She touched other controls. All but two dots on the screen turned from yellow to green. "Fishing boats from the other lodges that ring Patra. They have compatible instrumentation." She tapped the screen with a fingernail. "That pair that's stayed yellow? Moving, nonorganic, incompatible transponder. Who do you suppose that might be?"

Flinx said nothing, just stared at the tracking screen. Before long, he found himself staring over the bow that wasn't actually a bow. The twin hulls of the jet catamaran knifed through the surface of the lake as Lauren steadily increased their speed.

She glanced occasionally over at the tracker. "They're moving pretty well—must be pushing their mudders to maximum. Headed due north, probably looking to deplane at Point Horakov. We have to catch them before they cross, of course. This is no mudder. Useless off the water."

"Will we?" Flinx asked anxiously. "Catch them, I mean." His eyes searched the cloud-swept horizon, looking for the telltale glare of diffused sunlight on metal.

"No problem," she assured him. "Not unless they have some special engines in those mudders. I'd think if they did, they'd be using 'em right now."

"What happens when we catch them?"

"I'll try cutting in front of them," she said thoughtfully. "If that doesn't make them stop, well—" she indicated the rifle resting nearby. "We can pick them off one at a time. That rifle's accurate to a kilometer. The darts are gas-propelled, you see, and the gun has a telescopic sight that'll let me put a dart in somebody's ear if I have to."

"What if they shoot back?"

"Not a paralysis pistol made that can outrange that rifle, let alone cover any distance with accuracy. The effect is dispersed. It's only at close range that paralysis is effective on people. Or lethal to small animals," she added bitterly. "If they'll surrender, we'll take them in and turn them over to the game authorities. You can add your own charges at the same time. Wervils are an endangered species on Moth. Of course, I'd much prefer that the scum resist so that we can defend ourselves."

Such bloodthirstiness in so attractive a woman was no surprise to Flinx. He'd encountered it before in the marketplace. It was her motivation that was new to him. He wondered how old she was. Probably twice his own age, he thought, though it was difficult to tell for sure. Time spent in the wilderness had put rough edges on her that even harsh city life would be hard put to equal. It was a different kind of roughness; Flinx thought it very becoming.

"What if they choose to give themselves up?" He knew that was hardly likely, but he was curious to know what her contingency for such a possibility might be.

"Like I said, we take them back with us and turn them over to the game warden in Kalish."

He made a short, stabbing motion with one hand. "That could be awkward for me."

"Don't worry," she told him. "I'll see to it that you're not involved. It's not only the game laws they've violated. Remember that injured guest? Ms. Marteenson's a sick woman. The effect of a paralysis beam on her could be permanent. So it's not just the game authorities who'll be interested in these people.

"As to you and your mother, the two of you can disappear. Why has she been kidnapped? For ransom?"

"She hasn't any money," Flinx replied. "Not enough to bother with, anyway."

"Well, then, why?" Lauren's eyes stayed on the tracker, occasionally drifting to scan the sky for signs of rain. The jet boat had a portable cover that she hoped they wouldn't have to use. It would make aiming more difficult.

"That's what I'd like to know," Flinx told her. "Maybe we'll find out when we catch up with them."

"We should," she agreed, "though that won't do Sennar and Soba any good. You've probably guessed by now that my opinion of human beings is pretty low. Present company excepted. I'm very fond of animals. Much rather associate with them. I never had a wervil betray me, or any other creature of the woods, for that matter. You know where you stand with an animal. That's a major reason why I've chosen the kind of life I have."

"I know a few other people who feel the way you do," Flinx said. "You don't have to apologize for it."

"I wasn't apologizing," she replied matter-of-factly.

"Yet you manage a hunting lodge."

"Not a hunting lodge," she corrected him. "Fishing lodge. Strictly fishing. We don't accommodate hunters here, but I can't stop other lodges from doing so."

"You have no sympathy for the fish, then? It's a question of scales versus fur? The AAnn wouldn't like that."

She smiled. "Who cares what the AAnn think? As for the rest of your argument, it's hard to get cozy with a fish. I've seen the fish of this lake gobble up helpless young wervils and other innocents that make the mistake of straying too far out into the water. Though if it came down to it"—she adjusted a control on the instrument dash, and the jet boat leaped to starboard—"I'm not sure I wouldn't prefer the company of fish to that of people either."

"It's simple, then," Flinx said. "You're a chronic antisocial."

She shrugged indifferently. "I'm me. Lauren Walder. I'm happy with what I am. Are you happy with what you are?"

His smile faded. "I don't know what I am yet." He dropped his gaze and brooded at the tracker, his attention focused on the nearing yellow dot that indicated their quarry.

Odd thing for a young man like that to say, she thought. Most people would've said they didn't know *who* they were yet. Slip of the tongue. She let the remark pass.

The gap between pursued and pursuer shrank rapidly on the tracker. It wasn't long before Flinx was able to gesture excitedly over the bow and shout, "There they are!"

Lauren squinted and saw only water and cloud, then glanced down at the tracker. "You've got mighty sharp eyes, Flinx."

"Prerequisite for survival in Drallar," he explained.

A moment later she saw the mudders also, skittering along just above the waves and still headed for the northern shore. Simultaneously, those in the mudders reacted to the appearance of the boat behind them. They accelerated and for a moment moved out of sight again.

Lauren increased the power. This time they didn't pull away from the jet boat.

She nodded slightly. "I thought so. Standard mudder engines, no surprises. I don't think they're hiding anything from us." She glanced at her companion. "Think you can drive this thing for a little while?"

Flinx had spent the past half hour studying the controls as well as the image on the tracker. The instrumentation was no more complex than that of his mudder. On the other hand, he was used to driving over land. "I think so," he said. This was not the time for excessive caution.

"Good." She slid out of the pilot's chair and waited until he slipped in and took control over the wheel. "It's very responsive," she warned him, "and at the speed we're traveling, even a slight turn of the wheel will send us shooting off in another direction. So watch it."

"I'll be okay," he assured her. He could feel the vibration of the engine through the wheel. The sensation was exhilarating.

A flash of light suddenly marked the fleeing mudders, but it dissipated well shy of the jet boat's bow. Flinx maintained the gap between the three craft. The flash was repeated; it did no more damage to the boat or its crew than would a flashlight beam.

"No long-range weapons," Lauren murmured. "If they had 'em, now'd be the time to use 'em." Flinx saw she was hefting the dart rifle. It was nearly as tall as she was. She settled it onto a vacant bracket and bent over to peer through the complex telescopic sight. In that position, it resembled a small cannon more than a rifle.

Two more flares of light shot from the mudders, futile stabs at the pursuing jet boat. "I can see them," Lauren announced as she squinted through the sight. "They look confused. That's sensible. I don't see anything but hand weapons. Two of them seem to be arguing. I don't think they expected this kind of pursuit."

"They didn't expect to see me in the dining room, either," Flinx said confidentially. "I'll *bet* they're confused."

She looked over from the sight. "You're sure they weren't looking for you to follow?"

"I doubt it, or I'd never have come this close to them."

She grunted once and returned her eyes to the sight. "At this range, I can pick their teeth." She moved the rifle slightly. "Hold her steady, please." She pushed the button which took the place of a regular trigger. The gun went *phut!* and something tiny and explosive burst from the muzzle.

"Warning shot," she explained. "There—someone's pulling the dart out. I put it in the back of the pilot's chair. Now they're gathering around and studying it, except the driver, of course. Now they're looking back at us. One of them's keeping two hands on a little old lady. Your mother?"

"I'm sure," Flinx said tightly.

"She's giving the one restraining her fits, trying to bite him, kicking at him even though it looks like her feet are bound at the ankles."

"That's her, all right." Flinx couldn't repress a grin. "What are they doing now?"

Lauren frowned. "Uh oh. Putting up some kind of transparent shield. Now the regular vehicle dome over that. The dome we can penetrate. I don't know about the shield-thing. Well, that's no problem. Go to port."

"Port?" Flinx repeated.

"To your left," she said. "We'll cut around in front of them and block their course. Maybe when they see that we can not only catch them but run circles around them, they'll be willing to listen to reason."

Flinx obediently turned the wheel to his left and felt the catamaran respond instantly.

"Okay, now back to star—to your right, not too sharply." The boat split the water as he turned the wheel.

Suddenly, everything changed. A new sound, a deep humming, became audible.

"Damn," Lauren said in frustration, pointing upward.

Flinx's gaze went toward the clouds. The skimmer that had appeared from out of the northern horizon was of pretty good size. It was certainly more than big enough to hold its own crew in addition to the mudders' occupants. If there was any doubt as to the skimmer's intent, it was quickly eliminated as the versatile craft dipped low, circled once, and then settled toward the first mudder as it strove to match the smaller vehicle's speed.

"If they get aboard, we'll lose them permanently," said a worried Flinx. "Can you pick them off as they try to transfer?" Already the skimmer's crew had matched velocity with the mudder and was dropping a chute ladder toward the water.

Lauren bent over the rifle again. Her finger hesitated over the button; then she unexpectedly pulled back and whacked the butt of the gun angrily. "Lovely people. They're holding your mother next to the base of the chute. I can't get a clear shot."

"What are we going to do? We can't just keep circling them like this!"

"How the hell should I know?" She abandoned the rifle and rushed to a storage locker amidships. "Mudders, paralysis pistols, kidnapping, and now a skimmer sent out from the north. Who are these people, anyway?"

"I don't know," Flinx snapped. "I told you before that I don't understand any of this." He hesitated, trying to watch her and keep the jet boat circling the still-racing mudders and the skimmer hovering above them. "What are you going to do now?"

The device she had extracted from the storage locker was as long as the dart rifle but much narrower. "When I give the word," she said tightly, "I want you to charge them and pull aside at the last moment. I don't think they'll be expecting a rush on our part. They're much too busy transferring to the skimmer."

"What are you going to try and do?" he asked curiously. "Disable the skimmer?"

"With a dart gun? Are you kidding?" she snorted. "Just do as I say."

"So long as what you say continues making sense," he agreed, a bit put off by her tone.

"You're wasting time. Do it!"

He threw the wheel hard over. The catamaran spun on the surface so sharply that the portside hull lifted clear of the water. A high rooster tail obscured them from sight for a moment.

In seconds, they were on top of the mudder and the

skimmer drifting steadily above it. Activity on both craft intensified as the jet boat bore down on the mudder. As Lauren suspected, the last thing their opponents were expecting was a broadside charge. A couple of shots passed behind the onrushing boat, hastily dispatched and imperfectly aimed.

"Hard to port!" Lauren shouted above the roar of the engine. Those still on board the mudder had hunched down in anticipation of a collision. Flinx leaned on the wheel. Engine screaming, the catamaran spun to its left, nearly drowning those starting up the chute ladder toward the skimmer.

Lauren must have fired at least once, Flinx thought as the jet boat sped away. He turned the wheel, and they started back toward their quarry in a wide arc. To his surprise, the woman put the peculiar-looking weapon back in the storage locker and returned to the bracket-held dart rifle. "Now let's go back and take our best shots."

"A one-shot gun?" he murmured. "I didn't even hear it go off. What was the purpose of that crazy charge?" He wrestled with the wheel.

"That charge was our insurance, Flinx." She gestured back toward the storage locker where she had repositioned the narrow gun. "That gun was a Marker. We use it to help track injured fish that break their lines." She nodded toward the skimmer. "I think I hit it twice. The gun fires a capsule which holds a specially sensitized gel. Epoxied bonder, sticks to *anything* on contact, and it's not water soluble. As long as they don't think to check the underside of their skimmer for damage, and there's no reason for them to do so since it's operating perfectly, they'll never see the gel. It's transparent, anyway. Now we can track them."

"Not with this boat, surely."

"No. But there's a skimmer back at the lodge. Would've taken too long to ready it or we'd be on it now instead of on this boat. Wish we were. No reason to expect a skimmer to show up suddenly to help them, though." She gestured toward the mudder.

"As long as they don't get too far ahead of us, we'll be able to follow them—just like we did with this boat. But if we can hurt them now . . ." She looked back through the telescopic sight. "Ah, they've taken your mother up on a hoist. Strapped in. I'm sure she didn't make it easy for them."

"She wouldn't," Flinx murmured affectionately.

"Clear shooting now," Lauren said delightedly. A loud beeping sounded from the tracking unit.

"What's that?" Flinx gave the device a puzzled glance.

Lauren uttered a curse and pulled away from the rifle. A quick glance at the screen and Flinx found himself shoved none too gently out of the pilot's chair. He landed on the deck hard.

"Hey, what's—!"

Lauren wasn't listening to him as she wrenched the wheel hard to starboard. Flinx frantically grabbed for some support as the boat heeled over. He could just see the port hull rising clear of the water as something immense and silvery-sided erupted from the lake's surface.

Chapter Ten

Screams and shouts came from the vicinity of the mudders and the skimmer. A violent reactive wave nearly capsized the jet boat; only Lauren's skillful and experienced maneuvering kept them afloat.

Flinx saw a vast argent spine shot through with flecks of gold that shone in the diffused sunlight. It looked like a huge pipe emerging from beneath the waves, and it turned the sunlight to rainbows. Then it was gone, not endless as he first believed. Another wave shook the catamaran as the monster submerged once again. Flinx pulled himself up to where he could peer over the edge of the cabin compartment.

The mudders had vanished completely, sucked down in a single gulp by whatever had materialized from the depths of the lake. The skimmer itself just missed being dragged down by that great gulf of a mouth. It hovered above the disturbed section of lake where its companion craft had been only a moment ago. Then someone on the skimmer apparently made a decision, for it rose another twenty meters toward the clouds and accelerated rapidly northward.

"They're leaving," Flinx shouted. "We have to get back to the lodge, get the skimmer you mentioned, and hurry after them before—"

"We have to get out of here alive first." Lauren followed her announcement with another curse as her hands tore at the wheel. The silver mountain lifted from the lake just starboard of the jet boat. Flinx was gifted with a long, uncomfortable view down a throat wide enough to swallow several mudders intact. Or a jet boat. The jaws slammed shut, sending a heavy spray crashing over the gunwales. The monster was so close Flinx could smell its horrid breath. Then it was sinking back into the waters boiling behind the catamaran.

Something moved on his shoulder, and he reached up to grasp at the muscular form that was uncoiling. "No, Pip! Easy . . . this one's too big even for you." The snake struggled for a moment before relaxing. It bobbed and ducked nervously, however, sensing a threat not only to its master but to itself. Yet it responded to the pressure of Flinx's restraining fingers and held its position.

For a third time, the penestral struck, snapping in frustration at the spot where the jet boat had been only seconds earlier. Thanks to the tracker, which had first warned Lauren of the nightmare's approach, they were able to avoid its upward rush.

"This won't do," she murmured. "It'll keep working us until I make a mistake. Then it'll take us the way it took the poor souls still stuck on those mudders." She studied the tracker intently. "It's circling now. Trying to cut us off from shallow water and the shore. We'll let it think we're headed that way. Then we'll reverse back into deep water."

"Why?"

She ignored the question. "You didn't care for it when I had to shove you away from the wheel a few minutes ago, did you? Here, it's all yours again." She reached down and half pulled, half guided him back into the pilot's chair. "That's enough." She threw the wheel over, and the boat seemed to spin on its axis. Flinx grabbed for the wheel.

"It'll follow us straight now instead of trying to ambush us from below and will try to hit us from astern. Keep us headed out into the lake and let me know when it's tangent to our square." She indicated the red dot on the tracking screen that was closing on them from behind.

"But shouldn't we—?"

She wasn't listening to him as she made her way back to the pair of gantrylike structures protruding from the rear of the boat. She took a seat behind one, stretched it out so the arm hung free over the water, then checked controls.

"When I tell you," she shouted back at him over the roar of the engine and the spray, "go hard a-port. That's left."

"I remember," he snapped back at her. His attention was locked to the tracker. "It's getting awfully close."

"Good." She positioned herself carefully in the seat, touched a switch. Flexible braces snapped shut across her waist, hips, shoulders and legs, pinning her to the seat in a striped cocoon.

"*Awfully* close," Flinx reiterated.

"Not ready yet," she murmured. "A fisherman has to be patient." The water astern began to bubble, a disturbance more widespread than a mere boat engine could produce. "Now!" she shouted.

Flinx wrenched the wheel to his left. Simultaneously, the surface of the lake exploded behind them. With both hands on the wheel, there was nothing Flinx could do except cry out as Pip left its perch and launched itself into the air. A muffled explosion sounded from the stern, and a moment later its echo reached him as the harpoon struck the penestral just beneath one of the winglike fins that shielded its gills.

The soaring monster displaced the lake where the jet boat had been before Flinx had sent it screaming into a tight turn. A distant *crump* reached the surface as the harpoon's delayed charge went off inside the guts of the penestral. Polyline spewed from a drum inside the ship's hull, a gel coating eliminating dangerous heat buildup where line rubbed the deck.

"Cut the engine," came the command from astern.

"But then we won't have any—" he started to protest.

"Do it," she ordered.

Flinx sighed. He was not a good swimmer. He flicked

the accelerator until their speed dropped to nothing. The jet engine sank to an idle. Instantly, the catamaran began moving in reverse. The twin hulls were pointed aft as well as forward, and the boat moved neatly through the water as it was towed backward. The retreating polyline slowed from a blur to where Flinx could count space markings as it slid off the boat. Meanwhile, Lauren had reloaded the harpoon gun and was watching the surface carefully.

She called back to him. "Where's the penestral?"

"Still moving ahead of us, but I think it's slowing."

"That's to be expected. Keep your hands on the accelerator and the wheel."

"It's still slowing," he told her. "Slowing, slowing—I can't see it anymore. I think it's under the boat!"

"Go!" she yelled, but at that point he didn't need to be told what to do; he had already jammed the accelerator control forward. The jet boat roared, shot out across the lake. An instant later a geyser erupted behind them as the penestral tried to swallow the sky. Flinx heard the harpoon gun discharge a second time.

This time, the penestral was struck just behind one crystal-like eye the size of a telescope mirror. It collapsed back into the water like a tridee scene running in reverse, sending up huge waves over which the retreating catamaran rode with ease. The waves were matched in frequency if not intensity by the palpitations of Flinx's stomach.

This time, the fish didn't sink back into the depths. It stayed on the surface, thrashing convulsively.

"Bring us back around," Lauren directed Flinx. She was sweating profusely as she reloaded the harpoon cannon for the third time. Only the autoloading equipment made it possible for one person to manipulate the heavy metal shaft and its explosive charge.

This harpoon was slightly smaller and thinner than the two that had preceded it. As the boat swung back toward the penestral, Flinx heard the gun go off again. Several minutes passed. The penestral stopped fighting and began to sink.

Lauren touched another button. There was a hum as a compressor located inside the catamaran started up, pumping air through the plastic line that ran to the hollow shaft of the last harpoon. She unstrapped herself from the chair and began to oversee the reeling in of the colossal catch. "Air'll keep it afloat for days," she said idly, exchanging seats with Flinx once again. "Too big for darts, this one."

"Why bother with it?" Flinx stared as the silver-sided mountain expanded and drew alongside the catamaran.

"You might be right—it's not much of a fish. Bet it doesn't run more than fifteen meters." Flinx gaped at her. "But there are hungry people in Kaslin and the other towns south of the lake, and the penestral's a good food fish—lean and not fatty. They'll make good use of it. What they don't eat they'll process for resale further south. The credit will go to the lodge.

"Besides, we have guests staying with us who come up to Patra regularly, twice a year for many years, and who in all that time have never seen anything bigger than a five-meter minnow. Your first time and you've participated in a catch. You should feel proud."

"I didn't catch it," he corrected her quickly. "You did."

"Sorry, modesty's not permitted on this lake. Catching even a penestral's a cooperative effort. Dodging is just as important as firing the gun. Otherwise, *we* end up on *his* trophy wall." She jabbed a thumb in the direction of the inflated bulk now secured to the side of the catamaran.

A weight settled gently onto Flinx's left shoulder. "I'd hoped you hadn't gone off to try and attack it," he said to the minidrag as it slipped multiple coils around his arm. "It's good to know you have *some* instinct for self-preservation." The flying snake stared quizzically back at him, then closed its eyes and relaxed.

Flinx inspected what he could see of the penestral while the jet boat headed back toward the southern shore. "Those people in the mudders, they didn't stand a chance."

"Never knew what hit them," Lauren agreed. "I'm sure they weren't carrying any kind of tracking equipment. No reason for it. If our tracker had been out of order, we'd have joined the mudders in the penestral's belly."

A quick death at least, Flinx thought. Death was a frequent visitor to the unwary in the Drallarian marketplace, so he was no stranger to it. Thoughts of death reminded him of Mother Mastiff. Would his persistence result in her captors' deciding she wasn't worth the trouble anymore? What might they have in mind for her, now that her presence had caused the death of a number of them? Surely, he decided, they wouldn't kill her out of hand. They had gone to so much trouble already.

But the thought made him worry even more.

Exhilarated by the fight, Lauren's voice was slightly elevated and hurried. She had reason to be short of wind, Flinx thought. "One of these days, Flinx, after we've finished with this business, you'll have to come back up here. I'll take you over to Lake Hozingar or Utuhuku. Now those are respectable-sized lakes and home to some decent-sized fish. Not like poor little Patra, here. At Hozingar, you can see the real meaning of the name The-Blue-That-Blinded."

Flinx regarded the immense carcass slung alongside the jet boat in light of her words. "I know there are bigger lakes than this one, but I didn't know they held bigger penestrals."

"Oh, the penestral's a midrange predator," she told him conversationally. "On Hozingar you don't go fishing for penestral. You fish for oboweir."

"What," Flinx asked, "is an oboweir?"

"A fish that feeds regularly on penestrals."

"Oh," he said quietly, trying to stretch his imagination to handle the picture her words had conjured up.

Quite a crowd was waiting to greet them as they tied up at the lodge pier. Lauren had moored the inflated penestral to a buoy nearby. The carcass drew too much water to be brought right inshore.

Flinx slipped through the *oohing* and *ahhing* guests, leaving Lauren to handle the questions. Several of her employees fought their way to her and added questions of their own. Eventually, the crowd began to break up, some to return to their rooms, others to remain to gawk at the fish bobbing slowly on the surface.

Flinx had collapsed gratefully into a chair on the porch that encircled the main building. "How much do you want

for the use of the skimmer and a tracker?" he asked
Lauren when she was able to join him. "I'll need you to
show me how to use it, of course."

She frowned at him. "I'm not sure I follow you, Flinx."

"I told you, I'm going after them. You've made it possible for me to do that, and I'm very grateful to you."

She looked thoughtful. "Management will scream when
they find out I've taken out the skimmer for personal use.
They're a lot more expensive than a jet boat or mudder.
We'll have to be careful with it."

He still wasn't listening to her, his mind full of plans for
pursuing the kidnappers. "I don't know how I'll ever repay
you for this, Lauren."

"Don't worry about it. The lodge's share of profit from
the disposal of the penestral ought to defray all the operating expenses. Come on, get yourself and your snake out
of that chair. We have to gather supplies. The skimmer's
usually used for making quick runs between here and At-
tock. That's where we pick up our guests. We'll need to
stock some food, of course, and I want to make sure the
engine is fully charged. And if I don't take ten minutes to
comb my hair out, I'm going to die." She tugged at the
tangles of black ringlets that the action on the lake had
produced.

"Just a minute." This time it was Flinx who put out the
restraining hand as he bounded out of the chair. "I think
I've misunderstood. You don't mean you're coming with
me?"

"You don't know how to use the tracking equipment,"
she pointed out.

"I can figure it out," he assured her confidently. "It
didn't take me long to figure out how to handle the boat,
did it?"

"You don't know the country."

"I'm not interested in the country," he responded. "I'm
not going on a sightseeing trip. That's what the tracker's
for, isn't it? Just loan the stuff to me. I'll pay you back
somehow. Let me just have the tracker and a charge for
my mudder, if you're worried about the skimmer."

"You're forgetting about my wervils. Besides, you can't

track a skimmer with a mudder. What if you hit a canyon?"

"Surely you're not giving up your work here," he said, trying another tack, "just so you can seek revenge for the deaths of a couple of pets?"

"I told you, wervils are an endangered species on Moth. And I also told you how I feel about animals."

"I know," he protested, "but that still doesn't—"

He broke off his protest as she reached out to ruffle his hair. "You know, you remind me of another wervil I cared for once, though his fur wasn't quite as bright as yours. Near enough, though." Then she went on more seriously. "Flinx, I don't like these people, whoever they are. I don't like them because of what they've done to you, and I don't like them because of what they've done to me. Because of that, I'm going to help you as well as myself. Because I'd be going out after them whether you were here or not, for the sake of Sennar and Soba.

"Don't try to deny that you couldn't use a little help and don't give me any of that archaic nonsense about your not wanting me along because I'm a woman."

"Oh, don't worry," he told her crisply. "The last thing I'd try to do would be to inflict any archaic nonsense on you."

That caused her to hesitate momentarily, uncertain whether he was joking or not. "Anyway," she added, "if I can't go, not that you can stop me, then you couldn't go, either. Because I'm the only one who has access to the skimmer."

It was not hard for Flinx to give in. "I haven't got time to argue with you."

"And also the sense not to, I suspect. But you're right about the time. The tracker should pick up the gel underneath their skimmer right away, but let's not play our luck to the limit. I don't know what kind of skimmer they were using. I've never seen the like before, so I've no idea if it's faster than usual. We go together, then?"

"Together. On two conditions, Lauren."

Again, she found herself frowning at him. Just when she thought she could predict his actions, he would do something to surprise her again. "Say them, anyway."

"First, that Pip continues to tolerate you." He rubbed the back of the flying snake's head affectionately. It rose delightedly against the pressure. "You see, I have certain feelings toward animals myself."

"And the other condition?" she inquired.

"If you ever touch my hair like that again, you'd better be prepared for me to kick your lovely backside all the way to the Pole. Old ladies have been doing that to me ever since I can remember, and I've had my fill of it!"

She grinned at him. "It's a deal, then. I'm glad your snake isn't as touchy as you are. Let's go. I have to leave a message for my superiors in case they call in and want to know not only where their skimmer is but their lodge manager as well."

When she informed the assistant manager of the lodge, he was very upset. "But what do I tell Kilkenny if he calls from Attoka? What if he has guests to send up?"

"We're not expecting anyone for another week. You know that, Sal. Tell him anything you want." She was arranging items in a small sack as she spoke. "No, tell him I've gone to the aid of a traveler in distress across the lake. That's an acceptable excuse in any circumstance."

The assistant looked past her to where Flinx stood waiting impatiently, chucking Pip under its jaw and staring in the direction of the lake.

"He doesn't look like he's very distressed to me."

"His distress is well hidden," Lauren informed him, "which is more than I can say for you, Sal. I'm surprised at you. We'll be back real soon."

"Uh-huh. It's just that I'm not a very good liar, Lauren. You know that."

"Do the best you can." She patted his cheek affectionately. "And I'm not lying. He really is in trouble."

"But the *skimmer,* Lauren."

"You still have the lodge mudders and the boats. Short of a major catastrophe of some kind, I can see no reason why you'd need the skimmer. It's really only here to be used in case of emergency. To my mind"—she gestured toward Flinx—"this is an emergency."

The assistant kicked at the dirt. "It's your neck."

"Yes, it's my neck."

"Suppose they ask which way you went?"

"Tell them I've headed——" A cough interrupted her. She looked back at Flinx and nodded once. "Just say that I've had to go across Patra."

"But which way across?"

"Across the lake, Sal."

"Oh. Okay, I understand. You've got your reasons for doing this, I guess."

"I guess I do. And if I'm wrong, well, you always wanted to be manager here, anyway, Sal."

"Now hold on a minute, Lauren. I never said——"

"Do the best you can for me," she gently admonished him. "This means something to me."

"You *really* expect to be back soon?"

"Depends on how things go. See you, Sal."

"Take care of yourself, Lauren." He watched as she turned to rejoin the strange youth, then shrugged and started back up the steps into the lodge.

As Lauren had said, it was her neck.

It didn't take long for the skimmer to be checked out. Flinx climbed aboard and admired the utilitarian vehicle. For almost the first time since he left Drallar, he would be traveling totally clear of such persistent obstacles as mist-shrouded boulders and towering trees. The machine's body was made of black resin. It was large enough to accommodate a dozen passengers and crew. In addition to the standard emergency stores, Lauren provisioned it with additional food and medical supplies. They also took along the dart rifle and several clips and a portable sounding tracker.

Flinx studied the tracking screen and the single moving dot that drifted northwestward across the transparency. A series of concentric gauging rings filled the circular screen. The dot that represented their quarry had already reached the outermost ring.

"They'll move off the screen in a little while," he murmured to Lauren.

"Don't worry. I'm sure they're convinced by now that they've lost us."

"They're zigzagging all over the screen," he noted.

"Taking no chances. Doesn't do any good if you're

showing up on a tracker. But you're right. We'd better get moving."

She slid into the pilot's chair and thumbed controls. The whine of the skimmer's engine drowned out the tracker's gentle hum as the craft rose several meters. Lauren held it there as she ran a final instrument check, then pivoted the vehicle on an invisible axis and drove it from the hangar. A nudge of the altitude switch sent them ten, twenty, thirty meters into the air above the lodge. A touch on the accelerator and they were rushing toward the beach.

Despite the warmth of the cabin heater, Flinx still felt cold as he gazed single-mindedly at the screen.

"I told you not to worry," Lauren said with a glance at his expression as they crossed the shoreline. "We'll catch them."

"It's not that." Flinx peered out through the transparent cabin cover. "I was thinking about what might catch us."

"I've yet to see the penestral that can pick out and catch an airborne target moving at our speed thirty meters up. An oboweir might do it, but there aren't any oboweirs in Lake Patra. Leastwise, none that I've ever heard tell of."

Nevertheless, Flinx's attention and thoughts remained evenly divided between the horizon ahead and the potentially lethal waters below.

"I understand you've had some trouble here."

Sal relaxed in the chair in the dining room and sipped at a hot cup of toma as he regarded his visitors. They had arrived in their own mudder, which immediately stamped them as independent as well as wealthy. If he played this right, he might convince them to spend a few days at the lodge. They had several expensive suites vacant, and if he could place this pair in one, it certainly wouldn't do his record any harm. Usually, he could place an offworlder by accent, but not these two. Their words were clear but their phonemes amorphous. It puzzled him.

Routine had returned as soon as Lauren and her charity case had departed. No one had called from down south, not the district manager, not anyone. He was feeling very content. Unless, of course, the company had decided to send its own investigators instead of simply calling in a checkup. That thought made him frown at the woman.

"Say, are you two Company?"

"No," the woman's companion replied, smiling pleasantly. "Goodness no, nothing like that. We just like a little excitement, that's all. If something unusual's going on in the area, it kind of tickles our curiosity, if you know what I mean."

"You had a man killed here, didn't you?" the woman asked.

"Well, yes, it did get pretty lively here for a day." No accounting for taste, Sal mused. "Someone was killed during a fight. A nonguest," he hastened to add. "Right in here. Quite a melee."

"Can you describe any of those involved?" she asked him.

"Not really. I'm not even positive which guests were involved and which day visitors. I didn't witness the argument myself, you see, and by the time I arrived, most of the participants had left."

The woman accepted this admission with a disappointed nod. "Was there a young man involved? Say, of about sixteen?"

"Yes, him I did see. Bright-red hair?"

"That's the one," she admitted.

"Say, is he dangerous or anything?" The assistant manager leaned forward in his chair, suddenly concerned.

"Why do you want to know?" the man asked.

"Well, my superior here, the regular manager—Lauren Walder. She went off with him."

"Went off with him?" The pleasant expression that had dominated the woman's face quickly vanished, to be replaced by something much harder.

"Yes. Three, maybe four days ago now. I'm still not completely sure why. She only told me that the young man had a problem and she was going to try to help him out."

"Which way did their mudder go?" the man asked.

"North, across Lake Patra," Sal informed them. "They're not in a mudder, though. She took the lodge skimmer."

"A skimmer!" The woman threw up her hands in frustration and sat down heavily in a chair opposite the assistant. "We're losing ground," she told her companion, "instead of gaining on him. If he catches up with them before we do, we could lose him *and* the . . ." Her companion cut the air with the edge of his hand, and her words trailed away to an indecipherable mumble. The gesture had been quick and partly concealed, but Sal had noticed it nonetheless.

"Now you've really got me worried," he told the pair. "If Lauren's in some kind of trouble—"

"She could be," the man admitted, pleased that the assistant had changed the subject.

Sal thought a moment. "Would she be in danger from these people who had the fight here, or from the redhead?"

"Conceivably from both." The man was only half lying. "You'd better tell us everything you know."

"I already have," Sal replied.

"You said they went north, across the lake. Can't you be any more specific than that?"

Sal looked helpless. "Lauren wouldn't be any more specific than that."

"They might not continue heading north."

"No, they might not. Do you have a tracker for following other craft?" Sal asked.

The man shook his head. "We didn't think we'd need one. The last we knew, the young man we'd like to talk with was traveling on stupava-back."

"I think he arrived here in a mudder."

The woman looked surprised and grinned ruefully at her companion. "No wonder we fell behind. Resourceful, isn't he?"

"Too resourceful for my liking," the man murmured, "and maybe for his own good if he backs those you-know-whos into a corner."

The women sighed, then rose from her chair. "Well, we've wasted enough time here. We'll just have to return to Pranbeth for a skimmer and tracking unit. Unless you think we should try to catch up to them in the mudder."

The man let out a short, humorless laugh, then turned

back to the assistant manager. "Thanks, son. You've been helpful."

"I wish I could be more so," Sal told him anxiously. "If anything were to happen to Lauren—you'll see that nothing happens to her, won't you?"

"I promise you we'll do our best," the woman assured him. "We don't want to see innocent bystanders hurt. We don't even want to see noninnocents hurt." She favored him with a maternal smile, which for some reason did nothing to make the nervous assistant feel any better about the situation.

Chapter Eleven

The tracker hummed quietly, the single glowing dot showing clearly on its screen as the skimmer rushed northward. It was clipping the tops of the tallest trees, more than eighty meters above the bogs and muck that passed for the ground. They had crossed Lake Patra, then an intervening neck of dry land, then the much larger lake known as Tigranocerta and were once more cruising over the forest. A cold rain was falling, spattering off the skimmer's acrylic canopy to form a constantly changing wet topography that obscured much of the view outside. The skimmer's instruments kept its speed responsive, maintaining a predetermined distance between it and its quarry to the north.

Awfully quiet, Lauren Walder thought. He's awfully quiet, and maybe something else.

"No, I'm not too young," he said into the silence that filled the cabin, his tone softly defensive.

Lauren's eyebrows lifted. "You can read minds?"

He responded with a shy smile. "No, not that." Fingers stroked the head of the minidrag sleeping on his shoulder. "I just feel things at times. Not thoughts, nothing that elaborate. Just the way people are feeling." He glanced up at her. "From the way I thought you were feeling just now, I thought you were going to say something along that line."

"Well, you were right," she confessed, wondering what to make of the rest of his declaration.

"I'm not, you know."

"How old are you?" she asked.

"Sixteen. As best I know. I can't be certain."

Sixteen going on sixty, she thought sadly. During her rare visits to Drallar, she had seen his type before. Child of circumstance, raised in the streets and instructed by wrong example and accident, though he seemed to have turned out better than his brethren. His face held the knowledge withheld from his more fortunate contemporaries, but it didn't seem to have made him vicious or bitter.

Still she felt there was something else at work here.

"How old do you think I am?" she asked idly.

Flinx pursed his lips as he stared at her. "Twenty-three," he told her without hesitating.

She laughed softly and clapped both hands together in delight. "So that's what I'm helping, a sixteen-year-old vengeful diplomat!" Her laughter faded. The smile remained. "Tell me about yourself, Flinx."

It was a question that no stranger in Drallar would ever be so brazen as to ask. But this was not Drallar, he reminded himself. Besides, he owed this woman.

So he told her as much as he knew. When he finished his narrative, she continued to stare solemnly at him, nodding her head as if his words had done no more than confirm suspicions already held. She spared a glance to make sure the tracker was still functioning efficiently, then looked back at him. "You haven't exactly had a comfortable childhood, have you?"

"I wouldn't know," he replied, "because I only have hearsay to compare it with."

"Take my word for it, you haven't. You've also managed to get along with the majority of humanity even though they don't seem to want to have anything to do with you. Whereas I've had to avoid the majority of people who seem to want to have a lot to do with me."

Impulsively, she leaned over out of the pilot's chair and kissed him. At the last instant, he flinched, nervous at such unaccustomed proximity to another human being—especially an attractive member of the opposite sex—and the kiss, which was meant for his cheek, landed instead on his lips.

That made her pull back fast. The smile stayed on her face, and she only blinked once in surprise. It had been an accident, after all. "Take my word for something else, Flinx. If you live long enough, life gets better."

"Is that one of the Church's homilies?" He wondered if she wore some caustic substance to protect her lips from burning, because his own were on fire.

"No," she said. "That's a Lauren Walder homily."

"Glad to hear it. I've never had much use for the Church."

"Nor have I. Nor have most people. That's why it's been so successful, I expect." She turned her gaze to the tracker. "They're starting to slow down. We'll do the same."

"Do you think they've seen us?" Suddenly, he didn't really care what the people in the skimmer ahead of them decided to do. The fire spread from his lips to his mouth, ran down his throat, and dispersed across his whole body. It was a sweet, thick fire.

"I doubt it," she replied. "I'll bet they're close to their destination." Her hands manipulated controls.

"How far ahead of us are they?" He walked forward to peer over her shoulder at the screen. He could have stood to her left, but he was suddenly conscious of the warmth of her, the perfume of her hair. He was very careful not to touch her.

She performed some quick calculations, using the tracker's predictor. "Day or so. We don't want to run up their tail. There's nothing up in this part of the country. Odd place to stop, but then this whole business is odd, from what you've told me. Why bring your mother up here?"

He had no answer for her.

They dropped until the skimmer was rising and falling in concert with the treetops. So intent were they on the actions of the dot performing on the tracking screen that neither of them noticed that not only had the rain stopped but the cloud cover had cracked. Overhead, one of the wings of Moth, the interrupted ring which encircled the planet, shimmered golden against the ceiling of night.

"What makes you so sure they're stopping here instead of just slowing down for a while?" he asked Lauren.

"Because a skimmer operates on a stored charge, just like a mudder. Remember, they had to come from here down to Patra. Our own charge is running low, and we're not on the return leg of a round trip. I don't know what model they're flying, but I saw how big it was. It can't possibly retain enough energy to take them much farther than we've gone the past several days. They at least have to be stopping somewhere to recharge, which is good."

"Why is that?" Flinx asked.

"Because we're going to have to recharge, also." She pointed to a readout. "We've used more than half our own power. If we can't recharge somewhere around here, we're going to have some hiking to do on our way out."

Flinx regarded her with new respect, if that was possible; his opinion of her had already reached dizzying heights. "Why didn't you tell me when we reached the turnaround point?"

She shrugged slightly. "Why? We've gone to a lot of trouble to come as far as we have. You might have argued with me about turning back."

"No," Flinx said quietly, "I wouldn't have done that."

"I didn't think so. You're almost as determined to see this through as I am, and at least as crazy."

She stared up at him, and he stared back. Nothing more needed to be said.

"I vote *no*."

Nyassa-lee was firm in her disagreement. She sat on one side of the table and gazed expectantly at her colleagues. Brora was thoughtfully inspecting the fingernails of his left hand, while Haithness toyed with her eyelashes.

"Really," the tall black woman murmured to her compatriot, "to show such reluctance at this stage is most discouraging, Nyassa-lee." Her fingers left her eyes. "We may never have the chance to manipulate another subject as promising as this Twelve. Time and events conspire against us. You know that as well as I."

"I know." The shorter woman leaned forward in the chair and gazed between her legs at the floor. Cracks showed between the panels; the building had been assembled in haste. "I'm just not convinced it's worth the risk."

"What risk?" Haithness demanded to know. "We've still seen nothing like a demonstration of threatening power. Quite the contrary, I'd say. Certainly the subject had the opportunity to display any such abilities. It's evident he does not possess them, or he would doubtless have employed them against us. Instead, what did we see? Knife." She made it sound disgusting as well as primitive.

"She's right, you know." Brora rarely spoke, preferring to let the two senior scientists do most of the arguing. He stepped in only when he was completely confident of his opinion.

"We don't want another repeat of the girl," Nyassa-lee said. "The society couldn't stand another failure like that."

"Which is precisely why we must pursue this last opportunity to its conclusion," Haithness persisted.

"We don't know that it represents our last opportunity."

"Oh, come on, Nyassa-lee." Haithness pushed back her chair and stood; she began pacing nervously back and forth. Behind her, lights shone cold green and blue from the consoles hastily assembled. "Even if there *are* other subjects of equal potential out there, we've no guarantee that any of us will be around much longer to follow up on them."

"I can't argue with that," Nyassa-lee admitted. "Nor can I argue this Number Twelve's statistical promise. It's just those statistics which frighten me."

"Frighten you?" Haithness stopped pacing and looked over at her companion of many hard years. The tall woman was surprised. She had seen Nyassa-lee wield a gun with the cold-blooded efficiency of a qwarm. Fear seemed foreign to her. "But why? He's done nothing to justify such fear."

"Oh, no?" Nyassa-lee ticked off her points on the fingers of one hand. "One, his statistical potential is alarming. Two, he's sixteen, on the verge of full maturity. Three, he could cross into that at *any* time."

"The girl," Brora pointed out, "was considerably younger."

"Agreed," said Nyassa-lee, "but her abilities were precocious. Her advantage was surprise. This Number Twelve is developing slowly but with greater potential. He may be the kind who responds to pressure by reaching deeper into himself."

"Maybe," Brora said thoughtfully, "but we have no proof of it, nor does his profile predict anything of the sort."

"Then how do you square that," she responded, "with the fact that he has by himself—"

"He's not by himself," Brora interrupted her. "That woman from the lodge was helping him out on the lake."

"*Was* helping him. She didn't help him get to that point. He followed us all the way to that lake on his own, without any kind of external assistance. To me that indicates the accelerated development of a Talent we'd better beware of."

"All the more reason," Haithness said angrily, slapping the table with one palm, "why we must push ahead with our plan!"

"I don't know," Nyassa-lee murmured, unconvinced.

"Do you not agree," Haithness countered, forcing herself to restrain her temper, "that if the operation is a success we stand a good chance of accomplishing our goal as regards outside manipulation of the subject?"

"Possibly," Nyassa-lee conceded.

"Why just 'possibly'? Do you doubt the emotional bond?"

"That's not what concerns me. Suppose, just suppose, that because his potential is still undeveloped, he has no conscious control of it?"

"What are you saying?" Brora asked.

She leaned intently over the table. "With the girl Mahnahmi we knew where we stood, once she'd revealed herself. Unfortunately, that knowledge came as a surprise to us, and too late to counteract. We've no idea where we stand vis-à-vis this subject's Talents. Suppose that, despite the emotional bond, pressure and fear conspire to release his potential regardless of his surface feelings? Statistically, the subject is a walking bomb that may not be capable or mature enough to control itself. *That's* what worries me, Haithness. The emotional bond may be sufficient to control his conscious self. The unpredictable part of him may react violently in spite of it."

"We cannot abandon our hopes and work on so slim a supposition, one that we have no solid facts to support," Haithness insisted. "Besides, the subject is sixteen. If anything, he should have much more control over himself than the girl did."

"I know, I know," Nyassa-lee muttered unhappily. "Everything you say is true, Haithness, yet I can't help worrying. In any case, I'm outvoted."

"That you are," the tall woman said after a questioning glance at Brora. "And if Cruachan were here with us, you know he'd vote to proceed too."

"I suppose." Nyassa-lee smiled thinly. "I worry too much. Brora, are you sure you can handle the implant?"

He nodded. "I haven't done one in some time, but the old skills remain. It requires patience more than anything else. You remember. As to possible unpredictable results, failure, well"—he smiled—"we're all condemned already. One more little outrage perpetrated against society's archaic laws can't harm us one way or the other if we fail here."

Off in a nearby corner, Mother Mastiff sat in a chair, hands clasped in her lap, and listened. She was not bound. There was no reason to tie her, and she knew why as well as her captors. There was nowhere to run. She was in excellent condition for a woman her age, but she had had a good view of the modest complex of deceptive stone and wood structures as the skimmer had landed. Thousands of square kilometers of damp, hostile forest lay between the place she had been brought to and the familiar confines of Drallar. She was no more likely to steal a vehicle than she was to turn twenty again.

She wondered what poor Flinx was going through. That

had been him, out on the boat on the lake far to the south. How he had managed to trace her so far she had no idea. At first, her concern had been for herself. Now that she had had ample opportunity to listen to the demonic trio arguing in front of her—for demonic she was certain they were—she found herself as concerned for the fate of her adopted son as for her own. If she was lost, well, she had had a long and eventful life. Better perhaps that her brave Flinx lose track of her than stumble into these monsters again.

One of the trio, the short, toad-faced man, had spoken of "adjusting" her and of "implants." That was enough to convince her to prepare for something worse than death. Many of their words made no sense to her. She still had no idea who the people were, much less where they had come from or the reasons for their actions. They never spoke to her, ignoring her questions as well as her curses.

Actually, they did not treat her as a human being at all, but rather as a delicate piece of furniture. Their current conversation was the most peculiar yet, for one of them was expressing fear of her boy. She could not imagine why. True, Flinx had tamed a dangerous animal, that horrid little flying creature, but that was hardly a feat to inspire fear in such people. They knew he occasionally had the ability to sense what others were feeling. Yet far from fearing such erratic and minor talents, these people discussed them as if they were matters of great importance.

None of which explained why they'd kidnapped her. If their real interest lay with her boy, then why hadn't they kidnapped him? The whole affair was too complicated a puzzle for her to figure out. Mother Mastiff was not a stupid woman, and her deficiency in formal education did not blunt her sharp, inquiring mind; still she could not fathom what was happening to her, or why.

She let her attention drift from the argument raging across the table nearby to study the room to which she had been brought. Most of the illumination came from the impressive array of electronics lining the walls. Everything she could see hinted of portability and hurried installation. She had no idea as to the purpose of the instrumentation, but she had been around enough to know that such devices were expensive. That, and the actions of the people who had abducted her, hinted at an organization well stocked with money as well as malign intentions.

"I'm not even sure," Nyassa-lee was saying, "that the subject realizes how he's managed to follow us this far."

"There is likely nothing mysterious about it," Haithness argued. "Remember that he is a product of an intensely competitive, if primitive, environment. Urban youths grow up fast when left to their own resources. He may not have enjoyed much in the way of a formal education, but he's been schooled in the real world—something we've had to master ourselves these past years. And he may have had some ordinary, quite natural luck."

"These past years," Brora was mumbling sadly. "Years that should have been spent prying into the great mysteries of the universe instead of learning how to make contacts with and use of the criminal underworld."

"I feel as wasted as you do, Brora," the tall woman said soothingly, "but vindication lies at hand."

"If you're both determined to proceed, then I vote that we begin immediately." Nyassa-lee sighed.

"Immediately with what?" a crotchety voice demanded. For some reason, the question caused the trio to respond, whereas previous attempts to draw their attention had failed miserably.

Nyassa-lee left the table and approached Mother Mastiff. She tried to adopt a kindly, understanding expression, but was only partly successful. "We're scientists embarked on a project of great importance to all mankind. I'm sorry we've been forced to inconvenience you, but this is all necessary. I wish you were of a more educated turn of mind and could understand our point of view. It would make things easier for you."

"Inconvenienced!" Mother Mastiff snorted. "Ye pluck me out of my house and haul me halfway across the planet. That's inconvenience? I call it something else." Her bluster faded as she asked, "What is it you want with my boy Flinx?"

"Your *adopted* boy," Nyassa-lee said. While the small Oriental spoke, Mother Mastiff noted that the other two were studying her the way a collector might watch a bug on a park bench. That made her even madder, and the anger helped to put a damper on her fear. "I wouldn't make things any easier for you people if ye promised me half the wealth of Terra."

"I'm sorry you feel that way, but it's only what we have come to expect," Nyassa-lee said, turning icy once again. "Have you heard of the Meliorare Society?"

Mother Mastiff shook her head, too angry to cry, which is what she really wanted to do. Names, words they threw at her, all meaningless.

"We're part of an experiment," the Oriental explained, "an experiment which began on Terra many years ago. We are not only scientists, we are activists. We believe that the true task of science is not only to study that which exists but to forge onward and bring into existence that which does not exist but eventually will. We determined not to stand still, nor to let nature do so, either."

Mother Mastiff shook her head. "I don't understand."

"Think," Nyassa-lee urged her, warming to her subject, "what is there in Commonwealth society today that could most stand improvement? The government?" A bitter, derogatory laugh sounded behind her, from Haithness. "Not the government, then. What about the ships that carry us from star to star? No? Language, then, an improvement on Terranglo or symbospeech? What about music or architecture?"

Mother Mastiff simply stared at the woman ranting before her. She was quite certain now, quite certain. These three were all as insane as a brain-damaged Yax'm.

"No, none of those things!" Nyassa-lee snapped. It was terrible to see such complete assurance in one so diminutive. "It's us. We." She tapped her sternum. "Humankind. And the means for our improvement lie within." Her hand went to her head. "In here, in abilities and areas of our mind still not properly developed.

"We and the other members of the Society decided many years ago that something could and should be done about that. We formed a cover organization to fool superstitious regulators. In secret, we were able to select certain human ova, certain sperm, and work carefully with them. Our planning was minute, our preparations extensive.

Through microsurgical techniques, we were able to alter the genetic code of our humans-to-be prior to womb implantation. The result was to be, *will* be, a better version of mankind."

Mother Mastiff gaped at her. Nyassa-lee sighed and turned to her companions. "As I feared, all this is beyond her meager comprehension."

"Perfectly understandable," Brora said. "What I don't understand is why you trouble to try?"

"It would be easier," Nyassa-lee said.

"Easier for her, or for you?" Haithness wondered. The smaller woman did not reply. "It won't matter after the operation, anyway." At these words, the fine hair on the back of Mother Mastiff's neck began to rise.

"It might," Nyassa-lee insisted. She looked back down at Mother Mastiff, staring hard into those old eyes. "Don't you understand yet, old woman? Your boy, your adopted son: he was one of our subjects."

"No," Mother Mastiff whispered, though even as she mouthed the word, she knew the woman's words must be true. "What—what happened to your experiment?"

"All the children were provided with attention, affection, education, and certain special training. The majority of the subjects displayed nothing unusual in the way of ability or talent. They were quite normal in every way. We proceeded with great care and caution, you see.

"A few of the subjects developed abnormally. That is in the nature of science, unfortunately. We must accept the good together with the bad. However, in light of our imminent success, those failures were quite justified." She sounded as if she were trying to reassure herself as much as Mother Mastiff.

"A few of the children, a very small number, gave indications of developing those abilities which we believe to lie dormant in every human brain. We don't pretend to understand everything about such Talents. We are in the position of mechanics who have a good idea how to repair an imperfect machine without really knowing what the repaired machine is capable of. This naturally resulted in some surprises.

"An ignorant Commonwealth society did not feel as we

did about the importance of our activities. As a result, we
have undergone many years of persecution. Yet we have
persisted. As you can see, all of us who are original members of the Society are nearly as advanced in years as
yourself.

"The government has been relentless in its efforts to
wipe us out. Over the years, it has whittled away at our
number until we have been reduced to a dedicated few.
Yet we need but a single success, one incontrovertible
proof of the worthiness of our work, to free ourselves
from the lies and innuendo with which we have been
saddled.

"It was a cruel and uncaring government which caused
the dispersal of the children many years ago and which
brought us to our current state of scientific exile. Slowly,
patiently, we have worked to try and relocate those children, in particular any whose profiles showed real promise.
Your Flinx is one of those singled out by statistics as a potential Talent."

"But there's nothing abnormal about him," Mother
Mastiff protested. "He's a perfectly average, healthy young
man. Quieter than most, perhaps, but that's all. Is that
worth all this trouble? Oh, I'll admit he can do some par-
lor tricks from time to time. But I know a hundred street
magicians who can do the same. Why don't you go pick
on them?"

Nyassa-lee smiled that humorless, cold smile. "You're
lying to us, old woman. We know that he is capable of
more than mere tricks and that something far more important than sleight of hand is involved."

"Well, then," she continued, trying a different tack,
"why kidnap me? Why pull me away from my home like
this? I'm an old woman, just as ye say. I can't stand in
your way or do ye any harm. If 'tis Flinx you're so concerned with, why did ye not abduct *him*? I surely could
not have prevented ye from doing so."

"Because he may be dangerous."

Yes, they are quite mad, this lot, Mother Mastiff mused.
Her boy, Flinx, dangerous? Nonsense! He was a sensitive
boy, true; he could sometimes know what others were
feeling, but only rarely, and hardly at all when he most

wished to do so. And maybe he could push the emotions of others a tiny bit. But dangerous? The danger was to him, from these offworld fools and madmen.

"Also," the little Oriental continued, "we have to proceed very carefully because we cannot risk further harm to the Society. Our numbers have already been drastically reduced, partly by our too-hasty attempt to regain control of one subject child a number of years ago. We cannot risk making the same mistake with this Number Twelve. Most of our colleagues have been killed, imprisoned, or selectively mindwiped."

Mother Mastiff's sense of concern doubled at that almost indifferent admission. She didn't understand all the woman's chatter about genetic alterations and improving mankind, but she understood mindwiping, all right. A criminal had to be found guilty of some especially heinous crime to be condemned to that treatment, which took away forever a section of his memories, of his life, of his very self, and left him to wander for the rest of his days tormented by a dark, empty gap in his mind.

"You leave him alone!" she shouted, surprised at the violence of her reaction. Had she become so attached to the boy? Most of the time she regarded him as a nuisance inflicted on her by an unkind fate—didn't she?

"Don't you hurt him!" She was on her feet and pounding with both fists on the shoulders of the woman called Nyassa-lee.

Though white-haired and no youngster, Nyassa-lee was a good deal younger and stronger than Mother Mastiff. She took the older woman's wrists and gently pushed her back down into the chair.

"Now, we're not going to hurt him. Didn't I just explain his importance to us? Would we want to damage someone like that? Of course not. It's clear how fond you've become of your charge. In our own way, we're equally fond of him."

What soulless people these are, Mother Mastiff thought as she slumped helplessly in her chair. What dead, distant shadows of human beings.

"I promise you that we will not try to force the boy to

do anything against his will, nor will we harm him in any way."

"What do ye mean to do with him, then?"

"We need to guide his future maturation," the woman explained, "to ensure that whatever abilities he possesses are developed to their utmost. It's highly unlikely he can do this without proper instruction and training, which is why his abilities have not manifested themselves fully so far. Experience, however, has shown us that when the children reach puberty, they are no longer willing to accept such training and manipulation. We therefore have to guide him without his being aware of it."

"How can ye do this without his knowing what is being done to him?"

"By manipulating him through a third party whose suggestions and directions he will accept freely," the woman said. "That is where you become important."

"So ye wish for me to make him do certain things, to alter his life so that your experiment can be proven a success?"

"That's correct," Nyassa-lee said. "All this must be carried out in such a way that he cannot suspect he is being guided by an outside force." She gestured toward the far end of the room, past transparent doors sealing off a self-contained operating theater. In the dim blue and green light of the instrument readouts, the sterile theater gleamed softly.

"We cannot allow the possibility of interference or misdirection to hamper our efforts, nor can we risk exposure to the Commonwealth agencies which continue to hound us. It is vital that our instructions be carried out quickly and efficiently. Therefore, it will be necessary for us to place certain small devices in your brain, to ensure your complete compliance with our directives."

"Like hell," Mother Mastiff snapped. "I've spent a hundred years filling up this head of mine. I know where everything is stored. I don't want somebody else messing around up there." She did not add, as she glanced surreptitiously toward the operating room, that she had never been under the knife or the laser and that she had a deathly fear of being cut.

"Look," she went on desperately, "I'll be glad to help ye. I'll tell the boy anything ye wish, have him study anything ye want and avoid whatever matters ye wish him to avoid. But leave my poor old head alone. Wouldn't I be much more the help to ye if I did what ye require voluntarily instead of like some altered pet?"

Brora folded his hands on the table and regarded her emotionlessly. "That would certainly be true. However, there are factors which unfortunately mitigate against this.

"First, there are mental activities you will be required to carry out which involve complex processes you are not conversant with but which can be stimulated via direct implants. Second, there is no guarantee that at some future time you would not become discouraged or rebellious and tell the subject what you know. That could be a catastrophe for the experiment. Third, though you may direct the boy with surface willingness, his abilities may enable him to see your inner distress and know that something is amiss, whereas I do not think he can detect the implants themselves, as they are wholly mechanical. Lastly, I think you are lying when you say you would be willing to help us."

"But I don't want an operation!" she cried, pounding at the arms of the chair with her fists. "I tell you 'tis not necessary! I'll do anything ye ask of me if you'll but leave the boy alone and instruct me. Why should I lie to ye? You've said yourself that he's not my true child, only an adopted one. I'll be glad to help ye, particularly," she added with a sly smile, "if there be any money involved."

But the man Brora was shaking his head. "You lie forcefully, but not forcefully enough, old woman. We've spent most of our lives having to cope with traitors in our midst. We can't afford another one. I'm sorry." His attention was drawn to the main entrance and to the two men who'd just entered. He nodded toward Mother Mastiff.

"Restrain her. She knows enough now to do something foolish to herself."

One of the new arrivals held Mother Mastiff's right arm and glanced back toward Brora. "Anesthetic, sir?"

"No, not yet." Mother Mastiff stared at the horrid little

man and shuddered as he spoke quietly to the black woman. "What do you think, Haithness?"

She examined Mother Mastiff. "Tomorrow is soon enough. I'm tired. Better to begin fresh. We'll all need to be alert."

Brora nodded in agreement, leaving the two younger men to bind the raving Mother Mastiff.

Later that evening, over dinner, Nyassa-lee said to Haithness, "The woman's advanced age still gives me concern."

"She's not that old," the taller woman said, spooning down something artificial but nourishing. "With care, she has another twenty years of good health to look forward to."

"I know, but she hasn't the reserves of a woman of fifty anymore, either. It's just as well we haven't told her how complex tomorrow's operation is or explained that her mind will be permanently altered."

Haithness nodded agreement. "There's hardly any need to upset her any more than she already is. Your excessive concern for her welfare surprises me."

Nyassa-lee picked at her food and did not comment, but Haithness refused to let the matter drop.

"How many of our friends have perished at the hands of the government? How many have been mindwiped? It's true that if this old woman dies, we lose an important element in the experiment, but not necessarily a final one. We've all agreed that implanting her is the best way to proceed."

"I'm not arguing that," Nyassa-lee said, "only reminding you that we should be prepared for failure."

Brora leaned back in his chair and sighed. He was not hungry; he was too excited by the prospects raised by the operation.

"We will not fail, Nyassa-lee. This is the best chance we've had in years to gain control over a really promising Subject. We won't fail." He looked over at Haithness. "I checked the implants before dinner."

"Again?"

"Nothing else to do. I couldn't stand just waiting around. The circuitry is complete, cryogenic enervation constant. I anticipate no trouble in making the synaptic connections." He glanced toward Nyassa-lee. "The woman's age notwithstanding.

"As to the part of the old woman that will unavoidably be lost due to the operation"——he shrugged——"I've studied the matter in depth and see no way around it. Not that there seems a great deal worth preserving. She's an ignorant primitive. If anything, the implants and resulting excisions will result in an improved being."

"Her strongest virtues appear to be cantankerousness and obstinacy," Haithness agreed, "coupled to an appalling ignorance of life outside her immediate community."

"Typical speciman," Brora said. "Ironic that such a low example should be the key not only to our greatest success but our eventual vindication."

Nyassa-lee pushed away her food. Her colleague's conversation was upsetting to her. "What time tomorrow?"

"Reasonably early, I should think," Haithness murmured. "It will be the best time for the old woman, and better for us not to linger over philosophy and speculation."

Brora was startled at the latter implication. "Surely you don't expect the boy to show up?"

"You'd best stop thinking of him as a boy."

"He barely qualifies as a young adult."

"Barely is sufficient. Though he's demonstrated nothing in the way of unexpected talent so far, his persistent pursuit of his adopted mother is indication enough to me that he possesses a sharp mind in addition to Talent." She smiled thinly at Nyassa-lee. "You see, my dear, though I do not share your proclivity to panic in this case, I do respect and value your opinion."

"So you *are* expecting him?"

"No, I'm not," Haithness insisted, "but it would be awkward if by some miracle he were to show up here prior to the operation's successful completion. Once that is accomplished, we'll naturally want to make contact with him through his mother. When he finds her unharmed and seemingly untouched, he will relax into our control."

"But what if he does show up prior to our returning the old woman to Drallar?"

"Don't worry," Haithness said. "I have the standard story prepared, and our personnel here have been well coached in the pertinent details."

"You think he'd accept that tale?" Nyassa-lee asked. "That hoary old business of us being an altruistic society of physicians dedicated to helping the old and enfeebled against the indifference of government medical facilities?"

"It's true that we've utilized the story in various guises before, but it will be new to the subject," Haithness reminded her colleague. "Besides, as Brora says, he barely qualifies as an adult, and his background does not suggest sophistication. I think he'll believe us, especially when we restore his mother to him. That should be enough to satisfy him. The operation will, of course, be rendered cosmetically undetectable."

"I do better work on a full night's sleep." Brora abruptly pushed back from the table. "Especially prior to a hard day's work."

They all rose and started toward their quarters, Brora contemplating the operation near at hand, Haithness the chances for success, and only Nyassa-lee the last look in Mother Mastiff's eyes.

Chapter Twelve

They had to be close to their destination because their quarry had been motionless for more than an hour. That's when the pain hit Flinx; sharp, hot, and unexpected as always. He winced and shut his eyes tight while Pip stirred nervously on its master's shoulder.

Alarmed, Lauren turned hurriedly to her young companion. "What is it? What's wrong, Flinx?"

"Close. We're very close."

"I can tell that by looking at the tracker," she said.

"It's her, it's Mother Mastiff."

"She's hurt?" Already Lauren was dropping the skimmer into the woods. The minidrag writhed on Flinx's shoulder, hunting for an unseen enemy.

"She's—she's not hurting," Flinx mumbled. "She's—there's worry in her, and fear. Someone's planning to do something terrible to her. She fears for me, too, I think. But I can't understand—I don't know what or wh—"

He blinked. Pip ceased his convulsions. "It's gone. Damn it, it's gone." He kicked at the console in frustration. "Gone and I can't make it come back."

"I thought—"

He interrupted her; his expression was one of resignation. "I have no control over the Talent. No control at all. These feelings hit me when I least expect them, and never, it seems, when I want them to. Sometimes I can't even locate the source. But this time it was Mother Mastiff. I'm sure of it."

"How can you tell that?" Lauren banked the skimmer to port, dodging a massive emergent.

"Because I know how her mind feels."

Lauren threw him an uncertain look, then decided there was no point in trying to comprehend something beyond her ken.

The skimmer slowed to a crawl and quickly settled down among the concealing trees on a comparatively dry knoll. After cutting the power, Lauren moved to the rear of the cabin and began assembling packs and equipment. The night was deep around them, and the sounds of nocturnal forest dwellers began to seep into the skimmer.

"We have to hurry," Flinx said anxiously. He was already unsnapping the door latches. "They're going to hurt her soon!"

"Hold it!" Lauren said sharply. "You don't know what's going to happen to her. More important, you don't know when."

"Soon!" he insisted. The door popped open and slid back into the transparent outer wall. He stared out into the forest in the direction he knew they must take even though he hadn't checked their location on the tracking screen.

"I promise that we'll get to her as fast as is feasible," Lauren assured him as she slipped the sling of the dart rifle over her shoulder, "but we won't do her or ourselves any good at all if we go charging blindly in on those people, whoever they are. Remember, they carried paralysis weapons on their vehicles. They may have more lethal weapons here. They're not going to sit idly by while you march in and demand the return of the woman they've gone to a helluva lot of trouble to haul across a continent. We'll get her back, Flinx, just as quickly as we can, but recklessness won't help us. Surely you know that. You're a city boy."

He winced at the "boy," but otherwise had to agree with her. With considerable effort he kept himself from dashing blindly into the black forest. Instead, he forced himself to the back of the skimmer and checked out the contents of the backpack she had assembled for him. "Don't I get a gun, too?"

"A fishing lodge isn't an armory, you know." She patted the rifle butt. "This is about all we keep around in the way of a portable weapon. Besides, I seem to recall you putting away an opponent bigger than yourself using only your own equipment."

Flinx glanced self-consciously down at his right boot. His prowess with a knife was not something he was particularly proud of, and he didn't like talking about it. "A stiletto's not much good over distance, and we may not have darkness for an ally."

"Have you ever handled a real hand weapon?" she asked him. "A needler? Beam thrower, projectile gun?"

"No, but I've seen them used, and I know how they work. It's not too hard to figure out that you point the business end at the person you're mad at and pull the trigger or depress the firing stud."

"Sometimes it's not quite that simple, Flinx." She tightened the belly strap of her backpack. "In any case, you'll have to make do with just your blade because there isn't anything else. And I'm not going to give you the dart rifle. I'm much more comfortable with it than you'd be. If you're worried about my determination to use it, you should know me better than that by now. I don't feel like being nice to these people. Kidnappers and wervil killers."

She checked their course on the tracker, entered it into her little compass, and led him from the cabin. The ground was comparatively dry, soft and springy underfoot.

As they marched behind twin search beams, Flinx once more found himself considering his companion. They had a number of important things in common besides independence. Love of animals, for example. Lauren's hair masked the side of her face from him but he felt he could see it, anyway.

Pip stirred on its master's shoulder as it sensed strange emotions welling up inside Flinx, emotions that were new to the minidrag and left it feeling not truly upset but decidedly ill at ease. It tried to slip farther beneath the protective jacket.

By the time they reached their destination, it was very near midnight. They hunkered down in a thick copse and stared between the trees. Flinx itched to continue, knowing that Mother Mastiff lay in uneasy sleep somewhere in the complex of buildings not far below. The common sense that had served him so well since infancy did more to hold him back than logic or reason.

To all appearances, the cluster of dimly lit structures resembled nothing so much as another hunting or fishing lodge, though much larger than the one that Lauren managed. In the center were the main lodge buildings, to the left the sleeping quarters for less wealthy guests, to the right the maintenance and storage sheds. Lauren studied the layout through the thumb-sized daynight binoculars. Her experienced eye detected something far more significant than the complex's deceptive layout.

"Those aren't logs," she told Flinx. "They're resinated plastics. Very nicely camouflaged, but there's no more wood in them than in my head. Same thing goes for the masonry and rockwork in the foundations."

"How can you tell?" he asked curiously.

She handed him the tiny viewing device. Flinx put it to his eyes, and it immediately adjusted itself to his different vision, changing light and sharpening focus.

"Look at the corner joints and the lines along the ground and ceilings," she told him. "They're much too regular, too precise. That's usually the result when someone tries to copy nature. The hand of the computer, or just man himself, always shows itself. The protrusions on the logs, the smooth concavities on the 'rocks'—there are too many obvious replications from one to the next.

"Oh, they'd fool anyone not attuned to such stuff, and certainly anyone flying over in an aircraft or skimmer. But the materials in those buildings are fake, which tells us that they were put here recently. Anyone building a lodge for long-term use in the lake country always uses native materials."

Closest to their position on the little hillside was a pair

of long, narrow structures. One was dark; the other had several lights showing. Phosphorescent walkways drew narrow glowing lines between buildings.

To the right of the longhouses stood a hexagonal building, some three stories tall, made of plastic rock surmounted with more plastic paneling. Beyond it sprawled a large two-story structure whose purpose Flinx could easily divine from the tall doors fronting it and the single mudder parked outside: a hangar for servicing and protecting vehicles.

Nearby squatted a low edifice crowned with a coiffure of thin silvery cables. The power station wasn't large enough to conceal a fusion system. Probably a fuel cell complex, Flinx decided.

More puzzling was the absence of any kind of fence or other barrier. That was carrying verisimilitude a little too far, he thought. In the absence of any such wall, Flinx's attention, like Lauren's, was drawn to the peculiar central tower, the one structure that clearly had no place in a resort complex.

She examined it closely through the binoculars. "Lights on in there, too," she murmured. "Could be meant to pass as some kind of observation tower, or even a restaurant."

"Seems awfully small at the top for an eating room," he commented.

Searchlights probed the darkness between the buildings as the rest of the internal lights winked out. Another hour's wait in the damp, chilly bushes confirmed Lauren's suspicions about the mysterious tower. "There are six conical objects spaced around the roof," she told Flinx, pointing with a gloved hand. "At first, I thought they were searchlights, but not one of them has shown a light. What the devil could they be?"

Flinx had spotted them, too. "I think I recognize them now. Those are sparksound projectors."

She looked at him in surprise. "What's that? And how can you be sure that's what they are?"

He favored her with a wan smile. "I've had to avoid them before this. Each cone projects a wide, flat beam of high-intensity sound. Immobile objects don't register on the sensors, so it can be used to blanket a large area that includes buildings." He studied the tower intently.

"Just guessing from the angles at which the projectors are set, I'd say that their effective range stops about fifty meters out from the longhouses."

"That's not good," she muttered, trying to make out the invisible barrier though she knew that was impossible.

"It's worse than you think," he told her, "because the computer which monitors the beams is usually programed automatically to disregard anything that doesn't conform to human proportions. The interruption of the sonic field by anything even faintly human will generate a graphic display on a viewscreen. Any guard watching the screen will be able to tell what's entered the protected area and decide on that basis whether or not to sound further alarm." He added apologetically, "Rich people are very fond of this system."

"When we didn't see a regular fence, I was afraid of something like this. Isn't there any way to circumvent it, Flinx? You said you've avoided such things in the past."

He nodded. "I've avoided them because there's no way to break the system. Not from the outside, anyway. I suppose we might be able to tunnel beneath it."

"How deep into the ground would the sound penetrate?"

"That's a problem," he replied. "Depends entirely on the power being fed to the projectors and the frequencies being generated. Maybe only a meter, or maybe a dozen. We could tunnel inside the camp and strike it without knowing we'd done so until we came up into a circle of guns. Even if we made it, we'd have another problem, because the beams probably cover the entire camp. We'd almost have to come up inside one of the buildings."

"It doesn't matter," she murmured, "because we don't have any tunneling equipment handy. I'm going to hazard a guess that if they have the surface monitored so intently, the sky in the immediate vicinity will be even more carefully covered."

"I'd bet on that, too." Flinx gestured toward the tower. "Of course, we could just run the skimmer in on them.

There aren't that many buildings. Maybe we could find Mother Mastiff and get her out before they could react."

Lauren continued to study the complex. "There's nothing more expensive than a temporary facility fixed up to look permanent. I'd guess this setup supports between thirty and a hundred people. They're not going to make this kind of effort to detect intruders without being damn ready to repel them as well. Remember, there are only two of us."

"Three," Flinx corrected her. A pleased hiss sounded from the vicinity of his shoulder.

"Surprise is worth a lot," Lauren went on. "Maybe ten, but no more that. We won't do your mother any good as corpses. Keep in mind that no one else knows we're here. If we go down, so do her chances."

"I know the odds aren't good," he said irritably, "but we've got to do something."

"And do something we will. You remember that partially deforested section we flew over earlier today?"

Flinx thought a moment, then nodded.

"That was a trail line."

"Trail line for what?"

"For equalization," she told him. "For evening out the odds. For a better weapon than this." She patted the sling of the dart rifle. "Better even than that snake riding your shoulder. I don't share your confidence in it."

"You haven't seen Pip in action," he reminded her. "What kind of weapon are you talking about?"

She stood and brushed bark and dirt from her coveralls. "You'll see," she assured him, "but we have to be damn careful." She gazed toward the camp below. "I wish I could think of a better way, but I can't. They're sure to have guards posted in addition to monitoring the detection system you described. We don't even know which building your mother is in. If we're going to risk everything on one blind charge, it ought to be one hell of a charge.

"The weapon I have in mind is a volatile one. It can cut both ways, but I'd rather chance a danger I'm familiar with. Let's get back to the skimmer."

She pivoted and headed back through the forest. Flinx

rose to join her, forcing himself away from the lights of
the camp, which gleamed like so many reptilian eyes in
the night, until the trees swallowed them up.

They were halfway back to the little grove where they
had parked the skimmer when the sensation swept through
him. As usual, it came as a complete surprise, but this
time it was very different from his recent receptions. For
one thing, no feeling of pain was attached to it, and for
another, it did not come from the direction of the
camp. It arose from an entirely new source. Oddly, it carried overtones of distress with it, though distress of a confusing kind.

It came from Lauren and was directed at him.

There was no love in it, no grand, heated follow-up to
the casual kiss she had given him in the skimmer. Affection, yes, which was not what he had hoped for. Admiration, too, and something more. Something he had not
expected from her: a great wave of concern for him, and to
a lesser extent, of pity.

Flinx had become more adept at sorting out and identi-
fying the emotions he received, and there was no mistaking those he was feeling now. That kiss, then, had not only
carried no true love with it—it held even less than that.
She felt sorry for him.

He tried to reject the feelings, not only from disappointment but out of embarrassment. This was worse than looking into someone's mind. He was reading her heart, not her
thoughts. Though he tried hard, he could not shut off the
flow. He could no more stop the river of emotion than he
could willingly turn it on.

He made certain he stayed a step or two behind her so
she would not be able to see his face in the darkness, still
soaking up the waves of concern and sympathy that
poured from her, wishing they might be something else,
something more.

They hesitated before approaching the skimmer, circling
the landing area once. The quick search revealed that their
hiding place had remained inviolate. Once aboard, Lauren
took the craft up. She did not head toward the camp; instead, she turned south and began to retrace their course

over the treetops. Very soon they encountered the long, open gash in the woods. Lauren hovered above it for several minutes as she studied the ground, then decisively headed west. Flinx kept to himself, trying to shut the memory of that emotional deluge out of his mind. Then, quite unexpectedly, the open space in the trees came to a dead end.

"Damn," Lauren muttered. "Must have picked the wrong direction. I thought sure I read the surface right. Maybe it's the other way."

Flinx did not comment as she wheeled the skimmer around and headed southeast. When the pathway again ended in an unbroken wall of trees, she angrily wrenched the craft around a second time. This time when they encountered the forest wall, she slowed but continued westward, her gaze darting repeatedly from the darkened woods below to the skimmer's instrumentation.

"Maybe if you were a little more specific, I could help you look," he finally said, a touch of frustration in his voice.

"I told you. Weapons. Allies, actually. It comes to the same thing. No sign of them, though. They must have finished eating and entered semidormancy. That's how they live; do nothing but eat for several days in a row, then lie down to sleep it off for a week. The trouble is that once they've finished an eating period, they're apt to wander off in any direction until they find a sleep spot that pleases them. We haven't got the time to search the whole forest for the herd."

"Herd of what?" Flinx asked.

"Didn't I tell you? Devilopes."

Enlightenment came to Flinx. He had heard of Devilopes, even seen a small head or two mounted in large commercial buildings. But he had had no personal experience of them. Few citizens of Drallar did. There was not even one in the city zoo. As Flinx understood it, Devilopes were not zooable.

The Demichin Devilope was the dominant native life form on Moth. It was unusual for a herbivore to be the dominant life form, but excepting man, a fairly recent arrival, they had no natural enemies. They were comparatively scarce, as were the mounted heads Flinx had seen; the excessive cost of the taxidermy involved prevented all but the extremely wealthy from collecting Devilope.

The skimmer prowled the treetops, rising to clear occasional emergents topping ninety meters, dropping lower when the woods scaled more modest heights. Occasionally, Lauren would take them down to ground level, only to lift skyward again in disappointment when the omens proved unhelpful. There was no sign of a Devilope herd.

Meanwhile, another series of sensations swept through Flinx's active mind, and Pip stirred on his shoulder. He had continually tried to find Mother Mastiff's emotions, without success. Instead, his attempts seemed to be attracting the feelings of everyone but his mother-not. He wondered anew at his heightened perception since he had acquired his pet; though it was likely, he reminded himself that here in the vastness of the northern forests where minds were few and scattered, it might be only natural that his receptivity improved.

These latest sensations carried a female signature. They were also new, not of Mother Mastiff or Lauren. Cool and calm, they were vague and hard to define: whoever they belonged to was a particularly unemotional individual. He felt fear, slight but unmistakable, coupled with a formidable resolution that was cold, implacable—so hard and unyielding that it frightened Flinx almost as much as Mother Mastiff's own terror. Save for the slight overtones of fear, they might have been the emotions of a machine.

The feelings came from the camp where Mother Mastiff was being held. Flinx had little doubt that they belonged to one of those mysterious individuals who had abducted her. From the one brief, faint sensation he felt he could understand her fear. Then it was gone, having lasted less than a minute. Yet, in that time, Flinx had received a complete emotional picture of the person whose feelings he had latched onto. Never before had he encountered a mind so intent on a single purpose and so devoid of those usual emotional colorations that comprised common humanity. Pip hissed at the empty air as if ready to strike and defend its master.

"This isn't working," Lauren muttered, trying to see through the trees. "We'll have to—" She paused, frowning at him. "Are you all right? You've got the most peculiar expression on your face."

"I'm okay." The coldness was at last fading from his mind; evidently he hadn't been conscious of how completely it had possessed him. Her query snapped him back to immediacy, and he could feel anew the warmth of the skimmer's cabin, of his own body. Not for the first time did he find himself wondering if his unmanageable talent might someday do him harm as well as good. "I was just thinking."

"You do a lot of that," she murmured. "Flinx, you're the funniest man I've ever met."

"You're not laughing."

"I didn't mean funny ha ha." She turned back to the controls. "I'm going to set us down. This skimmer really isn't equipped for the kind of night-tracking we're doing. Besides, I don't know about you, but it's late, and I'm worn out."

Flinx was exhausted too, mentally as much as physically. So he did not object as Lauren selected a stand of trees and set the skimmer down in their midst.

"I don't think we need to stand a watch," she said. "We're far enough from the camp so that no one's going to stumble in on us. I haven't seen any sign of aerial patrol." She was at the rear of the skimmer now, fluffing out the sleeping bags they had brought from the lodge.

Flinx sat quietly watching her. He had known a few girls—young women—back in Drallar. Inhabitants of the marketplace, like himself, students in the harsh school of the moment. He could never get interested in any of them, though a few showed more than casual interest in him. They were not, well, not serious. About life, and other matters.

Mother Mastiff repeatedly chided him about his attitude. "There's no reason for ye to be so standoffish, boy. You're no older than them." That was not true, of course, but he could not convince her of that.

Lauren was a citizen of another dimension entirely. She

was an attractive, mature woman. A self-confident, thinking adult—which was how Flinx viewed himself, despite his age. She was already out of pants and shirt and slipping into the thin thermal cocoon of the sleeping bag.

"Well?" She blinked at him, pushed her hair away from her face. "Aren't you going to bed? Don't tell me you're not tired."

"I can hardly stand up," he admitted. Discarding his own clothing, he slipped into the sleeping bag next to hers. Lying there listening to the rhythmic patter of rain against the canopy, he strained toward her with his mind, seeking a hint, a suggestion of the emotions he so desperately wanted her to feel. Maddeningly, he could sense nothing at all.

The warmth of the sleeping bag and the cabin enveloped him, and he was acutely aware of the faint musky smell of the woman barely an arm's length away. He wanted to reach out to her; to touch that smooth, sun-darkened flesh; to caress the glistening ringlets of night that tumbled down the side of her head to cover cheek and neck and finally form a dark bulge against the bulwark of the sleeping bag. His hand trembled.

What do I do, he thought furiously. How do I begin this? Is there something special I should say first, or should I reach out now and speak later? How can I tell her what I'm feeling? I can receive. If only I could broadcast!

Pip lay curled into a hard, scaly knot near his feet in the bottom of the sleeping bag. Flinx slumped in on himself, tired and frustrated and helpless. What was there to do now? What could he possibly do except the expected?

A soft whisper reached him from the other sleeping bag. Black hair shuffled against itself. "Good night, Flinx." She turned to smile briefly at him, lighting up the cabin, then turned over and became still.

"Good night," he mumbled. The uncertain hand that was halfway out of his covering withdrew and clenched convulsively on the rim of the material.

Maybe this was best, he tried to tell himself. Adult though he believed himself to be, there were mysteries and passwords he was still unfamiliar with. Besides, there was that surge of pity and compassion he had detected in her.

Admiring, reassuring, but not what he was hoping to feel from her. He wanted—had to have—something more than that.

The one thing he didn't need was another mother.

Chapter Thirteen

He said nothing when they rose the next morning, downed a quick breakfast of concentrates, and lifted once again into the murky sky. The sun was not quite up, though its cloud-diffused light brightened the treetops. They had to find Lauren's herd soon, he knew, because the skimmer's charge was running low and so were their options. He did not know how much time Mother Mastiff had left before the source of fear he had detected in her came to meet her.

Perhaps they had been hindered by the absence of daylight, or perhaps they had simply passed by the place, but this time they found the herd in minutes. Below the hovering skimmer they saw a multitude of small hills the color of obsidian. Black hair rippled in the morning breeze, thick and meter-long. Where one of the hills shifted in deep sleep, there was a flash of red like a ruby lost in a coal heap as an eye momentarily opened and closed.

Flinx counted more than fifty adults. Scattered among them were an equal number of adolescents and infants. All lay sprawled on their sides on the damp ground, shielded somewhat from the rain by the grove they had chosen as a resting place.

So these were the fabled Demichin Devilopes!—awesome and threatening even in their satiated sleep. Flinx's gaze settled on one immense male snoring away between two towering hardwoods. He guessed its length at ten meters, its height when erect at close to six. Had it been standing, a tall man could have walked beneath its belly and barely brushed the lower tips of the shaggy hair.

The downsloping, heavily muscled neck drooped from between a pair of immense humped shoulders to end in a nightmarish skull from which several horns protruded. Some Devilopes had as few as two horns, others as many as nine. The horns twisted and curled, though most ended by pointing forward; no two animals' horns grew in exactly the same way. Bony plates flared slightly outward from the horns to protect the eyes.

The forelegs were longer than the hind—unusual for so massive a mammal. This extreme fore musculature allowed a Devilope to push over a fully grown tree. That explained the devastated trail that marked their eating period. A herd would strip a section of forest bare, pushing down the evergreens to get at the tender branches and needles, even pulling off and consuming the bark of the main boles.

The Devilopes shifted in their sleep, kicking tree-sized legs.

"They'll sleep like this for days," Lauren explained as they circled slowly above the herd. "Until they get hungry again or unless something disturbs them. They don't even bother to post sentries. No predator in its right mind would attack a herd of sleeping Devilopes. There's always the danger they'd wake up."

Flinx stared at the ocean of Devilope. "What do we do with them?" Not to mention how, he thought.

"They can't be tamed, and they can't be driven," Lauren told him, "but sometimes you can draw them. We have to find a young mare in heat. The season's right." Her fingers moved over the controls, and the skimmer started to drop.

"We're going into *that*?" Flinx pointed toward the herd.

"Have to," she said. "There's no other way. It ought to be okay. They're asleep and unafraid."

"That's more than I can say," he muttered as the skimmer dipped into the trees. Lauren maneuvered it carefully, trying to break as few branches and make as little noise as possible. "What do we need with a mare in heat?"

"Musk oil and blood," Lauren explained as the skimmer gently touched down.

Up close, the herd was twice as impressive: a seething, rippling mass of shaggy black hair broken by isolated clumps of twisted, massive horns, it looked more like a landscape of hell than an assembly of temporarily inanimate herbivores. When Lauren killed the engine and popped open the cabin door, Flinx was assailed by a powerful odor and the steady sonority of the herd's breathing. Earth humming, he thought.

Lauren had the dart rifle out and ready as they approached the herd on foot. Flinx followed her and tried to pretend that the black cliffs that towered over them were basalt and not flesh.

"There." She pointed between a pair of slowly heaving bulks at a medium-sized animal. Picking her spot, she sighted the long barrel carefully before putting three darts behind the massive skull. The mare stirred, coughing once. Then the head, which had begun to rise, relaxed, slowly sinking back to the surface. Flinx and Lauren held their breath, but the slight activity had failed to rouse any of their target's neighbors.

Lauren fearlessly strode between the two hulks that formed a living canyon and unslung her backpack next to the tranquilized mare. Before leaving the skimmer, she had extracted several objects from its stores. These she now methodically laid out in a row on the ground and set to work. Flinx watched with interest as knife and tools he didn't recognize did their work.

One container filled rapidly with blood. A second filled more rapidly with a green crystalline liquid. Lauren's face was screwed up like a knot, and as soon as the aroma of the green fluid reached Flinx, he knew why. The scent was as overpowering as anything his nostrils had ever encountered. Fortunately, the smell was not bad, merely overwhelming.

A loud, sharp grunt sounded from behind him. He turned, to find himself gazing in horrified fascination at a great crimson eye. An absurdly tiny black pupil floated in the center of that blood-red disk. Then the eyelid rolled like a curtain over the apparition. Flinx did not relax.

"Hurry up!" he called softly over his shoulder. "I think this one's waking up."

"We're not finished here yet," Louren replied, stoppering the second bottle and setting to work with a low-power laser. "I have to close both wounds first."

"Let nature close them," he urged her, keeping an eye on the orb that had fixed blankly on him. The eyelid rippled, and he feared that the next time it opened, it would likely be to full awareness.

"You know me better than that," she said firmly. Flinx waited, screaming silently for her to hurry. Finally, she said, "That's done. We can go."

They hurried back through the bulwark of black hair. Flinx did not allow himself to relax until they sat once more inside the skimmer. He spent much of the time trying to soothe Pip; in response to its master's worry, it had developed a nervous twitch.

Despite the tight seal, the miasma rising from the green bottle nearly choked him. There was no odor from the container of blood.

"The green is the oil," she explained unnecessarily. "It's the rutting season."

"I can see what you have in mind to do with that," Flinx told her, "but why the blood?"

"Released in the open air, the concentrated oil would be enough to interest the males of the herd. We need to do more than just interest them. We need to drive them a little crazy. The only way to do that is to convince them that a ready female is in danger. The herd's females will respond to that, too." She set to work with the skimmer's simple store of chemicals.

"You ought to be around sometime when the males are awake and fighting," she said to him as she mixed oil, blood, and various catalysts in a sealed container. Flinx was watching the herd anxiously. "The whole forest shakes. Even the tallest trees tremble. When two of the big males connect with those skulls and horns, you can hear the sound of the collision echo for kilometers."

Five minutes later, she held a large flask up to the dim early-morning light. "There, that should do it. Pheromones and blood and a few other nose-ticklers. If this doesn't draw them, nothing will."

"They'll set off the alarm when they cross the sonic fence," he reminded her.

"Yes, but by that time they'll be so berserk, nothing will turn them. Then it won't matter what they set off." She smiled nastily, then hesitated at the thought. "My only concern is that we find your mother before they start in on the buildings."

"We'd better," Flinx said.

"There should be enough confusion," she went on, "to distract everyone's attention. Unless they're downright inhuman, the inhabitants of the camp aren't going to be thinking of much of anything beyond saving their own skins.

"As to getting your mother out fast, I think we can assume that she's not in the hangar area or the power station or that central tower. That leaves the two long structures off to the west. If we can get inside and get her out before whoever's in charge comes to his senses, we should be able to get away before anyone realizes what's happening.

"Remember, we'll be the only ones ready for what's going to happen. A lot will depend on how these people react. They're obviously not stupid, but I don't see how anyone could be adaptable enough to react calmly to what we're going to do to them. Besides, I don't have any better ideas."

Flinx shook his head. "Neither do I. I can see one difficulty, though. If we're going to convince this herd that they're chasing after an injured Devilope in heat, we're going to have to stay on the ground. I don't see them following the scent up in the air."

"Quite right, and we have to make our actions as believable as possible. That means hugging the surface. Not only would tree-level flight confuse the herd, air currents would carry the scent upward too quickly and dissipate it too fast."

"Then what happens," Flinx pressed on, "if this idea works and the herd does follow us back toward the camp and we hit a tree or stall or something?"

Lauren shrugged. "Can you climb?"

"There aren't many trees in Drallar free for the climbing," he told her, "but I've done a lot of climbing on the outsides of buildings."

"You'll find little difference," she assured him, "with the kind of motivation you'll have if the skimmer stalls. If something happens, head for the biggest tree you can find. I think they'll avoid the emergents. The smaller stuff they'll just ignore." She hesitated, stared sideways at him. "You want to wait a little while to think it over?"

"We're wasting time talking," he replied, knowing that every minute brought Mother Mastiff closer and closer to whatever fate her abductors had planned for her. "I'm ready if you are."

"I'm not ready," she said, "but I never will be, for this. So we might as well go." She settled into the pilot's chair and thumbed a control. The rear of the cabin's canopy swung upward.

"Climb into the back. When I give the word, you uncap the flask and pour out, oh, maybe a tenth of the contents. Then hold it out back, keep it open, and pour a tenth every time I say so. Got it?"

"Got it," he assured her with more confidence than he felt. "You just drive this thing and make sure we don't get into an argument with a tree."

"Don't worry about that." She gave him a last smile before turning to the control console.

The skimmer rose and turned, heading slowly back toward the somnolent herd. When they were just ten meters from the nearest animal, Lauren pivoted the craft and hovered, studying the scanner's display of the forest ahead.

Violent grunts and an occasional bleating sound began to issue from the herd as Flinx held the still tightly sealed flask over the stern of the skimmer. He looked around until he found a piece of thin cloth and tied it across his nose and mouth.

"I should have thought of that," she murmured, watching him. "Sorry."

"Don't you want one?" he asked.

She shook her head. "I'm up here, and the wind will carry the scent back away from me. I'll be all right. You ready?" Her hands tightened on the wheel.

"Ready," he said. "You ready, Pip?"

The flying snake said nothing; it did not even hiss in response. But Flinx could feel the coils tighten expectantly around his left arm and shoulder.

"Open and pour," she instructed him.

Flinx popped the seal on the flask as Lauren slowly edged the skimmer forward. Even with the improvised mask and a breeze to carry the aroma away from him, the odor was all but overpowering. His eyes watered as his nostrils rebelled. Somehow he kept his attention on the task at hand and slowly measured out a tenth of the liquid.

A violent, querulous bellow rose from several massive throats. As the skimmer slipped past a cathedral-like cluster of hardwoods, Flinx could see one huge male pushing itself erect. It seemed to dominate the forest even though the great trees rose high above. The metallic red eyes were fully open now, the tiny black pupils looking like holes in the crimson.

The Devilope shook its head from side to side, back and forth, and thundered. It took a step forward, then another. Behind it, the rest of the herd was rising, the initial uncertain bellowing turning to roars of desire and rage. A second male started forward in the wake of the first; then a third took up the long, ponderous stride. At this rate, Flinx thought, it would take them days to reach the camp.

But even as he watched and worried, the pace of the awakening herd began to increase. It took time for such massive animals to get going. Once they did, they ate up distance. Not long after, Flinx found himself wishing for the skimmer to accelerate, and accelerate again.

The herd was bearing down on the weaving, dodging craft. Lauren had to avoid even the smaller trees, which the herd ignored in its fury to locate the source of that pungent, electrifying odor. She turned to yell something to him, but he couldn't hear her anymore.

Trees whizzed by as Lauren somehow managed to increase their speed without running into anything. Behind them sounded a rising thunder as the noise of hundreds of hooves pulverizing the earth mixed with the crackle of snapping tree trunks and the moan of larger boles being torn from their roots.

Red eyes and horns were all Flinx could see as he poured another tenth of the herd-maddening liquid from the flask, drawing the thunder down on the fragile skimmer and its even more fragile cargo. . . .

There was nothing in the small operating theater that had not been thoroughly sanitized. Mother Mastiff had no strength left to fight with as they gently but firmly strapped her to the lukewarm table. Her curses and imprecations had been reduced to whimpered pleas, more reflex than anything else, for she had seen by now that nothing would dissuade these crazy people from their intentions. Eventually, she lost even the will to beg and contented herself with glaring tight-lipped at her tormentors.

Bright lights winked to life, blinding her. The tall black woman stood to the right of the table, checking a palm-sized circle of plastic. Mother Mastiff recognized the pressure syringe, and looked away from it.

Like her companions, Haithness wore a pale surgical gown and a mask that left only her eyes showing. Nyassa-lee plugged in the shears that would be used to depilate the subject's skull. Brora, who would execute the actual implantation, stood off to one side examining a readout on the display screen that hung just above and behind Mother Mastiff's head. Occasionally, he would glance down at a small table holding surgical instruments and several square transparent boxes frosted with cold. Inside the boxes were the microelectronic implants that he would place in the subject's skull.

A globular metal mass hung from the ceiling above the operating table, gleaming like a steel jellyfish. Wiry arms and tendrils radiated from its underside. They would supply power to attachments, suction through hosing, and supplementary service to any organs that exhibited signs of failure during the operation. There were microthin filament arms that could substitute for cerebral capillaries, tendrils that could fuse or excavate bone, and devices that could by-pass the lungs and provide oxygen directly to the blood.

"I'm ready to begin." Brora smiled thinly across at Nyassa-lee, who nodded. He looked to his other colleague. "Haithness?" She answered him with her eyes as she readied the syringe.

"A last instrument check, then," he murmured, turning his attention to the raised platform containing the microsurgical instruments. Overhead, the jellyfish hummed expectantly.

"Now that's funny." He paused, frowning. "Look here." Both women leaned toward him. The instruments, the tiny boxes with their frozen contents, even the platform itself, seemed to be vibrating.

"Trouble over at power?" ventured Nyassa-lee. She glanced upward and saw that the central support globe was swaying slightly.

"I don't know. Surely if it was anything serious, we would have been told by now," Brora muttered. The vibration intensified. One of the probes tumbled from the holding table and clattered across the plastic floor. "It's getting worse, I think." A faint rumble reached them from somewhere outside. Brora thought it arose somewhere off to the west.

"Storm coming?" Nyassa-lee asked, frowning.

Brora shook his head. "Thunder wouldn't make the table shake, and Weather didn't say anything about an early storm watch. No quake, either. This region is seismically stable."

The thunder that continued to grow in their ears did not come down out of a distant sky but up out of the disturbed earth itself. Abruptly, the alarm system came to life all around the camp. The three surgeons stared in confusion at one another as the rumbling shook not only tables and instruments but the whole building.

The warning sirens howled mournfully. There came a ripping, tearing noise as something poured through the far end of the conference room, missing the surgery by an appreciable margin. It was visible only for seconds, though in that time it filled the entire chamber. Then it moved on, trailing sections of false log and plastic stone in its wake, letting in sky and mist and leaving behind a wide depression in the stelacrete foundation beneath the floor. Haithness had the best view as debris fell slowly from the roof to cover the mark: it was a footprint.

Nyassa-lee tore off her surgical mask and raced for the nearest doorway. Brora and Haithness were not far behind. At their departure, Mother Mastiff, who had quietly consigned that portion of herself that was independent to oblivion, suddenly found her voice again and began screaming for help.

Dust and insulation began to sift from the ceiling as the violent shaking and rumbling continued to echo around her. The multiarmed surgical sphere above the operating table was now swinging dangerously back and forth and threatening, with each successive vibration, to tear free of its mounting.

Mother Mastiff did not waste her energy in a futile attempt to break the straps that bound her. She knew her limits. Instead, she devoted her remaining strength to yelling at the top of her lungs.

As soon as they had entered the monitored border surrounding the camp, Lauren had accelerated and charged at dangerously high speed right past the central tower. Someone had had the presence of mind to respond to the frantic alarm siren by reaching for a weapon, but the hastily aimed and fired energy rifle missed well aft of the already fleeing skimmer.

At the same time, the wielder of the rifle had seen something flung from the rear of the intruder. He had flinched, and when no explosion had followed, leaned out of the third-story window to stare curiously at the broken glass and green-red liquid trickling down the side of the structure. He did not puzzle over it for very long because his attention—and that of his companions in the tower—was soon occupied by the black tidal wave that thundered out of the forest.

The frustrated, enraged herd concentrated all its attention on the strongest source of the infuriating odor. The central tower, which contained the main communications and defensive instrumentation for the encampment, was soon reduced to a mound of plastic and metal rubble.

Meanwhile, Lauren brought the skimmer around in a wide circle and set it down between the two long buildings on the west side of the camp. The camp personnel were too busy trying to escape into the forest and dodging massive horns and hoofs to wonder at the presence of the unfamiliar vehicle in their midst.

They had a fifty-fifty chance of picking the right building on the first try. As luck would have it, they choose correctly . . . no thanks, Flinx thought, to his resolutely unhelpful Talent.

The roof was already beginning to cave in on the operating theater when they finally reached that end of the building.

"Flinx, how'd ye—?" Mother Mastiff started to exclaim.

"How did he know how to find you?" Lauren finished for her as she started working on the restraining straps binding the older woman's right arm.

"No," Mother Mastiff corrected her, "I started to ask how he managed to get here without any money, I didn't think ye could go anywhere on Moth without money."

"I had a little, Mother." Flinx smiled down at her. She appeared unhurt, simply worn out from her ordeal of the past hectic, confusing days. "And I have other abilities, you know."

"Ah." She nodded somberly.

"No, not that," he corrected her. "You've forgotten that there are other ways to make use of things besides paying for them."

She laughed at that. The resounding cackle gladdened his heart. For an instant, it dominated the screams and the echoes of destruction that filled the air outside the building. The earth quivered beneath his feet.

"Yes, yes, ye were always good at helping yourself to whatever ye needed. Haven't I warned ye time enough against it? But I don't think now be the time to reprimand ye." She looked up at Lauren, who was having a tough time with the restraining straps.

"Now who," she inquired, her eyebrows rising, "be this one?"

"A friend," Flinx assured her. "Lauren, meet Mother Mastiff."

"Charmed, grandma." Lauren's teeth clenched as she fought with the recalcitrant restraints. "Damn magnetic catches built into the polyethelene." She glanced across to Flinx. "We may have to cut her loose."

"I know you'll handle it." Flinx turned and jogged toward the broken doorway, ducking just in time to avoid a section of roof brace as it crashed to the floor.

"Hey, where the hell do you think you're going?" Lauren shouted at him.

"I want some answers," he yelled back. "I still don't know what this is all about, and I'll be damned if I'm leaving here without trying to find out!"

" 'Tis you, boy!" Mother Mastiff yelled after him. "They wanted to use me to influence you!" But he was already out of earshot.

Mother Mastiff laid her head back down and stared worriedly at the groaning ceiling. "That boy," she mumbled, "I don't know that he hasn't been more trouble than he's worth."

The upper restraint suddenly came loose with a click, and Lauren breathed a sigh of relief. She was as conscious as Mother Mastiff of the creaking, unsteady ceiling and the heavy mass of the surgical globe swaying like a pendulum over the operating table.

"I doubt you really mean that, woman," she said evenly, "and you ought to stop thinking of him as a boy." The two women exchanged a glance, old eyes shooting questions, young ones providing an eloquent reply.

Confident that Lauren would soon free Mother Mastiff, Flinx was able to let the rage that had been bottled up inside him for days finally surge to the fore. So powerful was the suddenly freed emotion that an alarmed Pip slid off its master's shoulder and followed anxiously above. The tiny triangular head darted in all directions in an attempt to locate the as-yet-unperceived source of Flinx's hate.

The fury boiling within him was barely under control. "They're not going to get away with what they've done," he told himself repeatedly. "They're not going to get away with it." He did not know what he was going to do if he confronted these still-unknown assailants, only that he had to do *something*. A month ago, he would never have considered going after so dangerous an enemy, but the past weeks had done much for his confidence.

The herd was beginning to lose some of its fury even as its members still hunted for the puzzling source of their discomfort. Females with young were the first to break away, retreating back into the forest. Then there were only the solitary males roaming the encampment, venting their frustration and anger on anything larger than a rock. Occasionally, Flinx passed the remains of those who had not succeeded in fleeing into the trees in time to avoid the rampaging Devilopes. There was rarely more than a red smear staining the ground.

He was heading for the hangar he and Lauren had identified from their hilltop. It was the logical final refuge. It didn't take long for him to reach the building. As he strode single-mindedly across the open grounds, it never occurred to him to wonder why none of the snorting, pawing Devilopes paused to turn and stomp him into the earth.

The large doorway fronting the hangar had been pushed aside. Flinx could see movement and hear faint commands. Without hesitation, he walked inside and saw a large transport skimmer being loaded with crates. The loading crew worked desperately under the direction of a small, elderly Oriental woman. Flinx just stood in the portal, staring. Now that he had located someone in a position of authority, he really didn't know what to do next. Anger and chaos had brought him to the place; there had been no room in his thoughts for reasoned preparation.

A tall black lady standing in the fore section of the skimmer stopped barking orders long enough to glance toward the doorway. Her eyes locked on his. Instead of hatred, Flinx found himself thinking that in her youth this must have been a strikingly beautiful woman. Cold, though. Both women, so cold. Her hair was nearly all gray, and so were her eyes.

"Haithness." A man rushed up behind her. "We haven't got time for daydreaming. We—"

She pointed with a shaky finger. Brora followed her finger and found himself gaping at a slim, youthful figure in the doorway. "That boy," Brora whispered. "Is it him?"

"Yes, but look higher, Brora. Up in the light."

The stocky man's gaze rose, and his air of interested detachment suddenly deserted him. His mouth dropped open. "Oh, my God," he exclaimed, "an Alaspinian minidrag."

"You see," Haithness murmured as she looked down at Flinx, regarding him as she would any other laboratory subject, "it explains so much." Around them, the sounds of the encampment being destroyed continued to dominate everyone else's attention.

Brora regained his composure. "It may, it may, but the boy may not even be aware that—"

Flinx strained to understand their mumblings, but there was too much noise behind him. "Where did you come from?" he shouted toward the skimmer. His new-found maturity quickly deserted him; suddenly, he was only a furious, frustrated adolescent. "Why did you kidnap my mother? I don't like you, you know. I don't like any of you. I want to know why you've done what you've done!"

"Be careful," Nyassa-lee called up to them. "Remember the subject's profile!" She hoped they were getting this upstairs.

"He's not dangerous, I tell you," Haithness insisted. "This demonstrates his harmlessness. If he was in command of himself, he'd be throwing more than childish queries at us by now."

"But the catalyst creature." Brora waved a hand toward the flying snake drifting above Flinx.

"We don't know that it's catalyzing anything," Haithness reminded him, "because we don't know what the boy's abilities are as yet. They are only potentials. The minidrag may be doing nothing for him because it has nothing to work with as yet, other than a damnable persistence and a preternatural talent for following a thin trail." She continued to examine the subject almost within their grasp. "I would give a great deal to learn how he came to be in possession of a minidrag."

Brora found himself licking his lips. "We failed with the mother. Maybe we should try taking the subject directly in spite of our experience with the girl."

"No," she argued. "We don't have the authority to take that kind of risk. Cruachan must be consulted first. It's his decision to make. The important thing is for us to get out of here now with our records and ourselves intact."

"I disagree." Brora continued to study the boy, fascinated by his calm. The subject appeared indifferent to the hoofed death that was devastating the encampment. "Our initial plan has failed. Now is the time for us to improvise. We should seize the opportunity."

"Even if it's our last opportunity?"

Flinx shouted at them. "What are you talking about? Why don't you answer me?"

Haithness turned and seemed about to reply when a vast groaning shook the hangar. Suddenly, its east wall bulged inward. There were screams of despair as the loading crew flung cargo in all directions and scattered, ignoring Nyassa-lee's entreaties.

They didn't scatter fast enough.

Walls and roof came crashing down, burying personnel, containers, and the big cargo skimmer. Three bull Devilopes pushed through the ruined wall as Flinx threw himself backward through the doorway. Metal, plastic, and flesh blended into a chaotic pulp beneath massive hoofs. Fragments of plastic flew through the air around Flinx. One nicked his shoulder.

Red eyes flashing, one of the bulls wheeled toward the single figure sprawled on the ground. The great head lowered.

Coincidence, luck, something more: whatever had protected Flinx from the attention of the herd until now abruptly vanished. The bull looming overhead was half insane with fury. Its intent was evident in its gaze: it planned to make Flinx into still another red stain on the earth.

Something so tiny it was not noticed swooped in front of that lowering skull and spat into one plate-sized red eye. The Devilope bull blinked once, twice against the painful intrusion. That was enough to drive the venom into its bloodstream. The monster opened its mouth and let out a frightening bellow as it pulled away from Flinx. It started to shake its head violently, ignoring the other two bulls, which continued to crush the remains of the hangar underfoot.

Flinx scrambled to his feet and raced from the scene of destruction, heading back toward the building where he had left Lauren and Mother Mastiff. Pip rejoined him, choosing to glide just above its master's head, temporarily disdaining its familiar perch.

Behind them, the Devilope's bellowing turned thick and soft. Then there was a crash as it sat down on its rump. It sat for several moments more before the huge front legs slipped out from under it. Very slowly, like an iceberg calving from a glacier, it fell over on its side. The eye that had taken Pip's venom was gone, leaving behind only an empty socket.

Breathing hard, Flinx rushed back into the building housing the surgery and nearly ran over the fleeing Lauren and Mother Mastiff. He embraced his mother briefly, intensely, then swung her left arm over his shoulder to give her support.

Lauren supported the old woman at her other shoulder and looked curiously at Flinx. "Did you find who you were looking for?"

"I think so," he told her. "Sennar and Soba are properly revenged. The Devilopes did it for them."

Lauren nodded as they emerged from the remains of the building. Outside, the earth-shaking had lessened.

"The herd's dispersing. They'll reform in the forest, wonder what came over them, and likely go back to sleep. As soon as they start doing that, this camp will begin filling up with those who managed to escape. We need to improve our transportation, and fast. Remember, there's nowhere near a full charge in the skimmer. You and I could walk it, but—"

"I can walk anywhere ye can," Mother Mastiff insisted. Her condition belied her bravado—if not for the support of Flinx and Lauren, she would not have been able to stand.

"It's all right, Mother," Flinx told her. "We'll find something."

They boarded their skimmer. Lauren rekeyed the ignition, removed to prevent potential escapees from absconding with their craft, and they cruised around the ruined building back into the heart of the camp.

Their fear of danger from survivors was unfounded. The few men and women who wandered out of their way were too stunned by the catastrophe to offer even a challenging question. The majority of them had been administrative or maintenance personnel, quite unaware of the importance of Flinx or Mother Mastiff.

The Devilopes were gone. The power station was hardly damaged, perhaps because it lay apart from the rest of the encampment, perhaps because it operated on automatic and did not offer the herd any living targets. None of the camp personnel materialized to challenge their use of the station's recharge facility, though Lauren kept a ready finger on the trigger of the dart rifle until a readout showed that the skimmer once again rode on full power.

"I don't think we have to worry about pursuit," she declared. "It doesn't look like there's anyone left to pursue. If the leaders of this bunch got caught in that trampled hangar as you say, Flinx, then we've nothing to worry about."

"I didn't get my answers," he muttered disappointedly. Then, louder, he said, "Let's get out of this place."

"Yes," Mother Mastiff agreed quickly. She looked imploringly at Lauren. "I be a city lady. The country life doesn't agree with me." She grinned her irrepressible grin, and Flinx knew she was going to be all right.

Lauren smiled and nudged the accelerator. The skimmer moved, lifting above the surrounding trees. They crusied over several disoriented, spent Devilopes and sped south as fast as the skimmer's engine could push them.

"I didn't learn what this was all about," Flinx continued to mutter from his seat near the rear of the cabin. "Do you know why they abducted you, Mother? What did they want with you?"

It was on her lips to tell him the tale the Meliorares had told her the previous night—was it only last night? Something made her hesitate. Natural caution, concern for him. A lifetime of experience that taught one not to blunder ahead and blurt out the first thing that comes to mind, no matter how true it might be. There were things she needed to learn, things he needed to learn. There would always be time.

"You've said 'tis a long story as to how ye managed to trace me, boy. My tale's a long one, too. As to what they wanted with me, tis enough for ye to know now that it involves an old, old crime I once participated in and a thirst for revenge that never dies. Ye can understand that."

"Yes, yes I can." He knew that Mother Mastiff had enjoyed a diverse and checkered youth. "You can tell me all about it after we're back home."

"Yes," she said, pleased that he had apparently accepted her explanation. "After we're safely back home." She looked toward the pilot's chair and saw Lauren gazing quizzically back at her.

Mother Mastiff put a finger to her lips. The other woman nodded, not fully understanding but sensitive enough to go along with the older woman's wishes.

Chapter Fourteen

Several hours passed. The air was smooth, the mist thin, the ride comfortable as the skimmer slipped southward. Mother Mastiff looked back toward the rear of the craft to see Flinx sound asleep. His useful if loathsome pet was, as usual, curled up close to the boy's head.

She studied the pilot. Pretty, hard, and self-contained, she decided. Night was beginning to settle over the forest speeding by below. Within the sealed canopy of the skimmer, it was warm and dry. "What be your interest in my boy?" she asked evenly.

"As a friend. I also had a personal debt to pay," Lauren explained. "Those people who abducted you slaughtered a couple of rare animals who were long-time companions of mine. 'Revenge never dies.'" She smiled. "You said that a while ago, remember?"

"How did ye encounter him?"

"He appeared at the lodge I manage on a lake near here."

"Ah! The fight, yes, I remember. So that place was yours."

"I just manage it. That's where I'm heading. I can help you arrange return passage to Drallar from there."

"How do ye know we're from the city?"

Lauren gestured with a thumb back toward the sleeping figure behind them. "He told me. He told me a lot."

"That's odd," Mother Mastiff commented. "He's not the talkative kind, that boy." She went quiet for a while, watching the forest slide past below. Flinx slept on, enjoying his first relaxed sleep in some time.

" 'Tis an awful lot of trouble you've gone through on his behalf," she finally declared, "especially for a total stranger. Especially for one so young."

"Youth is relative," Lauren said. "Maybe he brought out the maternal instinct in me."

"Don't get profound with me, child," Mother Mastiff warned her, "nor sassy, either." Ironic, that last comment, though. Hadn't she once felt the same way about the boy many years ago? "I've watched ye, seen the way ye look at him. Do ye love him?"

"Love him?" Lauren's surprise was quite genuine. Then, seeing that Mother Mastiff was serious, she forced herself to respond solemnly. "Certainly not! At least, not in *that* way. I'm fond of him, sure. I respect him immensely for what he's managed to do on his own, and I also feel sorry for him. There is affection, certainly. But the kind of love you're talking about? Not a chance."

" 'Youth is relative,' " Mother Mastiff taunted her gently. "One must be certain. I've seen much in my life, child. There's little that can surprise me, or at least so I thought until a few weeks ago." She cackled softly. "I'm glad to hear ye say this. Anything else could do harm to the boy."

"I would never do that," Lauren assured her. She glanced back at Flinx's sleeping form. "I'm going to drop you at the lodge. My assistant's name is Sal. I'll make some pretense of going in to arrange your transportation and talk to him. Then I'll take off across the lake. I think it will be better for him that way. I don't want to hurt him." She hesitated. "You don't think he'll do anything silly, like coming after me?"

Mother Mastiff considered thoughtfully, then shook her

head. "He's just a little too sensible. He'll understand, I'm sure. As for me, I don't know what to say, child. You've been so helpful to him and to me."

" 'Revenge,' remember?" She grinned, the lights from the console glinting off her high cheekbones. "He's a funny one, your Flinx. I don't think I'll forget him."

"Ye know, child, 'tis peculiar," Mother Mastiff muttered as she gazed out into the clouds and mist, "but you're not the first person to say that."

"And I expect," Lauren added as she turned her attention back to her driving, "that I won't be the last, either."

The mudder circled the devastated encampment several times before leaving the cover of the forest and cruising among the ruined buildings. Eventually, it settled to ground near the stump of what had been a central tower.

The woman who stepped out was clad in a dark-green and brown camouflage suit, as was the man at the vehicle's controls. He kept the engine running as his companion marched a half-dozen meters toward the tower, stopped, and turned a slow circle, hands on hips. Then they both relaxed, recognizing that whatever had obliterated the installation no longer posed any threat. No discussion was necessary—they had worked together for a long time, and words had become superfluous.

The man killed the mudder's engine and exited to join his associate in surveying the wreckage. A light rain was falling. It did not soak them, for the camouflage suits repelled moisture. The field was temporary, but from what they could see of the encampment, they wouldn't be in the place long enough to have to recharge.

"I'm sick of opening packages, only to find smaller packages inside," the man said ruefully. "I'm sick of having every new avenue we take turn into a dead end." He gestured toward the destruction surrounding them; crumpled buildings, isolated wisps of smoke rising from piles of debris, slag where power had melted metal.

"Dead may be the right description, too, judging by the looks of things."

"Not necessarily." His companion only half heard him. She was staring at a wide depression near her feet. It was pointed at one end. A second, identical mark dented the ground several meters away, another an equal distance beyond. As she traced their progress, she saw that they formed a curving trail. She had not noticed them at first because they were filled with water.

She kicked in the side of the one nearest her boots. "Footprints," she said curtly.

"Hoof prints," the man corrected her. His gaze went to the mist-shrouded woods that surrounded the camp. "I wish I knew more about this backwater world."

"Don't criticize yourself. We didn't plan to spend so much time here. Besides, the urban center is pretty cosmopolitan."

"Yeah, and civilization stops at its outskirts. The rest of the planet's too primitive to rate a class. That's what's slowed us up from the beginning. Too many places to hide."

Her gaze swept the ruins. "Doesn't seem to have done them much good."

"No," he agreed. "I saw the bones on the way in, same as you did. I wonder if the poor monster died here, too?"

"Don't talk like that," she said uneasily. "You know how we're supposed to refer to him. You don't watch yourself, you'll put that in an official communiqué sometime and find yourself up for a formal reprimand."

"Ah, yes, I forgot," he murmured. "The disadvantaged child. Pardon me, Rose, but this whole business has been a lousy job from the beginning. You're right, though. I shouldn't single him out. It's not his fault. The contrary. He isn't responsible for what the Meliorares did to him."

"Right," the woman said. "Well, he'll soon be repaired."

"*If* he got away," her companion reminded her.

"Surely some of them did," the woman said.

The man pointed toward several long walls of rubble that might once have been buildings. "Speak of the devil."

A figure was headed toward them. It took longer than was necessary because it did not travel in a straight line. It attempted to, but every so often would stagger off to its right like a wheel with its bearings out. The man's clothes were filthy, his boots caked with mud. They had not been changed in several days. He waved weakly at the newcomers. Save for the limp with which he walked, he seemed intact. His stringy hair was soaked and plastered like wire to his face and head. He made no effort to brush it from his eyes.

He seemed indifferent to the identity of the new arrivals. His concerns were more prosaic. "Have you any food?"

"What happened here?" the woman asked him as soon as he had limped to within earshot.

"Have you any food? God knows there's plenty of water. That's all this miserable place has to offer is plenty of water. All you want even when you don't want it. I've been living on nuts and berries and what I've been able to salvage from the camp kitchen. Had to fight the scavengers for everything. Miserable, stinking hole."

"What happened here?" the woman repeated calmly. The man appeared to be in his late twenties. Too young, she knew, for him to be a member of the Meliorare's inner circle. Just an unlucky employee.

"Caster," he mumbled. "Name's Caster. Excuse me a minute." He slid down his crude, handmade crutch until he was sprawled on the damp earth. "Broke my ankle, I think. It hasn't healed too well. I need to have it set right." He winced, then looked up at them.

"Damned if I know. What happened here, I mean. One minute I was replacing communications modules, and the next all hell opened up. You should've seen 'em. Goddamn big as the tower, every one of 'em. Seemed like it, anyhow. Worst thing was those dish-size bloody eyes with tiny little black specks lookin' down at you like a machine. Not decent, them eyes. I don't know what brought 'em down on us like they came, but it sure as hell wasn't a kind providence."

"Are you the only survivor?" the man asked.

"I haven't seen anyone else, if that's what you mean." His voice turned pleading. "Hey, have you got any food?"

"We can feed you," the woman said with a smile. "Listen, who were you working for here?"

"Bunch of scientists. Uppity bunch. Never talked to us ordinary folk." He forced a weak laugh. "Paid well, though. Keep your mouth shut and do your job and see the countryside. Just never expected the countryside to come visiting me. I've had it with this outfit. Ready to go home. They can keep their damn severance fee." A new thought occurred to him, and he squinted up at the couple standing over him.

"Hey, you mean you don't know who they were? Who are you people, anyway?"

They exchanged a glance; then the woman shrugged. "No harm in it. Maybe it'll help his memory."

She pulled a small plastic card from an inside pocket and showed it to the injured man. It was bright red. On it was printed a name, then her world of origin: Terra. The eyes of the man on the ground widened slightly at that. The series of letters which followed added confusion to his astonishment.

FLT-I-PC-MO. The first section he understood. It told him that this visitor was an autonomous agent, rank Inspector, of the Commonwealth law enforcement arm, the Peaceforcers.

"What does 'MO' stand for?" he asked.

"Moral Operations section," she told him, repocketing the ident. "These scientists you worked for—even though you had little or no personal contact with them, you must have seen them from time to time?"

"Sure. They kept pretty well to themselves, but I sometimes saw 'em strolling around."

"They were all quite elderly, weren't they?"

He frowned. "You know, I didn't think much about it, but yeah, I guess they were. Does that mean something?"

"It needn't trouble you," the man said soothingly. "You've said you haven't seen anyone else around since this horde of beasts overwhelmed you. That doesn't necessarily mean you're the only survivor. I assume some form of transportation was maintained for local use here. You didn't see anyone get away in a mudder or skimmer?"

The man on the ground thought a moment, and his face brightened. "Yeah, yeah I did. There was this old lady and a younger one—good-looking, the younger one. There was a kid with 'em. I didn't recognize 'em, but there were always people coming and going here."

"How old was the kid?" the woman asked him.

"Damned if I know. I was running like blazes in one direction, and their skimmer was headed in the other, so I didn't stop to ask questions. Kid had red hair, though. I remember that. Redheads seem scarce on this ball of dirt."

"A charmed life," the older man murmured to his companion. There was admiration as well as frustration in his voice. "The boy leads a charmed life."

"As you well know, there may be a lot more than charm involved," the woman said tersely. "The old woman he refers to is obviously the adopting parent, but who was the other?" She frowned, now worried.

"It doesn't matter," her companion said. He spoke to the injured man. "Look, how well do you remember the attitudes of this trio? I know you didn't have much time. This younger woman, the attractive one. Did she give the appearance of being in control of the other two? Did it seem as if she was holding the boy and old lady under guard?"

"I told you, I didn't get much of a look," Caster replied. "I didn't see any weapons showing, if that's what you're talking about."

"Interesting," the woman murmured. "They may have enlisted an ally. Another complication to contend with." She sighed. "Damn this case, anyway. If it didn't carry such a high priority with HQ I'd ask to be taken off."

"You know how far we'd get with a request like that," her companion snorted. "We'll get 'em. We've come so damn close so many times already. The odds have to catch up with us."

"Maybe. Remember your packages inside packages," she taunted him gently. "Still, it might be easy now." She waved at the ruined camp. "It doesn't look like many, if any, of the Meliorares got away."

"Melio—Meliorares?" The injured man gaped at them. "Hey, I know that name. Weren't they the—?" His eyes widened with realization. "Now wait a second, people, I didn't—"

"Take it easy," the man in the camouflage suit urged him. "Your surprise confirms your innocence. Besides, you're too young. They've taken in smarter folk than you down over the years."

"We shouldn't have that much trouble relocating the boy." She was feeling confident now. "We should be able to pick them up at our leisure."

"I wish I were as sanguine," her associate murmured, chewing on his lower lip. "There's been nothing leisurely about this business from the start."

"I didn't know," the injured man was babbling. "I didn't know they were Meliorares. None of us did, none of us. I just answered an ad for a technician. No one ever said a word to any of us about—!"

"Take it easy, I told you," the older man snapped, disgusted at the other's reaction. People panic so easily, he though: you'll have to undergo a truth scan. There's no that leg set right. There's food in the mudder. One thing, though: you'll have to undergo a truth scan. There's no harm in that, you know. Afterwards, you'll likely be released."

The man struggled to his feet, using his crutch as a prop. He had calmed down somewhat at the other's reassuring words. "They never said a word about anything like that."

"They never do," the woman commented. "That's how they've been able to escape custody for so many years. The gullible never ask questions."

"Meliorares. Hell," the man mumbled. "If I'd known—"

"If you'd known, then you'd never have taken their money and gone to work for them, right?"

"Of course not. I've got my principles."

"Sure you do." He waved a hand, forestalling the other man's imminent protest. "Excuse me, friend. I've developed a rather jaundiced view of humanity during the eight years I've spent in MO. Not your fault. Come on," he said to the woman named Rose, "there's nothing more for us here."

"Me, too? You're sure?" The younger man limped after them.

"Yeah, you, too," the Peaceforcer said. "You're sure you don't mind giving a deposition under scan? It's purely a voluntary procedure."

"Be glad to," the other said, eager to please. "Damn

lousy Meliorares, taking in innocent workers like that. Hope you mindwipe every last one of 'em."

"There's food in back," the woman said evenly as they climbed into the mudder.

"It's strange," her companion remarked as they seated themselves, "how the local wildlife overran this place just in time to allow our quarry to flee. The histories of these children are full of such timely coincidences."

"I know," Rose said as the mudder's engine rose to a steady hum and the little vehicle slid forward into the forest. "Take this flying snake we've been told about. It's from where?"

"Alaspin, if the reports are accurate."

"That's right, Alaspin. If I remember my galographics correctly, that world's a fair number of parsecs from here. One hell of a coincidence."

"But not impossible."

"It seems like nothing's impossible where these children are concerned. The sooner we take this one into custody and turn him over to the psychosurgeons, the better I'll like it. Give me a good clean deviant murder any time. This mutant-hunting gives me the shivers."

"He's not a mutant, Rose," her companion reminded her. "That's as inaccurate as me calling him a monster." He glanced toward the rear of the mudder. Their passenger was gobbling food from their stores and ignoring their conversation. "We don't even know that he possesses any special abilities. The last two we tracked down were insipidly normal."

"The Meliorares must have thought differently," Rose challenged. "They've gone to a lot of trouble to try and catch this one and look what's happened to them."

They were well into the forest now, heading south. The ruined camp was out of sight, swallowed up by trees and rolling terrain behind them.

"Some big native animals did them in," her companion said. "A maddened herd that had nothing whatsoever to do with the boy or any imagined abilities of his. So far, his trail shows only that he's the usual Meliorare disturbed youth. You worry too much, Rose."

"Yeah. I know. It's the nature of the business, Feodor."

But their concerns haunted them as night began to over-take the racing mudder.

The woman manning the communications console was very old, almost as old and shaky as the small starship it-self, but her hands played the instrumentation with a con-fidence born of long experience, and her hearing was sharp enough for her to be certain she had not missed any portion of the broadcast. She looked up from her station into the face of the tall, solemn man standing next to her and shook her head slowly.

"I'm sorry, Dr. Cruachan, sir. They're not responding to any of our call signals. I can't even raise their tight-beam frequency anymore."

The tall man nodded slowly, reluctantly. "You know what this means?"

"Yes," she admitted, sadness tinging her voice. "Nyassa-lee, Haithness, Brora—all gone now. All those years." Her voice sank to a whisper.

"We can't be sure," Cruachan murmured. "Not one hundred percent. It's only that," he hesitated, "they ought to have responded by now, at least via the emergency unit."

"That stampede was terrible luck, sir."

"If it was bad luck," he said softly. "History shows that where the subject children are concerned, the unknown sometimes gives luck a push—or a violent shove."

"I know that, sir," the communicator said. She was tired, Cruachan knew; but then they were all tired. Time was running out for them and for the Meliorare Society as well as for its noble, much-misunderstood goals. There had been thoughts, years ago, of training new acolytes in the techniques and aims of genetic manipulation pioneered by the Society, but the onus under which they were forced to operate made the cooperation of foolish younger research-ers impossible to obtain, thanks to the unrelenting barrage of slanderous propaganda propagated by the Church and the Commonwealth government.

Curse them all for the ignorant primitives they were! The Society was not dead yet!

Haithness, Nyassa-lee, Brora—the names were a dirge

in his mind. If they were truly gone now, and it seemed that must be so, that left very few to carry on the Work. The conflict within him was strong. Should he press on-or flee to set up operations elsewhere? So many old friends, colleagues, great scientific minds, lost; was this one subject worth it? They still had no proof that he was. Only graphs and figures to which the computers held. But the computers didn't care. Nobody cared.

There was nothing to indicate that the subject had been in any way responsible for the unfortunate stampede that had destroyed the camp together with their hopes. Of course, it was quite possible that the subject had perished along with the others, Cruachan mused. If not, if he decided to pursue this one to a conclusion, then there could be no more external manipulation attempted. They would have to confront the subject directly, as they had years ago tried to do with the girl.

It was a long, roundabout course to their next "safe" station. Cruachan was not at all confident of working through another several years of hiding and seeking out another promising subject. If the long arm of the Peaceforcers had not caught up with him by then, time and old age were liable to do the job for the government. They had come a long way together, he and his associates. A great effort; many lives had been expended to keep the project alive. He and his few remaining colleagues had to follow this case to its conclusion.

"Thank you, Amareth," he told the woman waiting patiently at the console. "Keep the receiver open just in case."

"Of course, Dr. Cruachan, sir."

Turning, he headed slowly toward Conference. Halfway there, his step picked up, his stride became more brisk. This won't do, he told himself. As president of the Society, it was incumbent upon him to set an example for the others, now more than ever. By the time he reached the meeting room and strode inside, his initial despair at the reports from below had been replaced by icy determination.

Half a dozen elderly men and women sat waiting for him. So few, he thought, so few left. The last of the Society, the last supporters of a great idea. Their upturned faces all silently asked the same question.

"Still no word," he said firmly. "We must therefore assume that doctors Brora, Haithness, and Nyassa-lee have been lost." There were no outward expressions of grief, no wails or cries. They waited expectantly for him to continue, and their quiet vote of confidence redoubled his resolve.

"I recommend that we proceed with the attempt to regain control of Number Twelve."

"We have reason to believe that MO operatives are now working in this region," an old woman said from the far side of the comfortable room.

"What of it?" another woman asked sharply. "They've always been two steps behind us, and they always will be."

"I wish I was as positive of that as you, Hanson," the first woman said. "The longevity of the Society is the result of foresight and caution, not contempt for those who hold us in contempt." She looked up at their leader. "You're sure about continuing to operate here, Cruachan?"

"More so than ever," he told her. "We have too much invested in this Number Twelve *not* to continue." He proceeded to recite the long list of factors responsible for his decision.

When he finished, a thin little man seated in the far corner of the room spoke out sharply in an incongruously deep voice. He had an artificial leg and heart, but the look in his eyes was as blindly intense as it had been fifty years earlier.

"I concur! The promise still lies here. If the subject is still accessible—"

"We have no reason to believe he is not," Cruachan half lied.

"—then we have a chance to get to him before the MO insects do. As Cruachan says, we must balance the potential here against our own intensifying infirmities." He kicked the floor with his false leg.

"Very well," said the old lady who had raised the specter of Commonwealth interference. "I see that most of you are of a mind to continue with our work here. I must confess that I cannot muster an argument against Dr. Cruachan's many good points. But we now have a new problem to overcome which will not be solved by a vote.

"Is it true that the last report from the camp places the subject in proximity to an Alaspinian miniature dragon?"

Cruachan nodded slowly. "The presence of the catalyst creature close to the subject was alluded to, yes."

"Then how are we to proceed? Besides acting as a magnifying lens for any latent Talent the subject may possess, this particular animal is deadly in and of itself. If it has formed an emotional bond with the subject, it will be a much more dangerous opponent than any dozen MO officers."

Cruachan waved her worries aside. "I've given the matter proper consideration. The snake will be taken care of, I promise you. If we cannot neutralize a mere reptile, then we have no business pretending to the ideals of our Society."

"It is not a reptile," a man near the back put in. He was glassy-eyed because of the thick contact lenses he was forced to wear. "It is reptilian in appearance, but warm blood flows in its veins, and it should more properly be classified as—"

"I don't give a damn what Order it fits into," Cruachan broke in impatiently. "The beast will be handled." His brows drew together at a sudden thought. "In fact, if such a mental bond now exists, it is likely stronger than that which ties the subject to his adoptive parent."

"Another chance for external control!" a woman exclaimed.

"Yes. Instead of presenting us with a new threat, it's possible this creature may be our key to subject control. So you all see how seeming difficulties may be turned to our advantage."

"Too bad about Haithness and the others," one of the old men murmured. "I'd known Haithness for forty-five years."

"So did I," Cruachan reminded him. "We must not let her and Nyassa-lee and Brora down. If, as now seems likely, they have sacrificed themselves for the cause, they provide us with still another reason to press onward. As we shrink in numbers, so must we grow in determination."

Murmurs of assent rose from around the conference room.

"We will not abandon this subject," Cruachan continued forcefully. "He will be brought under our wing by whatever means is required. I call for a formal vote for proceeding."

Cruachan was gratified to see the decision to continue confirmed unanimously. Such decisions usually were; dissent had no place in an organization bent to such a singular purpose.

"Thank you all," he said when the hands dropped. "Remember, this Number Twelve may hold the key to our vindication. We should proceed with that hope in mind. From this moment on, our entire energy will be devoted to gaining control over him." He turned toward the doorway.

"We have to hurry. If the MOs find him first, they will ruin him for our purposes."

The group dissolved in a rush of activity and fresh resolve that was matched in intensity only by the desperation that gave it life.

Chapter Fifteen

The city stank of human and other beings, of animals and exotic cooking, of resins and building materials old and new, all affected by the eternal dampness that permeated organic and inorganic materials alike. But it was all flowers and spice to Flinx. The transport car hissed to a halt outside the paneled exterior of the little bar and with the little credit remaining to him, he paid the machine. It responded with a mechanical "Thank you, sir" before drifting off up the street in search of its next fare.

Mother Mastiff leaned heavily against him as they made their way inside. Her ordeal had left her feeling her age, and she was very tired. So tired that she did not pull away from the snake riding high on Flinx's shoulder.

Once inside, Pip uncoiled from its perch beneath the slickertic Lauren Walder had provided and made a snakeline for the bar itself. This place he knew. On the counter ahead sat bowls of pretzels, tarmac nuts, and other interesting salty delicacies that were almost as much fun to play with as to eat.

Flinx had deliberately brought them back to the marketplace via a zigzag, roundabout course, changing transports frequently, trying until the last moment to travel with other citizens. Try as he might, he had been unable to see any indication that they had been followed, nor had the minidrag reacted negatively to any of the travelers who had looked askance at the exhausted youth and the old woman with him. Still, it was this caution that prompted them to visit this bar before returning to the shop. It would be wise not to go home alone, and Small Symm, the bar owner, would be good company to have around when they again set palm print to the front-door lock. To some degree his physical talents matched those of Flinx's mind.

As giants go, Small Symm was about average. He had been a friend of Flinx since the day of the boy's adoption. He often bought interesting utensils from Mother Mastiff for use in his establishment.

An enormous hand appeared and all but swept the two travelers into a booth. At the long metal bar, patrons nervously moved aside to allow the acrobatic flying snake plenty of access to the pretzels.

"I've heard," the young giant said by way of greeting, his voice an echo from deep within a cavernous chest, "that you were back. Word travels fast in the market."

"We're okay, Symm." Flinx favored his friend with a tired smile. "I feel like I could sleep for a year, but other than that, we're all right."

The giant pulled a table close to the booth and used it for a chair. "What can I get for the two of you? Something nice and hot to drink?"

"Not now, boy," Mother Mastiff said with a desultory wave of one wrinkled hand. "We're anxious to be home. 'Tis your good company we'd make use of, not your beverages." She turned quiet and let Flinx do the majority of the explaining.

Small Symm frowned, his brows coming together like clouds in the sky. "You think these people might still be after you?"

She almost started to say, "'Tis not me they're after," and just did manage to hold her tongue. She still believed it was too soon to reveal to Flinx everything she had learned. Much too soon. "Unlikely but possible, and I'm not the type to tempt fate, the unkind bastard."

"I understand." Symm stood, his head just clearing the ceiling. "You would like some friendly companionship on your way home."

"If you could spare the time," Flinx said gratefully. "I really believe that we're finished with these people." He did not explain that he thought they were all dead. No need to complicate matters. "But we'd sure be a lot more comfortable if you'd come with us while we checked out the shop."

"I'll be just a moment," Symm assured him. "Wait here." He vanished into a back room. When he returned, it was in the company of a tall young woman. He spoke softly to her for a minute, she nodding in response, then rejoined his visitors. He was wearing a slickertic not quite large enough to protect a medium-sized building.

"I'm ready," he told them. "Nakina will watch business until I return. Unless you'd rather rest a while longer."

"No, no." Mother Mastiff struggled to her feet. "I'll rest when I'm back home in my shop."

It was not far from Small Symm's place to the side street where Mother Mastiff's stall was located. With Symm carrying her, they made good time.

"Seems empty," the giant commented as he gently set the old woman on her feet. It was evening. Most of the shops were already shuttered, perhaps because the rain was falling harder than usual. In the marketplace, weather was often the most profound of economic arbiters.

"I guess it's all right." Mother Mastiff stepped toward the front door.

"Wait a minute." Flinx put out an arm to hold her back. "Over there, to the left of the shop."

Symm and Mother Mastiff stared in the indicated direction. "I don't see anything," the giant said.

"I thought I saw movement." Flinx glanced down at Pip. The flying snake dozed peacefully beneath the cover of the slickertic. Of course, the snake's moods were often unpredictable, but his continued calm was a good sign. Flinx gestured to his right. The giant nodded and moved off like a huge shadow to conceal himself in the darkness next to the vacant shop off to the left. Flinx went to his right—to starboard, as Lauren might have said. It had taken him awhile to forgive her for leaving—and Mother Mastiff for letting her leave—while he was still sound asleep. He wondered what she was doing, yet the memory of her was already beginning to fade. It would take somewhat longer to escape his emotions.

Mother Mastiff waited and watched as friend and son moved off in opposite directions. She did not mind standing in the rain. It was Drallarian rain, which was different somehow from the rain that fell anywhere else in the universe.

Flinx crept warily along the damp plastic walls of the shop fronts, making his way toward the alley that meandered behind their home. If the movement he thought he had spied signified the presence of some scout awaiting their return, he did not want that individual reporting back to his superiors until Flinx had drained him of information.

There—movement again, and no mistaking it this time! It was moving away from him. He increased his pace, keeping to the darkest shadows. The stiletto that slept in his boot was in his right hand now, cold and familiar.

Then a cry in the darkness ahead and a looming, massive shape. Flinx rushed forward, ready to help even though it was unlikely the giant would need any assistance. Then something new, something unexpected.

Nervous laughter?

"Hello, Flinx-boy." In the dim light, Flinx made out the friendly face of their neighbor Arrapkha.

"Hello, yourself." Flinx put the stiletto back where it belonged. "You gave me reason to worry. I thought we were finished with shapes in the night."

"I gave *you* reason to worry?" The craftsman indicated the bulk of Small Symm standing behind him.

"I'm sorry," Symm said apologetically. "We couldn't see who you were."

"You know now." He looked back toward Flinx. "I've been watching your shop for you." Symm went to reassure Mother Mastiff. "You know, making sure no one broke in and tried to steal anything."

"That was good of you," Flinx said as they started back toward the street.

"It's good to see you back, Flinx-boy. I'd given you up not long after you left."

"Then why have you kept watching the shop?"

The older man grinned. "Couldn't stop hoping, I guess. What was it all about, anyway?"

"Something illegal that Mother Mastiff was involved in many years back," Flinx explained. "She didn't go into the details. Just told me that revenge was involved."

"Some people have long memories," Arrapkha said, nodding knowingly. "Since you have returned well and safe, I presume that you made a peace with the people who kidnaped your mother?"

"We concluded the business," Flinx said tersely.

They returned to the street, where Small Symm and Mother Mastiff waited to greet them.

"So it was you, Arrapkha. Ye ignorant fleurm, worrying us like that." She smiled. "Never thought I'd be glad to see ye, though."

"Nor I you," the woodworker confessed. He gestured toward Flinx. "That boy of yours is as persistent as he is foolhardy. I did my best to try and convince him not to go rushing off after you."

"I would have told him the same," she said, "and he would have ignored me, too. Headstrong, he be." She allowed herself a look of pardonable pride. Flinx was simply embarrassed. "And fortunate it is for me."

"Old acquaintances and bad business." Arrapkha waggled an admonishing finger at her. "Beware of old acquaintances and bad business and deeds left unresolved."

"Ah, yes." She changed the subject. "Been watching the old place for me, eh? Then I'd best check the stock carefully as soon as we're inside." They both laughed.

"If you think it's all right for me to leave," Small Symm murmured. "Nakina has a bad temper, and that's not good for business."

Mother Mastiff looked thoughtful. "If our friend here insists he's kept a close eye on the shop . . ."

"I've watched and watched," Arrapkha insisted. "Unless they've tunneled in, no one's gone inside since your boy left to look for you."

"No tunneling under these streets," she observed with a

grin. "They'd hit the sewers." She looked back up at their escort. "Thank ye, Symm. Ye can run back to your lovely den of iniquity."

"It's hardly that," he replied modestly. "Someday if I work hard, perhaps."

Flinx extended a hand, which vanished in the giant's grasp. "My thanks, also, Symm."

"No trouble. Glad to help." The giant turned and lumbered away into the night.

The three friends moved to the front door. Mother Mastiff placed her right palm against the lock plate. It clicked immediately, and the door slid aside, admitting them. Flinx activated the lights, enabling them to see clearly that the stall area was apparently untouched. Stock remained where they had left it, gleaming and reassuringly familiar in the light.

"Looks to be the same as when I left," Mother Mastiff observed gratefully.

"Looks to be the same as it did ten years ago." Arrapkha shook his head slowly. "You don't change much, Mother Mastiff, and neither does some of your stock. I think you're too fond of certain pieces to sell them."

"There be nothing I'm too fond of not to sell," she shot back, "and my stock changes twice as fast as that pile of beetle-eaten garbage ye try to pass off on unsuspecting customers as handicrafts."

"Please, no fighting," Flinx implored them. "I'm tired of fighting."

"Fighting?" Arrapkha said, looking surprised.

"We're not fighting, boy," Mother Mastiff told him. "Don't ye know by now how old friends greet one another? By seeing who can top the other's insults." To show him that she meant what she said, she smiled fondly at Arrapkha. The woodworker wasn't a bad sort at all. Only a little slow.

The living quarters they found likewise untouched: in total chaos, exactly as Flinx had last seen it.

"Housekeeping," Mother Mastiff grumbled. "I've always hated housekeeping. Still, someone has to get this place cleaned up, and better me than ye, boy. Ye have no touch for domesticity, I fear."

"Not tonight, Mother." Flinx yawned. His initial sight of his own bed had expanded until it filled the whole room.

"No, not tonight, boy. I must confess to being just the slightest bit tired." Flinx smiled to himself. She was on the verge of physical collapse, quite ready to go to sleep wherever her body might fall, but she was damned if she would show weakness in front of Arrapkha lest it damage her image of invincibility.

"Tomorrow we'll put things to rights. I work better in the daytime, anyway." She tried not to look toward her own bedroom, waiting on Arrapkha.

"Well, then, I will leave you," the craftsman said. "Again, it's good to see you back and healthy. The street wasn't the same without you."

"We monuments are hard to get rid of," Mother Mastiff said. "Perhaps we'll see ye tomorrow."

"Perhaps," Arrapkha agreed. He turned and left them, making certain that the front door locked behind him.

Once outside, Arrapkha drew his slickertic tight around his head and shoulders as he hurried back to his own shop. He had no more intention of turning his friends over to the authorities, as he had been instructed, than he did of cutting the price of his stock fifty percent for some rich merchant. He would not hinder the police, but he would do nothing to assist them, either. He could always plead ignorance, for which he was famed in this part of the marketplace.

So tired; they looked so tired, he thought. It was the first time he could remember Mother Mastiff looking her age. Even the boy, who, though slight of build, had never before seemed exhausted by any labor, appeared completely worn out. Even that lethal pet that always rode his shoulder had looked tired.

Well, he would give them a few days to get their house in order and regain their strength. Then he would surprise them by taking them to Magrim's for some tea and tall sandwiches and would tell them of the mysterious visit of the two Peaceforcers to their little street. It would be interesting to see what Mother Mastiff would make of that. She might welcome the interest of the authorities in her

case—and then again, she might not. Not knowing the details of her history, Arrapkha could not be sure, which was
why he had elected not to help those offworld visitors.

Yes, he decided firmly. Wait a few days and let them
rest up before springing that new information on them. No
harm in that, surely. He opened the door to his own shop
and shut it against the night and the rain.

One day passed, then another, and gradually the shop
again assumed the appearance of home as the mess the
kidnapers had made was cleaned up. Comfortable in such
familiar surroundings, Mother Mastiff regained her
strength rapidly. She was such a resilient old woman,
Flinx thought with admiration. For his part, by the second
day he was once again venturing out into his familiar
haunts, greeting old friends, some of whom had heard of
the incident and some of whom had not, but never straying far from the shop lest even at this late date and in
spite of his beliefs some surviving members of the organization that had abducted Mother Mastiff return, still seeking their revenge.

Nothing materialized, however, to give any credence to
such anxieties. By the third day, he had begun to relax
mentally as well as physcially. It was amazing, he thought,
as he settled in that night, the things that one misses the
most during a long absence. Odd how familiar and
friendly one's own bed becomes when one has had to sleep
elsewhere. . . .

It was the hate that woke Pip. Cold and harsh as the
most brutal day winter could muster on the ice world of
Tran-ky-ky, it shook the flying snake from a sound sleep.
It was directed not at the minidrag but at its master.

Pink and blue coils slid soundlessly clear of the thermal
blanket. Flinx slept on, unaware of his pet's activity.
Several hours remained until sunrise.

Pip rested and analyzed. Examining the minidrag lying
at the foot of the bed, an observer might have believed it
to be a reasoning being. It was not, of course, but neither
was its mental capacity inconsequential. Actually, no one
was quite sure how the mind of the Alaspinian miniature
dragon worked or what profound cogitations it might be

capable of, since no xenobiologist dared get close enough to study it.

Blue and pink wings opened, pleats expanding, and with a gentle whirr the snake took to the air. It hovered high over its master's head, worried, searching, trying to pinpoint the source of the unrelenting malignancy that was poisoning its thoughts. The hate was very near. Worse, it was familiar.

There was a curved roof vent that Pip had appropriated for its own private comings and goings. The snake darted toward it, the wings folding up at the last second to allow the slim body to slip through the curving tube. Nothing much bigger than a mouse could have slipped through that vent. With wings folded flat against its muscular sides, the minidrag made the passage easily.

Pip emerged atop the roof into the light, early-morning rain. Up that way the hate lay, to the north, up the alley. Wings unfolded and fanned the air. The minidrag circled once above the shop, paused to orient itself, then buzzed determinedly into the opening nearby where the alley emerged into cloudlight.

It braked to a halt and hovered, hissing at the mental snarl that had drawn it.

"Over here pretty, pretty," coaxed a voice. "You know who hates your master, don't you? And you know what we'll do to him if we get the chance."

The flying snake shot through the partly open doorway into the hate-filled room beyond. Two humans awaited it with deadly calm. Never would they have the chance to harm the minidrag's master. Never!

A thin stream of venom spewed from the roof of the flying snake's upper jaw and struck toward the nearest of the vicious bipeds. It never reached the man. Something was between him and Pip, something hard and transparent. The venom contacted it, hissed in the still air as it started to eat at the transparent shield. Startled, the two monsters seated behind the shield flinched and began to rise.

But the door opening on the alley had already slammed shut behind the minidrag. Suddenly, a strange, sweet smell filled the room. Wingbeats slackened and grew weak. Twin eyelids fluttered and closed. The flying snake flopped about on the floor like a fish out of water, wings beating futilely against the plastic as it gasped for breath.

"Be careful," a distant voice warned. "We don't want to overdose it. It's no good to us dead."

"I'd sooner see it dead and take our chances with the subject," another said.

"We need every hold we can manage, including the possibility raised by this little devil."

The voices faded. Soon the flying snake had stopped moving. Long minutes passed before a man dared to enter the sealed room. He was dressed head to toe in a protective suit. His eyes were anxious behind the transparent visor. With the long metal prod he carried he poked once, twice at the comatose minidrag. It jerked convulsively in response to the touches, but otherwise displayed no sign of life.

The man took a deep breath and set the long prod aside as he bent to pick up the thin body. It hung limply in his gloved hands as he inspected it.

"Still breathing," he declared to the people pressed close to the transparent wall.

"Good. Get it in the cage quick," said the shorter of the two observers. Her companion was studying the hole where the venom had finally eaten through the protective shield.

"I'd like to see a molecular breakdown on this stuff," he murmured, careful to keep his fingers clear of the still-sizzling edges of the ragged gap. "Anything that can eat through pancrylic this fast . . ." He shook his head in disbelief. "I don't see how the venom sacs can contain the stuff without dissolving right through the creature's jaw."

"You'd need a toxicologist and biochemist to explain it, if they could," said the woman standing next to him, likewise taking a moment to examine the hole. "Perhaps there's more to it than just a straightforward poison. The snake's mouth may hold several separate sacs whose contents mix only when it's spraying someone."

"Makes sense." The man turned away from the shield that had nearly failed them. "We better get moving. The subject may awaken any minute now. Be sure you keep the monster thoroughly narcotized."

"Is that necessary?" She frowned. "Surely the cage will hold it."

"That's what we thought about the wall. The cage is tougher, but we don't want to take any chances. I don't want our guest spitting his way free while we're asleep in our beds."

"No, we sure as hell don't." The woman shuddered slightly. "I'll take charge of it myself."

"I was hoping you'd say that." Cruachan smiled to himself. He was intimately familiar with the theories that attempted to explain the special bonds that could spring into being between a catalyst creature such as the minidrag and one of the Talented. Certainly the link that existed between this creature and the boy known as Number Twelve was as powerful as any of the imperfectly recorded cases he had studied. It was not unreasonable to suppose that it could be stronger than the affection bond between the boy and his adoptive mother.

They came at him without warning during his final period of REM sleep, when he was defenseless. They sprang into existence out of emptiness, laughing at him, tormenting him with feelings and sensations he could not define or understand.

Nightmares.

Someone was twisting a wire around his brain, compressing it tighter and tighter until it seemed certain that his eyes would explode out of his head and fly across the room. He lay in his bed, twitching slightly, his eyelids quivering, as they did their work on him and took advantage of his helpless, unconscious mind.

This batch was worse than most; twisting, abstract forms, dark swirling colors, and himself somehow in the middle of them all, racing down a long, ominous corridor. At the end of that corridor lay his salvation, he knew, and almost as important, answers. Understanding and safety.

But the faster he ran, the slower he advanced. The floor that was not a floor dissolved beneath his feet, dropping him like some relativistic Alice down a rabbit hole of space-time distortions, while the far end of the corridor and its promises of light and comprehension receded into the wastes overhead.

He woke up with a silent start and glanced rapidly around the room. Only after he convinced himself of its reality did he begin to relax.

It was the right room, his room, the one he had lived in most of his life: tiny, spartan, comfortable. The patter of morning rain was music on the roof, and faint daylight filtered through the window above his bed. He swung his legs out clear of the blanket and rubbed both throbbing eyes with his fingers.

The fingers abruptly ceased their ministrations, and he looked back to the bed. Something was wrong.

"Pip?" The flying snake was not coiled in its familiar position at the top of the pillow, nor was it underneath. Flinx pulled back the blanket, then bent to peer under the bed. "C'mon boy, don't hide from me this morning. I'm worn out, and my head is killing me."

There was no familiar hissing response to his confession. He prowled the room's meager confines, at first puzzled, then concerned. At last, he stood on the bed and shouted toward the air vent overhead.

"Pip, breakfast!"

No comforting hum of brightly hued wings reached him from beyond. He found a piece of wire and used it to probe the vent. It was clear to the outside.

He left his room and frantically started an inspection of the rest of the living quarters. Mother Mastiff stood by the convection stove, cooking something redolent of pepper and less exotic spices. "Something the matter, boy?"

"It's Pip." Flinx peered beneath recently righted furniture, moved bowls, and dropcloths.

"I gathered as much from the hollering ye were doing in your bedroom," she said sardonically. "Disappeared again, has he?"

"He never stays out through morning when he takes a solo night flight. Never."

"Always a first time, even for monsters," Mother Mastiff said, shrugging and concentrating on her cooking. "Wouldn't upset me if the little nastiness never did come back."

"Shame on you, Mother!" Flinx said, his tone agonized. "He saved my life, and probably yours, too."

"So I'm an ungrateful old Yax'm," she snorted. "Ye know my feelings toward your beast."

Flinx finished inspecting her room, then resolutely stormed back to his own and began dressing. "I'm going out to look for him."

Mother Mastiff frowned. "Breakfast ready soon. Why bother yourself, boy? Likely it'll be back soon enough, more's the pity. Besides, if it has got its slimy little self stuck someplace, you're not likely to find him."

"He could just be in the alley behind the shop," Flinx argued, "and I can hear him even when I can't see him."

"Suit yourself, boy."

"And don't wait breakfast on me."

"Think I'll starve meself on your account? Much less on account of some devil-wing." She had long ago given up arguing with him. When he made up his mind about something—well, one might as well wish for the planet's rings to be completed. He was a dutiful-enough son in most ways, but he simply refused to be restricted.

"It'll be here when ye get back," she said softly, checking the containers and lowering their ambient temperatures fifty degrees. "Ye can warm it up for your shiftless self."

"Thanks, Mother." Despite her contorting attempt to avoid him, he managed to plant a hurried kiss on one leathery cheek. She wiped at it, but not hard, as she watched him dash from the shop.

For an instant, she thought of telling him about what she had learned days ago up in the forest. About those strange Meliorare people and their intentions toward him. Then she shrugged the idea off. No, they were well clear of the horrid folk, and from the glimpse she had of their camp, they would not be bothering her boy ever again.

As to what she had learned of his history, it would be better to keep that secret for a few years yet. Knowing his stubborn impulsiveness, such information might send him running off in all sorts of dangerous directions. Much better not to say anything for a while. When he reached a reasonable age, twenty-three or so, she could let on what she had learned about his background. By then, he would have taken over management of the shop, perhaps married. Settled down some to a nice, sensible, quiet life.

She tasted the large pot, winced. Too little saxifrage. She reached for a small shaker.

"Pip! To me, boy!" Still no blue and pink flash enlivening the sky, still no rising hum. Now where would he get to? Flinx mused. He knew the minidrag was fond of the alley behind the shop. That was where he had first encountered the flying snake, after all, and to a snake's way of thinking, the alley was usually full of interesting things to eat. For all the minidrag's aerial agility, a box tumbling from the crest of a garbage heap or a rolling container could easily pin it to the ground. Flinx knew that no stranger was likely to get within ten meters of a trapped snake.

Might as well try the first, he decided. Slipping down the narrow space separating Mother Mastiff's shop from the vacant structure next to it, he soon found himself in the alley-way. It was damp and dark, its overall aspect dismal as usual.

He cupped his hands to his mouth, called out, "Pip?"

"Over here, boy," said a soft voice.

Flinx tensed, but his hand did not grab for the knife concealed in his boot. Too early. A glance showed that his retreat streetward was still unblocked, as was the section of alley behind him. Nor did the individual standing motionless beneath the archway in front of him look particularly threatening.

Flinx stood his ground and debated with himself, then finally asked, "If you know where my pet is, you can tell me just as easily from where you're standing, and I can hear you plainly from where *I'm* standing."

"I know where your pet is," the man admitted. His hair was entirely gray, Flinx noted. "I'll take you to it right now, if you wish."

Flinx stalled. "Is he all right? He hasn't gotten himself into some kind of trouble?"

The little man shook his head and smiled pleasantly. "No, he isn't in trouble, and he's just fine. He's sleeping, in fact."

"Then why can't you bring him out?" Flinx inquired. He continued to hold his position, ready to charge the man or race for the street as the situation dictated.

"Because I can't," the man said. "Really, I can't. I'm just following orders, you know."

"Whose orders?" Flinx asked suspiciously. Suddenly, events were becoming complicated again. The speaker's age and attitude abruptly impacted on him. "Are you with the people who abducted my mother? Because if you're trying to get revenge on her for whatever she was involved in years ago by harming me, it's not going to work."

"Take it easy, now," the man said. A voice Flinx could not hear whispered to the speaker from behind the door.

"For heaven's sake, Anders, don't get him excited!"

"I'm trying not to," the elderly speaker replied through clenched teeth. To Flinx he said more loudly, "No one wants to harm you or your pet, boy. You can have my word on that even if you don't think it's worth anything. My friends and I mean you and your pet only well." He did not respond to Flinx's brief allusion to his adoptive mother's past.

"Then if you mean us only well," Flinx said, "you won't object if I take a minute to go and reassure—"

The speaker took a step forward. "There's no need to disturb your parent, boy. In a moment she'll have her shop open and the crowd will ensure her safety, if that's what you're concerned about. Why alarm her needlessly? We just want to talk to you. Besides," he added darkly, taking a calculated risk, "you don't have any choice but to listen to me. Not if you want to see your pet alive again."

"It's only a pet snake." Flinx affected an air of indifference he didn't feel. "What if I refuse to go with you? There are plenty of other pets to be had."

The speaker shook his head slowly, his tone maddeningly knowledgeable. "Not like this one. That flying snake's a part of you, isn't it?"

"How do you know that?" Flinx asked. "How do you know how I feel about him?"

"Because despite what you may think of me right now," the speaker said, feeling a little more confident, "I am wise in the ways of certain things. If you'll let me, I'll share that knowledge with you."

Flinx hesitated, torn between concern for Pip and a sense of foreboding that had nothing to do with his peculiar Talents. But the man was right: there was no choice. He wouldn't chance Pip's coming to harm even though he couldn't have said why.

"All right." He started toward the speaker. "I'll go with you. You'd better be telling the truth."

"About not wishing to harm you or your pet?" The smile grew wider. "I promise you that I am."

Try as he might, Flinx couldn't sense any inimical feelings emanating from the little man. Given the erratic nature of his abilities, that proved nothing—for all Flinx could tell, the man might be planning murder even as he stood there smiling. Up close, the speaker looked even less formidable. He was barely Flinx's height, and though not as ancient as Mother Mastiff, it was doubtful he would be much opposition in a hand-to-hand fight.

"This is my friend and associate Stanzel," the man said. An equally elderly woman stepped out of the shadows. She seemed tired but forced herself to stand straight and look determined.

"I don't want to hurt you, either, boy." She studied him with unabashed curiosity. "None of us do."

"So there are still more of you," Flinx murmured in confusion. "I don't *understand* all this. Why do you have to keep persecuting Mother Mastiff and me? And now Pip, too? Why?"

"Everthing will be explained to you," the woman assured him, "if you'll just come with us." She gestured up the alley.

Flinx strode along between them, noting as he did so that neither of them appeared to be armed. That was a good sign but a puzzling one. His stiletto felt cold against his calf. He looked longingly back toward the shop. If only he could have told Mother Mastiff! But, he reminded himself, as long as he returned by bedtime, she wouldn't worry herself. She was used to his taking off on unannounced explorations.

"Mark me words," she would declaim repeatedly, "that curiosity of yours will be the death of ye!"

If it didn't involve striking against Mother Mastiff, though, then what did these people want with him? It was important to them, very important. If not, they wouldn't have risked an encounter with his deadly pet. Despite their age, he still feared them, if only for the fact that they had apparently managed to capture Pip, a feat beyond the capabilities of most.

But something, an attitude perhaps, marked these people as different from the usual run-of-the-mill marketplace cutthroats. They were different from any people he had ever encountered. Their coolness and indifference combined with their calm professionalism to frighten him.

They alley opened onto a side street, where an aircar waited. The old man unlocked it and gestured for him to enter. As Flinx started to step into the little cab, he experienced one of those mysterious, unannounced bursts of emotional insight. It was brief, so brief he was unsure he had actually felt it. It wiped out his own fear, leaving him more confused and uncertain than ever.

He might be afraid for Pip and perhaps even a little for himself, but for some unknown reason, these two outwardly relaxed, supremely confident individuals were utterly terrified of him!

Chapter Sixteen

Cruachan studied the readouts carefully. The section of the old warehouse in which they had established themselves was a poor substitute for the expensively outfitted installation they had laboriously constructed far to the north. He did not dwell on the loss. Years of disappointment had inured him to such setbacks. The machines surrounding him had been hastily assembled and linked together. Wiring was exposed everywhere, further evidence of haste and lack of time to install equipment properly. It would have to do, however.

He was not disappointed. In spite of all their problems, they appeared on the verge of accomplishing what they had intended to do on this world, albeit not in the manner originally planned. It seemed that the presence of the Alaspinian immigrant was going to turn to their advantage. For the first time since they had placed themselves in orbit around the world, he felt more than merely hopeful. His confidence came from Anders' and Stanzel's last report. The subject, accompanying them quietly, seemed reluctantly willing to cooperate, but had thus far displayed no sign of unexpected threatening abilities.

While a potentially lethal act, the taking of the subject's pet had turned out far more successful than the attempted adjustment of the subject's adoptive parent. Cruachan now conceded that that had been a mistake. If only their information had included mention of the catalyst creature in the first place! He did not blame the informant, though. It was likely that the minidrag came into the subject's possession subsequent to the filing of the informant's report.

He felt like an old tooth, cracked and worn down by overuse and age. But with the semisymbiotic pet now under their control, the subject would have to accede to their wishes. There could no longer be any consideration of attempting to influence the boy externally. They would have to implant the electronic synapses intended for his parent in the lad's own brain. Direct control posed some risks, but as far as Cruachan and his associates could see, they had no other choice. Cruachan was glad the case was nearing conclusion. He was very tired.

It was raining harder than usual for the season when the little aircar pulled up outside the warehouse. Flinx regarded the place with distaste. The section of Drallar out toward the shuttleport was bloated with stark, blocky monuments to bad business and overconsumption, peopled mostly with machines—dark, uninviting, and alien.

He had no thought of changing his mind, of making a break for the nearest side street or half-open doorway. Whoever these people were, they were not ignorant. They had correctly surmised the intensity of his feelings for Pip, which was why they had not bound him and carried no arms.

He still couldn't figure out what they wanted with him. If they were not lying to him and truly meant him no harm, then of what use could he be to them? If there was one thing he couldn't stand, it was unanswered questions. He wanted explanations almost as badly as he wanted to see Pip.

They seemed very sure of themselves. Of course, that no weapons were in evidence did not mean no weapons were around. He could not square their fear of him with the absence of armament. Perhaps, he mused, they were afraid of him because they feared he might reveal what he knew of the kidnaping to the local authorities. Maybe that was what they wanted from him: a promise to remain silent.

But somehow that didn't make much sense, either.

"I wish you'd tell me what you want with me," he said aloud, "and what's going on."

"It's not our place to explain." The man glanced at his companion and then said, as if unable to suppress his own curiosity, "Have you ever heard of the Meliorare Society?"

Flinx shook his head. "No. I know what the word means, though. What's it got to do with me?"

"Everything." He seemed on the verge of saying more, but the old woman shushed him.

The building they entered was surrounded by similarly nondescript edifices. They were off the main shuttleport accessway. Flinx had seen only a few people about from the time they had entered the area. No one was in the dingy hallway.

They rode an elevator to the third floor. His escorts led him through broad, empty corridors, past high-ceilinged storage rooms filled with plasticine crates and drums. Finally, they halted before a small speaker set into the plastic of an unmarked door. Words were exchanged between Flinx's escort and someone on the other side, and the door opened to admit them.

He found himself in still another room crammed full of bundles and boxes. What set it apart from a dozen similar rooms was the right-hand wall. Stacked against it was an impressive array of electronics. Empty crates nearby hinted at recent and hasty unpacking and setup. The consoles were powered-up and manned. Their operators spared curious glances for the new arrivals before returning their attention to their equipment. Save for their uniformly grim expressions, they looked like retirees on a holiday outing.

Two people emerged from a door at the rear of the room. They were soon joined by a third—a tall, silverhaired, ruggedly handsome man. He carried himself like a born leader, and Flinx concentrated on him immediately. The man smiled down at Flinx. Even though he was close to Mother Mastiff's age, the man held himself straight. If he was subject to the infirmities of old age, he did a masterful job of concealing them. Vanity or will? Flinx wondered. He sought the man's emotions and drew the usual blank. Nor could he feel anything of Pip's presence in the room or nearby.

Even as the tall senior was shaking his hand and mouthing platitudes, Flinx was searching for the most likely escape route. There seemed to be only one exit: the door through which he had entered. He had no idea where the door at the far end of the room led, but suspected that freedom was not one of the possibilities.

"What a great pleasure to finally meet you, my boy," the old man was saying. His grip was firm. "We've gone to a great deal of trouble to arrive at this meeting. I would rather not have had to proceed in this fashion, but circumstances conspired to force my hand."

"It *was* you, then"—Flinx gestured at the others—"who were responsible for abducting my mother?"

Cruachan relaxed. There was no danger in this skinny, innocent boy. Whatever abilities he might possess remained dormant, awaiting proper instruction and development. Certainly his attitude was anything but threatening.

"I asked him," the man who had brought Flinx from the marketplace reported, "if he'd heard of the Society. He said no."

"No reason for him to," Cruachan observed. "His life has been restricted, his horizons limited."

Flinx ignored that appraisal of his limitations. "Where's Pip?"

"Your pet, I assume? Yes." The tall man turned and called out toward the rear doorway. The section of wall containing the door creaked as hidden winches pulled it aside. Beyond lay still another of the endless series of storage chambers, packed with the usual containers and drums and crates. On a table in the forefront stood a transparent cube, perhaps a meter square, topped with several small metal tanks. Hoses ran from the tanks into the cube.

To the left of the table stood a nervous-looking old man holding a small, flat control box. His thumb was pressed hard against one of the buttons set in the box. His eyes shifted regularly from the cube to Flinx and back to the cube.

Pip lay in the bottom of the cube, coiled into itself apparently deep in sleep. Flinx took a step forward. Cruachan put out a hand to hold him back.

"Your pet is resting comfortably. The air in the cage has been mixed with a mild soporific. Westhoff is regulating the mixture and flow of gases even as we speak. If you were to try anything foolish, he would increase the flow from the tanks before you could possibly free your pet. You see, the cage has been weld-sealed. There is no latch.

"The adjusted normal atmosphere inside the cube will be completely replaced by the narcoleptic gas, and your pet will be asphyxiated. It would not take long. All Westhoff has to do is press violently on the button his thumb is caressing. If necessary, he will throw his body across it. So you see, there is nothing you could do to prevent him from carrying out his assignment."

Flinx listened quietly even as he was gauging the distance between himself and the cage. The elderly man holding the control box gazed grimly back at him. Even if he could somehow avoid the hands that would surely reach out to restrain him, he did not see how he could open the cage and free Pip. His stiletto would be useless against the thick pancrylic.

"You've made your point," he said finally. "What do you want from me?"

"Redemption," Cruachan told him softly.

"I don't understand."

"You will eventually, I hope. For now, suffice for you to know that we are interested in your erratic but unarguable abilities: your Talent."

All Flinx's preconceived ideas collapsed like sand castles in a typhoon. "You mean you've gone through all this, kidnaping Mother Mastiff and now Pip, just because you're curious about *my* abilities?" He shook his head in disbelief. "I would have done my best to satisfy you without your having to go through all this trouble."

"It's not quite that simple. You might say one thing, even believe it, and then your mind might react otherwise."

Crazier and crazier, Flinx thought dazedly. "I don't know what the hell you're talking about."

"Just as well," Cruachan murmured. "You are an emotional telepath, is that not correct?"

"I'm sensitive sometimes to what other people are feeling, if that's what you mean," Flinx replied belligerently.

"Nothing else? No precognitive abilities? Telekinesis? True telepathy? Pyrokinesis? Dimensional perceptivity?"

Flinx laughed at him, the sound sharpened by the tension that filled the room. "I don't even know what those words mean except for telepathy. If by that you mean can I read other people's minds, no. Only sometimes their feelings. That other stuff, that's all fantasy, isn't it?"

"Not entirely," Cruachan replied softly, "not entirely. The potentials lie within every human mind, or so we of the Society believe. When awakened, further stimuli, provided through training and other means, can bring such abilities to full life. That was the—" He paused, his smile returning.

"As I said, someday you will understand everything, I hope. For now, it will be sufficient if you will permit us to run some tests on you. We wish to measure the probable limits of your Talent and test for other possible hidden abilities as yet undeveloped."

"What kinds of tests?" Flinx regarded the tall man warily.

"Nothing elaborate. Measurements, electroencephalotopography."

"That sounds elaborate to me."

"I assure you, there will be no discomfort. If you'll just come with me . . ." He put a fatherly hand on Flinx's shoulder. Flinx flinched. There should have been a snake there, not an unfamiliar hand.

Cruachan guided him toward the instruments. "I promise you, give us twenty-four hours and you'll have your pet restored to you unharmed, and you'll never have to go through this again."

"I don't know," Flinx told him. "I'm still not sure of what you want from me." It seemed to him that there was an awful lot of instrumentation around for just a few simple tests, and some of it looked almost familiar. Where had he seen that tendriled globe before?

Over a table in a room far to the north, he realized suddenly.

What do I do? he thought frantically. He could not lie down on that table, beneath those waiting tentacles. But if he hesitated, what might they do to Pip out of impatience and anger?

Unexpectedly, as his thoughts were tied in knots and he tried to decide what to do next, a sudden surge of emotion burst into his brain. There was hate and a little fear and a self-righteous anger that bordered on the paranoiac. He looked up at Cruachan. The older man smiled pleasantly down at him, then frowned as he saw the expression that had come over the subject's face. "Is something wrong?"

Flinx did not reply, methodically searching every face in the room. None of them seemed to be the source of the feelings he was receiving. And they were getting steadily stronger, more intense. They came—they came from—

He looked sharply toward the main entrance.

"Nobody move!" snapped a determined voice. The couple who burst through the door, having quietly circumvented the lock, were complete strangers to Flinx. A middle-aged pair dressed like offworld tourists, each holding a gun bigger than a pistol and longer than a rifle carefully balanced in both hands, they surveyed the startled occupants of the storage chamber.

Flinx did not recognize their weapons. That was unusual. His learning expeditions through the marketplace had made him familiar with most personal armament. But these were new to him. As new as this couple. They looked unrelentingly average. There was nothing average about the way they moved, however, or gave commands or held those peculiar guns. The Meliorares certainly seemed familiar with them.

"MO Section, Commonwealth Peaceforce," the man barked. "All of you are under government detention as of this moment." He grinned crookedly, almost savagely. "The charges against you, the specifics of which I'm sure you're all quite familiar with, are many and varied. I don't think I have to go into details."

Flinx started gratefully toward them. "I don't know how you people found me, but I'm sure glad to see you."

"Hold it right there." The woman shifted her weapon toward him. The expression on her face assured Flinx she was ready to shoot him if he took so much as another half step toward her. He froze, hurt and confused.

There was something new there, partly in her eyes but also in her mind: not so much fear as a kind of twisted hatred, a loathing. The emotion was directed squarely at him. It was so new, so alien and sickening, that he didn't know how to react. He knew only that his would-be saviors held no more affection for him, and perhaps even less in the way of good intentions, than this insane society of Meliorare people.

His confusion was being replaced by anger, a frantic fury born of frustration and despair, compounded by helplessness and desperation. Through no fault of his own, desiring only to be left alone, he had become the focal point of forces beyond his control, forces that extended even beyond his world. And he didn't know how, couldn't begin to think how to deal with them.

Through all the confusion came one lucid realization: he wasn't as grown-up as he had thought.

Near the back room the man named Westhoff had gone unnoticed by the Peaceforcers. He did not linger. Putting aside the control box he commenced a cautious retreat, utilizing crates and containers to make good his escape.

Pressure removed, the button he had been holding down rebounded.

"Over against that empty packing and away from the consoles. All of you," the woman commanded them, gesturing meaningfully with her gun. Rising from their seats and showing empty hands, the Meliorares hurried to comply with her order.

"Anybody touches a switch," the other Peaceforcer warned them, "it'll be the last thing he ever touches."

The woman threw Flinx a hard look. "Hey, you too. Move it." Revulsion emanated from her. Disgust and pity washed over Flinx in waves. She was broadcasting them all. Flinx tried to squeeze the degrading emotions out of his mind.

"I'm not with them," he protested. "I'm not part of this."

"I'm afraid that you are, boy, whether you like it or not," she told him. "You've caused a lot of trouble. But don't worry." She tried to smile. The result was a discomfiting parody. "Everything's going to be all right. You're going to be fixed up so you can live a normal life."

A buzzer suddenly roared to life on one of the unattended consoles, filling the room with insistent discordance. Cruachan stared dumbly at it, then at Flinx, then at the Peaceforcers.

"For heaven's sake, don't threaten him!"

"Threaten me?" Flinx was almost crying now, ignoring Cruachan's sudden terror, the buzzing, everything, as he spoke to the female Peaceforcer. "What does he mean, threaten me? What did you mean when you said you're going to have me fixed up? I'm *fine*."

"Maybe you are, and maybe you aren't," she replied, "but these *Meliorares*," she spat the word out, "seem to think otherwise. That's good enough for me. I'm no specialist. They're the ones who'll decide what's to be done with you."

"And the sooner the better," her companion added. "Did you call for backup?"

"As soon as we were sure." She nodded. "It'll take them a few minutes to get here. This isn't Brizzy, you know."

Flinx felt unsteady on his feet as well as in his mind. Where he had expected rescue, there was only new hurt, fresh indifference. No, worse than indifference, for these people saw him only as some kind of deformed, unhealthy creature. There was no understanding for him here in this room, not from his ancient persecutors or these new arrivals. The universe, as represented by organizations illegal and legitimate, seemed wholly against him.

Fixed, the woman had said. He was going to be *fixed*. But there was nothing wrong with him. Nothing! Why do they want to do these unnamable things to me? he thought angrily.

The pain and confusion produced results unnoticed by the anxious antagonists facing each other across the floor. Prodded by the powerful emotions emanating from his master, half-awakened by the thinning quantity of soporific gas entering its cage, the flying snake awoke. It did not need to search visually for Flinx—his outburst of hurt was a screaming beacon marking his location.

The snake's wings remained folded as it quickly examined its prison. Then it rose up and spat. In the confused babble that filled the opposite end of the room, the quiet hissing of dissolving pancrylic went unnoticed.

"Let's get them outside." The male Peaceforcer moved to his right, separating from his companion to stand to one side of the entrance while she moved to get behind the shifting group gathered in the middle of the room.

"Single file now," she ordered them, gesturing with her gun. "All of you. And please keep your hands in the air. No dramatic last-minute gestures, please. I don't like a mess."

Cruachan pleaded with her. "Please, we're just a bunch of harmless old scholars. This is our last chance. This boy"—and he indicated Flinx—"may be our last opportunity to prove—"

"I've studied your history, read the reports." The woman's voice was icy. "What you did is beyond redemption or forgiving. You'll get just what you deserve, and it won't be a chance to experiment further on this poor, malformed child."

"Please, somebody," Flinx said desperately, "I don't know what you're talking about! Won't somebody tell me—?"

"Somebody probably will," she told him. "I'm not privy to the details, and explanations aren't my department." She shuddered visibly. "Fortunately."

"Rose, look out!" At the warning cry from her companion, the woman whirled. There was something in the air, humming like a giant bumblebee, moving rapidly from place to place: a pink and blue blur against the ceiling.

"What the hell's that?" she blurted.

Flinx started to answer, but Cruachan spoke first, taking a step out of the line and toward the Peaceforcer. "That's the boy's pet. I don't know how it got out. It's dangerous."

"Oh, it is, is it?" The muzzle of the short rifle came up.

"No!" Cruachan rushed toward her, the console buzzer screaming in his ears. "Don't!"

The Peaceforcer reacted instinctively to the unexpected charge. A brief burst of high-intensity sound struck the leader of the Meliorares. His stomach exploded through his spine. No sound had come from the gun. There had been only a slight punching noise when the burst had struck home.

One of the elderly women screamed. The Peaceforcer cursed her overanxiousness and took aim at the source of her embarrassment. As she pointed her weapon at Pip, all the fury and pain and anguish crashed together inside Flinx's head.

"Pip! No!" he yelled, rushing the woman. The other Peaceforcer moved to cover his companion. Pip darted toward the rear of the storage room. The woman's gun tracked the minidrag as her finger started to tighten on the trigger.

Something happened. Cruachan's eyes were still open. A smile of satisfaction appeared on his face. Then he died.

Night descended unexpectedly.

Flinx was floating inside a giant bass drum. Someone was pounding on it from both sides. The rhythm was erratic, the sound soul-deafening. It hurt.

Something was resting on his chest. I am lying on my back, he thought. He raised his head to look down at himself. Pip lay on the slickertic, bruised but alive. The flying snake looked dazed. As consciousness returned with a vengeance, the narrow tongue darted out repeatedly to touch Flinx's lips and nose. Content, the minidrag ceased its examination and crawled from chest to shoulder. Flinx fought to sit up.

There was something wrong with his balance. It made the simple act of changing from a prone to a sitting position into a major operation. Two things he noted immediately; it was cold, and rain was soaking his face. Then his vision cleared and he saw the old man bending over him.

For an instant the fear returned, but this was no Meliorare. It was a kindly, unfamiliar face. The oldster was dressed very differently from the Society members. There hadn't been anything shabby about their attire. This stranger was a refugee from a simpler life.

"Are you all right, boy?" He looked over his shoulder. "I think he's all right."

Flinx looked past the old man. Several other strangers were gathered behind him. It occurred to Flinx that he was the center of their concerned curiosity. Strong arms reached toward him and helped him to his feet. There were comments about the flying snake riding his shoulder.

A younger man stepped forward. "You okay?" He searched Flinx's face. "I've had a little medical training."

"I'm not—I think—" Funny, his mouth wasn't working right. He swallowed. "What happened?"

"You tell me," said the unsmiling young man. He was dressed neatly, much more so than the oldster who had first examined Flinx. A yellow-and-green-striped slickertic covered what Flinx could see of a brightly colored business suit.

"I'm a factotum for the Subhouse of Grandier. I was just coming down to check on the arrival of a recent shipment from Evoria." He turned and pointed. "That's our warehouse over there. I nearly tripped over you."

"Me, too," the oldster said, "though I'm no factotum for anybody 'cept my own house." He grinned, showing missing teeth.

Flinx brushed wet strands of hair from his eyes and forehead. How had he gotten so wet? He couldn't remember lying down in the street. He couldn't remember lying down at all.

Now that those around him had quieted, the roar that had filled his ears since he had regained consciousness assumed deafening proportions. Sirens sounded in counterpart.

A couple of blocks away, flames shot skyward from the top of a warehouse in defiance of the steady, light rain. A fire-control skimmer hovered off to one side, its crew spraying the flames with fire-retardant chemical foam. It combined with the rain to knock the blaze back into itself.

"Anyway," the younger man next to Flinx continued as they both watched the dying inferno, "I was just entering our office over there when that building"—he nodded toward the flames—"blew up. If I remember aright, it was four or five stories tall. There are only two left, as you can see. Top three must've been incinerated in the first seconds. There's charred debris all over the streets. Knocked me right off my feet, just like you." Flinx's gaze roved over the crowd that had gathered to watch the unusual sight. Large fires were rare in Drallar.

"Somebody's let themselves in for a nest o' trouble," the oldster muttered. "Storing explosives or volatiles inside the city limits. Bad business. Bad."

"Someone told me they felt it all the way to the inurbs," the younger man said conversationally. "I wonder what the devil was stored in there to cause an explosion like that? Piece of building went past me like a shot. It's stuck in our front door, no less, if you want to see it. As I was getting up, I saw you lying there in the street. Either something mercifully small hit you or else you got knocked out when your head hit the pavement."

"I didn't see him get hit," the oldster said.

"Doesn't mean anything, as fast as stuff was flying." The executive looked at Flinx. "I'll bet you never even felt it."

"No," Flinx admitted, still terribly confused. "I didn't. But I'm okay now."

"You're sure?" The man looked him over. "Funny. Whatever it was that knocked you down must have whizzed right past. I don't see any bruises or cuts, though it looks like your pet got a little banged up."

"Can do you like that," the oldster said. " 'Nother centimeter and maybe you'd have a piece of metal sticking out of your head. Conversation piece." He chuckled.

Flinx managed a weak grin. "I feel all right now." He swayed a moment, then held steady.

The executive was still studying the minidrag coiled around Flinx's left shoulder. "That's an interesting pet, all right."

"Everybody thinks so. Thanks for your concern, both of you." He staggered forward and joined the ring of spectators gawking at the obliterated building.

Slowly, reluctantly, his brain filled in the blank spaces pockmarking his memory. Third floor, he'd been up there, and the Meliorares . . . Yes, the Meliorares—that was their name—were getting ready to run some tests on him. Then the Peaceforcers had broken in, and Pip had gotten loose, and one of them had been ready to shoot it, and the head Meliorare—Flinx couldn't remember his name, only his eyes—had panicked and rushed the Peaceforcer, and Flinx remembered screaming desperately for the woman not to fire, not to hurt Pip, not to, not to—!

Then he had awakened, soaked and stunned in the street, an old man bending solicitously over him and Pip licking his mouth.

His hand went to the back of his head, which throbbed like the drum he had dreamed of being imprisoned inside. There was no lump there, no blood, but it sure felt like something had whacked him good, just as the executive had surmised. Only the pain seemed concentrated *inside* his head.

People were emerging from the burning warehouse: medical personnel in white slickertics. They were escorting someone between them. The woman's clothes were shredded, and blood filled the gaps. Though she walked under her own power, it took two medics to guide her.

Suddenly, Flinx could feel her, for just an instant. But there was no emotion there, no emotion or feelings of any kind. Then he noticed her eyes. Her stare was vacant, blank, without motivation. Probably the exposion had stunned her, he thought. She was the Peaceforcer who had been about to shoot Pip.

In a hospital that blankness would doubtless wear off, he thought. Though it was almost as if she had been mind-wiped, and not selectively, either. She looked like a walking husk of a human being. Flinx turned away from her, uncomfortable without really knowing why, as she was put in a hospital skimmer. The vehicle rose above the crowd and headed downtown, siren screaming.

Still he fought to reconstruct those last seconds in the warehouse. What *had* happened? That unfortunate woman had been about to kill Pip. Flinx had started toward her, protesting frantically, and her companion had started to aim his own weapon at him. The weapons themselves functioned noiselessly. Had the woman fired? Had the man?

The instrumentation that had filled the storage chamber required a lot of power. If the Peaceforcer had missed Flinx, perhaps deliberately firing a warning shot, the bolt might have struck something equally sensitive but far more volatile than human flesh. As a rule, warehouses did not draw much power. There might have been delicately attuned fuel cells in the room. The shot might have set them off.

Or had one of the Meliorares—perhaps the one who had fled from Pip's cage—set off some kind of suicide device to keep his colleagues from the disgrace of an official trial? He felt much better as he considered both reasonable explanations. They fit what had happened, were very plausible.

The only thing they failed to explain was how he had landed two blocks away, apparently unhurt except for a raging headache.

Well, he *had* been moving toward the door, and explosions could do funny things. The streets of the industrial district were notorious for their potholes, which were usually full of rain water. And he was soaked. Could the force of the explosion have thrown him into one deep enough to cushion his fall and cause him to skip out again like a stone on a pond? Obviously, that was what had happened. There was no other possible explanation.

His head hurt.

Local gendarmes were finally beginning to show up. At their arrival Flinx instinctively turned away, leaving the crowd behind and cradling Pip beneath his slickertic. He was glad that he hadn't been forced to use his own knife, felt lucky to be alive. Maybe now, at last, external forces would leave him and Mother Mastiff and Pip in peace.

He thought back a last time to that final instant in the warehouse. The rage and desperation had built up in him until he had been unable to stand it any longer and had charged blindly at the Peaceforcer about to kill Pip. He hoped he would never be that angry again in his life.

The crowd ignored the boy as he fled the scene; he vanished into the comforting shadows and narrow alleys that

filtered back toward the central city. There was nothing remarkable about him and no reason for the gendarmes to
stop and question him. The old man and the executive
who had found him lying in the street had already forgotten him, engrossed in the unusual sight of a major fire in
perpetually damp Drallar.

Flinx made his way back toward the more animated
sections of the city, toward the arguing and shouting and
smells and sights of the marketplace and Mother Mastiff's
warm, familiar little shop. He was sorry. Sorry for all the
trouble he seemed to have caused. Sorry for the funny old
Meliorares who were no more. Sorry for the overzealous
Peaceforcers.

Mother Mastiff wouldn't be sorry, he knew. She could
be as vindictive as an AAnn, especially if anything close to
her had been threatened.

For himself, however, he regretted the deaths of so
many. All for nothing, all because of some erratic,
harmless, usually useless emotion-reading ability he
possessed. Their own fault, though. Everything that happened was their own fault, Meliorares and Peaceforcers
alike. He tried to warn them. Never try to come between a
boy and his snake.

The damp trek homeward exhausted his remaining
strength. Never before had the city seemed so immense, its
byways and side streets so convoluted and tortuous. He
was completely worn out.

Mother Mastiff was manning the shop, waiting for him
as anxiously as she awaited customers. Her thin, aged arm
was strong as she slipped it around his back and helped
him the last agonizing steps into the store.

"I've been worried like to death over ye, boy! Damn ye
for causing a poor old woman such distress." Her fingers
touched his bruised cheeks, his forehead, as her eyes
searched for serious damage. "And you're all cut up and
bleeding. What's to become of ye, Flinx? Ye have got to
learn to stay out of trouble."

He summoned up a grin, glad to be home. "It seems to
come looking for me, Mother."

"Hmpnh! Excuses. The boy's wit is chock full of excuses. What happened to ye?"

He tried to marshal his thoughts as he slid Pip out from beneath the slickertic. Mother Mastiff backed away. The minidrag was as limp as a piece of rope. It lay curled up in its master's lap, if not asleep then giving a fine scaly imitation of some similar state.

"Some people kidnaped Pip. They called themselves Meliorares. But they really wanted me. They—" His expression screwed tight as he remembered, "One of them said something about wanting to fix me. Fix what? What did they want with me?"

She considered a long moment, studying the boy. Truly, it appeared that he was telling the truth, that he had learned no more than what he said. Ignoring the proximity of the hated flying snake, she sat down and put an arm around his shoulders.

"Now mark me well, boy, because this is vital to ye. I don't have to tell ye that you're different. You've always been different. Ye have to hide that as best ye can, and we'll have to hide ourselves. Drallar's a big place. We can move the shop if need be. But you're going to have to learn to live quietly, and you're going to have to keep your differences to yourself, or we'll be plagued with more of this unwelcome and unwholesome attention."

"It's all so silly, Mother. Just because I can sometimes sense what other people are feeling?"

"That. And maybe more."

"There isn't anything more. That's all I can do."

"Is it, boy? How did ye get away from these people." She looked past him toward the street, suddenly concerned. "Will they be coming after ye again?"

"I don't think so. Most of them were kind of dead when I left. I don't know how I got away from them. I think one of them shot at something explosive and it blew up. I was blown clear out of a building and into the street."

"Lucky to be alive ye are, it seems, though by what providence I wonder. Maybe 'tis best this way. Maybe 'tis best ye don't know too much about yourself just yet. Your mind always was advanced of your body, and maybe there's something more that's advanced even of that."

"But I don't *want* to be different," he insisted, almost crying. "I just want to be like everyone else."

"I know ye do, boy," she said gently, "but each of us must play the cards fate deals us, and if you've been stuck with the joker, you'll just have to learn to cope with it, turn it to your advantage somehow."

"I don't want any advantage! Not if it's going to cause us this kind of trouble."

"I'll have none of that, boy! A difference can always be to one's advantage. 'Tis time ye chose a profession. I know you've no like for running a shop like this one. What is it ye like to do?"

He mulled it over a while before replying. "All I enjoy doing is making other people happy."

She shook her head sadly. "Sometimes I think you've not enough self-interest to keep yourself alive. However, if that's what ye like, then you'll have to find some way to earn a living at it."

"Sometimes I dream of becoming a doctor and healing people."

"I'd advise ye to set your sights a bit lower, boy."

"All right. An actor, then."

"Nay, not that low. Be sensible. Set yourself to something ye can do *now*, without years of study."

"I could perform right here in the marketplace," he said thoughtfully. "I can juggle pretty good. You've seen me."

"Aye, and yelled at ye often enough for practicing with my expensive baubles. But 'tis a sound thought. We must find ye a good street corner. Surely ye can't get into trouble performing before these simple locals."

"Sure! I'll go and practice right now."

"Easy, boy, easy. You're nearly asleep on your feet, and I'll not have ye breaking either my goods or yourself. Go inside and lie down. I'll be in soon to fix ye something to eat. Go on now, boy, and be sure and take your monster with ye."

Cradling the exhausted Pip in his hands, Flinx rose and made his way through the displays to the section of the shop that served as their home. Mother Mastiff's eyes followed him.

What *was* to become of the boy? Somehow he had come to the attention of powerful, dangerous people. At least there was a good chance they wouldn't be bothered for a while. Not if he had left them "kind of dead."

How had he escaped? Sometimes he still frightened her. Oh, not because he would ever harm a hair of her old head. Quite the contrary, as his dogged pursuit and rescue of her these past days had proven. But there were forces at work within that adolescent body, forces beyond the comprehension of a simple shopkeeper, forces he might not be able to control. And there was more to it than reading the emotions of others. Of that she was certain. How much more she could only suspect, for it was clear enough the boy had little awareness of them himself.

Well, let him play at the trade of jongleur for a while. Surely that was harmless. Surely he could not find much trouble plying so simple an occupation.

She told herself that repeatedly all the rest of the afternoon and on into evening as she sat watching him sleep. When she finally slipped into her own bed, she thought she had put such imaginary fears beyond her, but such was not the case.

She sensed that the boy lying content and peaceful in the room opposite hers was destined for more than an idle life of entertaining on street corners. Much more. She knew somehow that a damnable universe, which was always sticking its cosmic nose into the destinies of innocent citizens, would never let anyone as unique as Flinx alone.

**DON'T MISS THE CONTINUING
ADVENTURES OF FLINX AND PIP IN:**

**THE TAR-AIYM KRANG
ORPHAN STAR
THE END OF THE MATTER
and
BLOODHYPE**

About the Author

Born in New York City in 1946, Alan Dean Foster was raised in Los Angeles, California. After receiving a bachelor's degree in political science and a Master of Fine Arts in motion pictures from UCLA in 1968–69, he worked for two years as a public relations copywriter in a small Studio City, California, firm.

His writing career began in 1968 when August Derleth bought a long letter of Foster's and published it as a short story in his biannual *Arkham Collector Magazine*. Sales of short fiction to other magazines followed. His first try at a novel, *The Tar-Aiym Krang*, was published by Ballantine Books in 1972.

Foster has toured extensively through Asia and the isles of the Pacific. Besides traveling, he enjoys classical and rock music, old films, basketball, body surfing, and karate. He has taught screenwriting, literature, and film history at UCLA and Los Angeles City College.

Currently, he resides in Arizona with his wife JoAnn (who is reputed to have the only extant recipe for Barbarian Cream Pie).